Strong Feather

by

Richard J. D. Regnier

Richard J. D. Regnier

10-18-06

Cover Design by

Chris Hieb

To: Theresa Haskins
Seek and you shall find
The True meaning of your life

II Timothy 2:15

Authors' Publishing House
Midland, Texas

ISBN: 0-9772221-6-0

For more information, contact:

        Authors' Publishing House
        2908 Shanks Drive
        Midland, Texas 79705

        Or visit our website at:

www.authorspublishinghouse.com

Dedication

This book is dedicated to

my wife Gwendolyn Joy

The Joy of my life

About The Author

Richard J. D. Regnier is a coal miner's son and was raised in a small town in Colorado. He is a veteran of World War II and Vietnam, with fifteen years of military service.

He has a bachelor's degree from Southwest Texas State University, and a master's degree from Sul Ross State University, both in Education.

Mr. Regnier has been a teacher, as well as a probation officer, and is retired from both professions. He spends his retirement time as an artist, poet and author.

Strong Feather

CHAPTER I

Gasping for breath, Jimmy bent over and closed his eyes. After running for about a quarter of a mile, he was out of breath. Jimmy was a young Indian lad of thirteen. As his breath returned, he slowly raised his head and looked around. He was halfway up the side of a hill behind his grandparents' house. There was a worried look on Jimmy Warrior's face as he walked along, not paying attention to his surroundings. The gentle slope of the grassy hill was interrupted now and then by small depressions. The fluid motion of his body adjusted to them as he moved along. His thoughts were miles away from the small town of Mercer, Colorado.

Four days earlier, he was in a damp, dimly lit jail cell in Newark, New Jersey. Now, he walked up the side of a hill with nothing but clear blue skies above him. He was glad to be here, but this was not home. How could he have let Officer Brown trick him into leaving his hometown, and come out here where he didn't know anybody but his grandparents? As he climbed up the side of the grassy hill, his eyes saw none of the beauty about him. Even though almost six feet tall, he was barely a teenager. He always wanted to be six feet tall like his dad, but quickly found out that growing up means one has more responsibilities, which bothered him. He walked along shaking his head.

It was the first week in June and at any other time (except in Newark) he felt great. School was out, which always gave him a feeling of freedom. In Newark, he felt different, maybe freer: maybe better, maybe worse. He wasn't sure.

The Colorado knee-high grass he walked through parted as he passed, then returned to its original position. Only the slightest trail through the grass could be seen where he walked. That would soon be gone.

1

Strong Feather

Nearing the top of the hill, Jimmy stopped and sat down. Perched on the back of his head was a black baseball cap. His grandpa gave it to him an hour earlier when he got off the bus from Newark. The word, "Tigers", was sewn on the front of it in large orange letters. "It stands for Mercer High Tigers," his grandpa, Tom, told him.

"What a dumb name," he thought at the time. Sitting there, his eyes took in everything around him, but nothing seemed to register. His mind was elsewhere.

Jimmy worried about the things that happened to him. Everything happened so fast. For a young lad of thirteen, deep furrows slowly etched in his brow from all the worrying he did lately. No matter what he tried to do, or how hard he tried not to worry, he couldn't shake it. "What was he going to do?" he thought, as he sat there looking at the tall grass about him. Why did things like this happen to him? It just wasn't fair. He thought about running away, but knew it would hurt his grandparents if he did. He tried to run away on the bus trip to Mercer, but it didn't work out like he planned. He thought about sticking it out with his grandparents, but he knew it wasn't going to work. He had to do something, but what?

As he wondered what to do, he was looking at the back of his grandparents' house. It needed painting and lots of work, just to make it look half decent. He knew his grandparents didn't have the money to fix it up. Even if they did, they'd probably expect him to do all the work. He surely would run away then.

Sitting there thinking about it bothered him. He knew earlier that most Indians didn't have much money. If he had money right now, he'd blow this hick town of Mercer, Colorado and head back to his hometown, the big city of Newark, New Jersey. Why he agreed to come to this nowhere town irritated him. Then he recalled being in that

Strong Feather

damp jail cell two floors below the police station in Newark, and he cringed. Even though he was sitting in the warm sunshine now, he still felt that cell's dampness. Cold shivers ran over his body.

"It isn't fair," he told himself. All he'd taken was a couple of apples.

The sun's heat finally won out and the chills left. He wiped his forehead, and to his surprise, the back of his sleeve came away dry. In Newark, it would have been wet with sweat on a warm day like this. This place had some advantages, but it wasn't anything like the big city. Nothing was. Jimmy heard a low whispering sound off to his left. He turned to see what it was. Pleasantly surprised, he saw it was the sound of the wind headed in his direction. He was amazed that he could both see and hear the wind. He watched the tops of the tall grasses sway back and forth as the wind gently caressed them. It looked as if a large unseen hand was gently moving across the tops of the grasses. The sound grew until it was now a loud whisper in his ears as it came closer. Then, with a gentle touch, it caressed him for only a moment and moved on, making him wish it had stayed a little longer.

A smile flickered across his face as he sat there watching the wind move off the side of the hill. It quickly moved towards the small creek below. Then it was gone. Sitting there, he held his breath as he wondered what happened to it. It seemed to vanish. He breathed a sigh. On the far side of the creek the grasses began to move. Their bending tattled on the wind as it moved on across the fields towards his grandparents' house. Then as quickly as it had come, it was gone. Not a blade of grass moved within his sight. The gentle wind that had come for an instant, caressed him, then went on its way, had felt good.

3

Strong Feather

The sun was now high in the sky, and its warmth helped Jimmy to relax. His eyelids began to grow heavier and heavier. Lying backwards into the tall grass, he soon found himself surrounded by the sweet smell of the green grass. The coolness of the grass made him feel good. A soft hedge of grass now engulfed him, hiding the world from his sight. Looking upward, all he could see was the deep-blue Colorado sky above. It was so blue it caused him to squint. Sitting up, he looked up at the sky all around him. Far off to his right, near the horizon, he saw a small group of white fluffy clouds. Returning to his lair, he placed his hands behind his head. "At least all of the sky," he thought, "wasn't blue." He'd never seen a place like this where there were so few clouds.

Pulling the bill of his baseball cap down to block out the sun, and most of the blue sky, he closed his eyes. The frown was still on his forehead as he lay there trying to decide what he would do. His eyelids fluttered now and then as his mind raced along, trying to sort it all out. Then, oh so slowly, his breathing became slower and slower. A slight smile flickered across his face as he sank deeper and deeper into sleep. He was back in Newark.

The streets of Newark were home to Jimmy Warrior most of his life. For over two years now they were his gold mine. Jimmy was a good-looking thirteen year old, with wavy black hair, brown eyes, and nice even white teeth. It was almost three years since his dad, Tommy, took off and left him and his mother. His mother, Mabel, stayed around the house for about two months, not knowing what to do, hoping he'd come back. Then one day she realized he would probably never show up again.

She went out and found a job working at a cafe. It wasn't the best job, but it was only two blocks from their

Strong Feather

third floor cold-water flat. Even with her working, money was very scarce in the Warrior household. One day Jimmy asked one of their neighbors for some money. To his surprise, he gave Jimmy a quarter. That was how it all started. It wasn't long until Jimmy asked strangers on the street for money, and got it. This was great. Jimmy went from being the poorest kid on the block, to the richest. He always had change in his once empty pockets.

Mabel realized she wasn't making enough money to pay the bills, so she changed jobs and started working nights at a nearby Bar-N-Grill. This left Jimmy free on weekends, and he roamed the streets at night. When school was out for the summer, he was free all day while his mother slept. He asked for handouts on busy streets a few blocks away from their house. He was so good at it that he expanded into one of the nearby parks. The park turned out to be his best moneymaker. It didn't take him long to discover he could get money from just about anyone he asked, except his mother. Somehow she knew what he was after before he asked. She always told him not to ask her for any money, because she would give him what he needed.

One day she gave him a quarter for his lunch at school. He looked at it and gave it back. "I've got a friend at school that has lots of money, and he buys all of my meals for me," he told her. It made his mother so mad that she started yelling and hitting him. "You're a liar and a thief!" she yelled.

Beginning that day, she called him a no-good thief. She never offered him money for his meals again. If Jimmy wanted money from her, he had to beg for it. The next summer when school was out, he spent most of his time at the movie houses downtown. When he watched all

5

the new movies each week, he went over to a diner near his home and played the pin-ball machines.

Jimmy just had the gift of conning people out of money. One day when passing a grocery store, he asked the owner for some fruit and got it. He could get food as easy as he could get money. So, instead of buying his food at the cafes and markets, they gave it to him. His friends, of course, were guys just like himself, but they didn't work as hard at it as Jimmy did. His buddies didn't hesitate to ask him for money when they didn't have any. He, of course, wouldn't give them a dime unless they kept after him. Eventually he would give in just to get rid of them. He didn't want them to think he was stuck up, but he did want them to know he was better at getting money than they were.

Jimmy liked school a lot and found it a place to have lots of fun. Good grades were easy for him, but not long after his dad left, his grades started slipping. It wasn't long until he was barely passing. He told anyone who would listen that he thought school was a waste of time for him. Those who listened agreed with him, because they felt the same way he did, especially when he supplied them with a little change now and then.

That fall when school started, he was in the seventh grade. Jimmy was irritated that he couldn't continue the free life he was accustomed to. He hadn't thought much about it, but he grew about five inches that summer. He no longer was that cute little boy asking for money. Jimmy found it harder and harder to get money from people. Instead of them giving him food, he now had to take it when they weren't looking. On the second day of school as he walked along, he decided to quit. Instead of going to school, he turned and walked over to the near by park to see if he could pick up some change.

Strong Feather

Instead of getting money from the people in the park, he got a lot of advice. "Go back to school," they all told him instead of giving him money. He left the park without a dime and started working the streets, but again no luck. Not being able to get any money was beginning to worry him. There had to be another place where he could pick up some change. Then it came to him. He knew exactly what he would do. He'd go downtown to one of the busiest streets and see what he could do there. He hadn't tried his luck there, but he felt there were lots of people who would give him a quarter if he asked.

A half hour later, Jimmy found himself walking down Broad Street, with five dollars in quarters in his pockets. "This place was a gold mine," he told himself, as he walked along asking people for quarters. Why hadn't he thought of this before? He had a big smile on his face when he spotted a well-dressed man heading towards him. He was about to ask him for some change when two hands grabbed him from behind, one by the arm, and the other by the back of his shirt, and dragged him into a nearby alley.

Before he knew what happened, something hit him on the left side of his head and he saw stars. Putting his hands up to protect himself, he ducked. As he stood there trying to clear his head, he was hit in the pit of the stomach. All the air in his lungs gushed out through his mouth, and he doubled over gasping for air. Again the fist hit him on the head. Then again. Once again he raised his arms over his head to ward off the blows that followed. Whoever was hitting him soon tired, and the blows ceased. Looking up, Jimmy swung at the attacker. Instead of hitting him, he was hit in the nose. Blood gushed from his nose and down his chin as he backed up. He pinched his nose trying to stop the bleeding and keep the blood off his clothes. His head was roughly jerked upright and a face appeared a few inches from his. To his surprise, it was a kid about three inches shorter than him.

"You stay off my street, you dumb jerk!" the face said. "I work this street and no punk like you is gonna cut in on my territory! If I see you around here again, I'll break both of your legs!"

He shoved Jimmy to the ground. He walked out of the alley and disappeared around the corner of the building. Jimmy was glad he was gone. Still holding his nose, Jimmy pulled out his handkerchief and put it up to his nose. Standing up, he ran towards the other end of the alley. As he ran, he could hear the jingling of coins in his front pockets. A smile flickered across his face as he ran along with a bloody nose. He knew he had made enough money to last him the rest of the week.

After his experience downtown, school looked pretty good to Jimmy. But the money he'd gotten was soon gone, and he had little success getting any handouts. Growing up like this sure wasn't helping. He now had to ask his mother for money so he could eat at school. She usually refused, which meant a long day without anything to eat.

Mabel would tell him to get his rich friend at school to buy his lunch. Occasionally he talked the local market managers out of some fruit and vegetables, but it was a job. They also told him to get a job if he wanted food. His buddies laughed at him when he asked them for money, especially now that they knew he couldn't make it on his own. He ate more and more of his meals at home. It seemed like everyone he asked for money told him he was too big to be begging for handouts. Looking in the mirror each day, he could almost see himself getting taller. He was too lazy to work and too tall to beg.

Strong Feather

During the lunch period at high school one day, a bully took Jimmy's lunch money from him. As he started to walk away, he heard the bully laughing at him. In a flash he turned, lowered his head and ran at the bully, but instead of knocking him down, Jimmy was thrown to the ground and kicked in the sides. He was in big trouble and he knew it. He rolled back and forth trying to get away from the kicks that followed. Rolling around on the ground Jimmy wanted to yell for help, but he was afraid and nothing came out. If only his mom were there to help him. She'd know what to do. With all of his strength he tried harder and harder to yell for his mother.

Moans and groans were coming from Jimmy as he rolled back and forth in the soft grass on the hillside. His face was distorted as his eyelids fluttered, then opened. "Mom! Help me!" he yelled, sitting up with a start. Sitting there with his eyes and mouth wide open, he looked around.

He realized where he was. He was still lying on the side of a hill behind his grandparent's house. He had been dreaming. "It seemed so real," he thought. Jimmy picked up his cap, lay back down and closed his eyes. Placing his cap back over his face, he slowly closed his eyes. It wasn't long until his eyelids once more fluttered. His breathing became slower and slower. Once again he was asleep, and back in Newark.

Jimmy walked along one of the streets near his house in Newark, New Jersey, heading towards the police station. As he walked, he unknowingly passed four of his buddies. They were each leaning up against the side of a building. He was deep in thought as he walked along, so

9

deep that he didn't notice them until one of them called his name.

"Hey, Jimmy," the short one said. "You too good to say hi?"

Jimmy looked at him. "No," he said. Returning to his thoughts, he walked on, leaving them standing there looking at him. Looking at one another they all laughed. The one who'd spoken moved his right index finger round and round next to his ear making the sign that means one is crazy. They all laughed.

Jimmy was oblivious to what they were doing as he walked down the street with an old suitcase swinging back and forth in his hand. His four friends shook their heads, turned and disappeared into a nearby alley.

When Jimmy reached the end of the block, he realized what he'd done and turned to say something to his friends. To his surprise, they were nowhere in sight. Scratching his head, he stood there for a moment wondering what was going on.

"Oh well," he thought, "he had more important things to worry about than those guys." Turning, he walked on wondering what he would have to eat on his bus trip. He was broke. His mother didn't give him a dime all week. He knew if he wanted to eat he would have to get some money somewhere. The next alley he came to, he turned in. He placed his suitcase behind two large trash cans. No one would ever think of looking behind trash cans for a suitcase. Turning towards the street, he froze. A police car drove slowly by the alley opening. The two officers inside glanced at him and drove on.

Shivers ran up his back as goose pimples popped out all over his body. Leaning up against the building next to the trash cans, he stood there and didn't move. The palms of his hands and his back were flat against the building behind him, as he slid down the wall and sat on the ground. With his elbows on his knees and face in his hands, he sat there not moving. He was scared. It was only yesterday morning when he'd been picked up by the police for stealing something to eat. Officer Bob Brown's voice still rung in his ears. His whole body cringed as he recalled what happened.

"So you're Jimmy Warrior, the Indian thief we've heard so much about around here," Officer Brown said. He spoke so loud that everyone in the police station office stopped and looked at the young lad. If Jimmy could have crawled under something, he would have. But there was no place to hide. With everyone looking at him, he pulled himself together and gave the officer his best grin, then smiled. Jimmy's even white teeth seemed to sparkle as he stood there. There were very few people who wouldn't give in to that smile, and he knew it. His ruddy complexion, dark wavy hair, and big smile got him out of tough jams before, and they would again. "This policeman was tough, but not that tough," he thought, as he stood there smiling at him.

He was taken back a little when he saw it wasn't working. For the last two weeks his luck had changed. It happened slowly, and hadn't bothered him at first, but it was now becoming a serious problem. All the other policemen he'd dealt with before were pushovers. But this guy was different. Something made him mad. But what? Jimmy felt he hadn't done a thing to make him mad. But everything he tried to do or say seemed to be wrong. He didn't know how to handle this guy. His smile faded when he decided it wasn't going to work.

"I'm going to put you away for good, Indian. You're going to be in jail so far under this building you'll think you're in your grave. I'm going to throw away the keys, and you'll never get out of here to steal again. You hear me, punk?"

"Yes, I hear you," Jimmy unconsciously stammered.

Officer Bob Brown walked back and forth in front of his desk like a lion in a cage. His hands were clasped together behind his back as he walked. His light-blue piercing eyes never looked away from Jimmy. Bob was six feet three inches tall, and almost skinny. His white shirt loosely hung on him, with some of it hanging over his belt.

Stopping in front of Jimmy, he poked his shirt into his pants. A couple strands of his straight brown hair fell into his eyes. He quickly ran the fingers of his right hand through his hair a couple of times until it was half combed back on his head. Some of his shirt had come back out, so he poked it back in. All this time his eyes never left Jimmy's eyes.

"Where's your mother, boy?" he asked. Then, not waiting for an answer from Jimmy, he continued. "We've been trying to call her ever since we picked you up. Where is she?"

"She works nights at Pete's Bar-N-Grill," Jimmy replied with a steadier voice, but there was now contempt in it as his eyes flashed. After he spoke he pulled back, expecting to be hit. He would have gotten a good one from his mom if he'd answered her like that. Seeing there was no response to what he said, he regained his composure and went on. "She didn't have to work last night. So she got up early this morning and went off somewhere before I got up. If I know her, she won't be back until late tonight."

Officer Brown saw how Jimmy stepped back when he talked back to him. He felt certain the boy was abused, but decided he needed to scare him so badly that he would quit taking things. He knew his brash street talk was just a put on. Looking at Jimmy, his face got sterner.

"You Indians are all alike," he said angrily and deliberately. "Your mother just lets you run wild on the streets with your pals. She don't care what you do. Well, that's going to change, punk. You're going to jail. I'm not going to call her anymore. Not today. If she's home tomorrow, I'll tell her we got you down here in jail and she can come down and get you. If she's not home tomorrow you'll just have to stay here until she comes looking for you. I kinda hope no one comes looking for you for a couple of weeks. That would serve you right, Indian. We don't like thieves around here. Do you hear me?"

Jimmy didn't answer him, which made Bob madder.

"Do you hear me?" he said louder, acting like he was going to hit him.

"Yeah," Jimmy said real low, ducking. "I hear you."

Tears came and ran down his cheeks. Jimmy worked the streets of Newark for about the past three years, and he felt nothing could bother him. But he found out that he wasn't as tough as he thought he was. As he stood there, he got mad at himself. The beating he'd taken from that creep downtown bothered him, but instead of letting anyone know it, he just acted tougher. But this policeman was something else. He was more than Jimmy could handle. Everything in his easy-going life was falling apart, and he had a hard time dealing with it.

An officer over near the far wall started walking toward Jimmy, but Bob held his hand up. Bob saw the look in the officer's eyes and knew he thought he was going too far with this boy. The officer stopped, shook his head, turned, and went back to his desk.

"Save the tears for the jail cell, Indian," Brown said, spitting the words out through his teeth. His harsh words stopped the tears as quickly as they had started, leaving two sad brown eyes looking up at him. "This boy could win his heart if he didn't watch out," Bob thought.

Walking to his desk, Bob opened the middle drawer. Taking out a large ring of keys, he briefly looked at the keys in his hand, then turned towards Jimmy with a scowl on his face.

"Follow me," he said, as he walked past Jimmy.

Jimmy turned, and followed Bob out of his office over to a door at the back of the room. The door quickly opened, and then just as quickly, closed behind them. They moved from a brightly lit room into a dimly lit hallway. When the door closed behind Jimmy, he heard a solid click he'd never heard before. Turning, he looked at the door and realized there was no doorknob. The only way to open it was with a key. He was trapped and there was no way out. The feeling of suffocating came over him. He found it hard to breathe. A shove from Officer Brown sent him down the steps.

Quickly grabbing onto the hand rails, he stopped his downward plunge. Footsteps passed him on the staircase and once again he found himself following the officer on a downward spiral. Step by step they descended lower and lower under the building. Jimmy's steps became slower and slower as he descended the staircase behind Officer Brown, until they were two floors below ground level.

Damp, musty air greeted them at the bottom of the stairs. Bob unlocked the door in front of them and dampness engulfed both of them like a wet blanket. He still found it hard to breathe, only now it was from the dampness that filled his lungs. As they walked down a dark passageway, Jimmy could see steel cells on either side.

Electric wires hung from the ceiling every 20 feet or so with a small bulb that gave just enough light to see.

Strong Feather

Even though it was dim, Jimmy saw a few faces looking through the bars at him. At the last cell, Bob stopped, opened the door and stepped aside.

Jimmy stopped outside the cell and started to back up. Bob's firm hand grabbed him by the arm and flung him into the cell. Jimmy put his hands out in front of himself to stop from running into the back of the cell. The door slammed behind him with a clang. There was a dull click as the key turned in the cell door lock. Jimmy couldn't move as he stood there with his hands against the back wall with his head lowered. He couldn't believe this was happening to him. But it was. He was in jail and he didn't like it. A few of his friends had told him about the times they'd been in jail. But he never thought it would happen to him, especially, for just taking some apples from that old fruit stand. He took apples from there before, but the owner only yelled at him when he caught him. Being put in jail for a few apples wasn't fair.

As he stood there, he had an eerie feeling. Then he realized what it was. It was Officer Brown's eyes on his back. Turning, he saw him standing outside the cell looking at him. He didn't know whether to laugh or tell him off. It wouldn't take much to hate this guy, but before he could make up his mind, he was gone.

"You're going to rot in there, Indian," Bob's voice echoed up and down the hall, finally ending in the cell where Jimmy stood. Placing his hands over his ears he tried to stop the echo, but the echo was now inside his head. Shaking his head, he looked around the cell and saw a steel bunk beside him. It sure looked good. Lying down he pulled the blanket up over his head and turned towards the wall. As he lay there, a deep sob came from within. Memories of his childhood came back. Times when his mom put him in a dark closet when he didn't mind her.

Strong Feather

The thought of those times caused him to draw up into a tight ball.

He didn't know how long he'd been lying there, but his mind slowly cleared. As it did, his body straightened out. Off in the distance he could hear strange sounds coming from outside his cell. Sitting up with a jerk, he listened, trying to figure out what it was. Then he knew. It was people shouting.

"Shut up that bawling, Injun," one voice said.

"If I ever get ahold of your neck you'll shut up," a raspy voice closer yelled.

Scooting up against the wall, Jimmy didn't utter another sound. When the voices stopped he felt better. He decided he wasn't going to let this place get to him. It wouldn't be easy in a damp cell like this, but he could do it. The first thing he had to do was get out. But how? Then he thought of his mom. She would get him out as soon as she found out he was in jail. She wouldn't let her only son stay in jail. Just the thought of his mom coming to get him out of this mess made him feel a lot better. "She'll tell them a thing or two when she does," he thought, and then smiled.

Jimmy was two floors underground and no windows where he could see outside. There was no way that he could tell what time it was, so he just looked at the bars on his cell. When he sat down and tried to sort it out, he fell asleep.

A loud clanging noise woke Jimmy up. He jumped off the bunk and onto the floor. Standing there half awake he looked all around his cell wondering what made the noise. Then something moved outside his cell. Squinting, he saw what it was that had made the noise. A small, skinny, gray-headed old man opened his cell door and placed a tray of food on the floor in front of him. With a quick jump backwards he closed the door, locked it, turned, and was gone.

Jimmy rubbed his eyes as he walked over to the cell door and picked up the tray. He couldn't believe what he saw. It looked like the awful food he got at school in Newark.

"What kind of a mess is this?" he yelled after the old man. "I want some food, not stuff like this." To his surprise he got an answer.

"If you don't want it, cry baby, just pass it around the bars and I'll eat it," a raspy voice said from the next cell. Then he laughed.

"Shut up," several others yelled.

Jimmy looked at the food and decided to eat it. He didn't know when he'd get another meal around this place. He sat down on his bunk and ate his first meal in jail.

When he finished, he slipped the tray through the bars and onto the floor outside his cell door. He walked back to the bunk and lay down. Pulling the thin blanket up over him he closed his eyes. It sure felt good to have something in his belly. Jimmy's mind flitted a lot as he lay with his hands behind his head. Now and then he caught himself dozing off, but the dampness of the cell woke him. He was chilled to the bone and he started shivering, which woke him each time he dozed off. Unknown to him, each time he drifted off to sleep, low sobs came from inside.

Jimmy was really scared, but didn't want anyone yelling at him, so he suppressed it. Half asleep, he pulled the blanket over his head. His shaking stopped as his breath kept the chill of the cell at bay. Again he fell asleep, only this time it was a deep, deep sleep. This time Jimmy dreamed, and it was so real he thought he was wide awake. In his dream he was at last nice and warm, and it felt so good. He was lying on the side of a hill looking up at the clear sky above him. It felt so good just to lie there in the warm sun.

He smelled the sweetness of the grass about him, and its softness under him. Shading his eyes from the sun, he looked at something up in the sky. High above him in the deep blue of the sky, flew a large bird. "It must be a large hawk," he thought, as he watched. It looked as if the hawk was standing still above him in the air. "How could it do that?" he wondered. Even though the hawk was high above him, he could tell it was big by its large wingspan. Then, as if by magic, the hawk began a slow circle going round and round. "Wow!" he thought, "It sure would be great to be able to fly high up in the sky like that."

A loud clanging brought Jimmy out of his sleep with a start. The noise was coming from outside his cell again. Bleary-eyed, he sat up and looked around trying to figure out what was going on. He was back in his dimly lit, cold, damp cell. The clattering noise was made by the old man who came to pick up his tray. He stood outside Jimmy's cell laughing as he banged the tray against the bars to wake him up.

Jimmy quickly lay back down. The old man quit, seeing he wasn't going to get a rise out of him. Again he hit the bars with the tray, but Jimmy just covered his ears with his hands and closed his eyes.

Lying there he tried to remember that great bird he saw flying high and free above him, but it was gone. He lay there thinking about that beautiful large bird that was free to fly anywhere it wanted to. Oh, how he wished he could fly out of this cell he was in. It wasn't right to be treated like he was being treated. With a frown on his forehead, he drifted off to sleep.

Strong Feather

A large hairy hand shook Jimmy back and forth causing him to finally open his eyes. He lay there blinking at Officer Brown standing beside his bunk.

"Get up, Jimmy," Bob said.

"What?" Jimmy said, not realizing where he was.

Brown grabbed him, pulling him up and off the bunk and stood him up in one motion. "Your mother is upstairs. Let's go!"

Shivers surged throughout Jimmy's body as he stood there. The dampness had chilled him throughout. The old bunk blanket had kept some of the dampness out, but not all. "I'll probably catch a cold," he thought, standing there half asleep. "That's all I need."

A quick shove sent him through the open cell door. Bob followed, closing the door behind them with a bang. Another shove directed him down the hallway towards the door.

"I'm glad you're taking that cry baby out of here, Brown," the guy in the next cell said. "It's bad enough being down here in your rat hole without having a crying kid making it worse."

Brown was about to answer the barb directed at him, but decided it would probably be the best kind of medicine he could give Jimmy, so he said nothing. Jimmy needed to feel that hatred other prisoners had. This kind of treatment had worked on some other juvenile offenders he worked with, and he was hoping it would work on Jimmy Warrior.

They quickly retraced the steps they took the day before. When they reached the top of the stairs, they entered the police room. The brightness of the lights hurt Jimmy's eyes. He stood there with his hands shading his eyes as he looked around the large room. His eyes darted back and forth around the room but he didn't see his mother. He wanted to run to her, have her take him into her arms and hug him.

"Where's my mother?" he asked, looking up at Brown.

"She's in my office," he replied, pointing.

Jimmy ran over to the office door and opened it. His mother was standing by the window with her back to him. Running across the room to her he stopped, smiled, and waited for her to greet him with a big hug. With a jerking motion, Mabel turned around. She looked him in the eye, and slapped him hard.

Jimmy's world fell apart as tears filled his eyes and ran down his cheeks. With that slap he thought he lost his only true friend, and now he knew the whole world hated him, even his mother.

Tears dripped from his chin, but he didn't make a sound. Officer Brown followed Jimmy into the room and stood there not believing what he just saw. He walked to his desk, stopped, looked at the two of them, but didn't say a word. He felt a twinge of pride as he stood there looking at the young lad acting like a man. He was quite a lad, he thought, and he liked him. Making his way around his desk he sat down. Sitting there looking at Jimmy's mother, he wondered why she couldn't see that in her son.

Mabel Warrior's black hair fell about her shoulders in waves. She had deep brown eyes and a creamy complexion. She was slightly plump, but carried her extra weight well on her five feet seven-inch frame. She could be nice when she wanted, but this wasn't one of those times.

"You're a good for nothing just like your father!" she yelled. "Look at you in jail for stealing. Well, I'm through with you. I hope they put you away somewhere where I won't have to worry about you anymore. I've told you over and over you'd turn out like this, and you have. You're no good."

She lunged at him with her right hand raised. Jimmy stepped aside and she stumbled past. She caught herself, stopped, turned and looked at him, breathing hard. Jimmy turned his head and put his hand to his nose.

"You've been drinking again, Mom," he said.

"What if I have?" she said. "At least I didn't steal it."

Brown stood up when she headed toward him again. Seeing Bob out of the corner of her eye, she stopped. She looked at him as if nothing happened and smiled. Everything was fuzzy to her. Shaking her head she walked over to the window and stood there.

"Officer Brown," she said, turning and looking at Jimmy. "I want you to send my boy to some kind of a juvenile place where he can be taught not to steal."

Brown said nothing as he stood there looking at one of them, and then the other. Not getting a response from him, she turned.

"What's the matter, Officer?" she asked. She started to say more, but Brown held up his hand, which stopped her.

Sitting down, Brown opened the middle drawer of his desk and put the ring of keys inside and closed it.

Smiling at Mabel he said, "Do you have any relatives Jimmy can stay with while you're working?"

"No," Mabel replied gruffly. "I don't want him freeloading on anyone I know. His father's somewhere in a veteran's hospital. He got shell shock during World War II, and now he's an alcoholic. The only relatives Jimmy has is his grandparents out west in Colorado. They're too old to take care of a kid like him, and besides that, they're broke.

Strong Feather

All they have to their name is the old house they live in. They sure wouldn't want to be bothered with a thief."

Brown thought a moment. "Would you call them so I can talk to them?"

"Not me, buster," she replied. "I'm not spending another dime on that kid."

Brown opened a drawer in his desk, took out a small metal box and opened it. Reaching inside he brought out some change.

"What's their number?" he asked, looking at Mabel.

She shrugged her shoulders, opened her purse and began digging through it. It took awhile but she finally found her address book and gave him their number. She watched as he copied it down. He left the office and went over to a wall pay phone in an outer office. They both watched as Brown dialed the phone and began talking to someone. Mabel looked at Jimmy. She shook her head as she headed toward him. Jimmy backed up towards the wall when she got close.

"Stealing again! After all I've done for you. You don't love me and this is what you do to prove it."

"I love you, Mom," Jimmy said. "Don't let them send me away. I don't want to go to Colorado, Mom. I want to stay with you. I won't steal anymore. Honest."

"Don't give me that," she replied. "You've told me that lie once too often. I don't believe you anymore. I know you really don't love me. This is your way of getting back at me for being good to you. Well, that's over. You're going to a juvenile jail. Your grandparents don't want a kid like you. They're dirt poor and barely have enough food for themselves, let alone all the food it takes to feed a kid like you."

Mabel made another move at Jimmy, but he stepped aside and she missed. Just then the door opened behind her and she smiled. Her head was beginning to clear, so she turned and looked at Officer Brown as if nothing happened.

"Jimmy, your grandparents don't have a phone, but they were both at the number your mother gave me. They will be glad to have you come stay with them for a while," Brown said, looking at Mabel for her reaction.

Her face turned red and she looked mad. Then, as quickly as it started it was gone, and she calmed down. "You go ahead and go to them, and stay there," Mabel said looking at Jimmy. "I don't ever want to see you again."

She walked out of the office into the other room. She stopped at the door, turned and looked at Jimmy. Her face was twisted. She was about to cry and stood there fighting what she was doing.

Jimmy's eyes were glued on his mother, standing there grasping the door handle until her knuckles turned white. His heart screamed for her not to go, but not a word came from his lips. Then, with a sad look, he watched his mother jerk open the door and slam it behind her.

Jimmy fought back the tears. This trying to act like a man was getting to him.

Bob walked over to Jimmy. Placing his hand on his shoulder, he stood there looking at him.

"Don't ever be too big to cry, Jimmy," he said. "The toughest guys I know have cried some time during their life. In fact, I cry every now and then myself."

Jimmy couldn't believe what he heard. This big bad cop standing beside him, this guy who had given him a hard time ever since they had met, had the nerve to stand there and tell him that he cries. What kind of a jerk was he? What kind of a jerk did he think Jimmy was?

Bob saw the look on Jimmy's face but he didn't let it stop him. He'd seen it on other kid's faces. "Your grandparents said they would be glad to have you come stay with them for a test period of six months. After that, if you want to come back to Newark, you can. But on the other hand, if you choose to stay with them after the six month trial period, that, too, would be fine with them. You can talk that over with them when the six months is over."

Sitting down in his chair, he motioned for Jimmy to sit down, while he waited for Jimmy's answer. Jimmy sat down, but didn't say a word. He didn't know what to say or do. Bob saw the puzzled look on his face.

"Jimmy, I've seen lots of kids like you pass through here. They come through here by the dozens, and they sit down in the same chair you're sitting in. This I know for sure, Jimmy. If you don't get out of this city, you'll be back. You'll be sitting in that chair, or in that cell downstairs. Is that what you want?"

"No, sir!" Jimmy said, sitting up and wiping his eyes.

"I don't want to see you grow up like you're having to grow up, Jimmy. You won't like the life you're going to have to live if you stay here in Newark. Your grandparents are offering you a chance to change all of that. You're only thirteen years old, and it's hard for you to understand most of this, but you've got some street sense."

"I'd advise you to go out to Colorado and see how it is out there for six months. It will be like a vacation. School's out for the summer tomorrow, and I've found out you're passing all your subjects. I think you'll like it out there, Jimmy. What do you say?"

"Okay," Jimmy said slowly. "I'll try it for six months, Officer Brown."

"The name is Bob, Jimmy," he said. "I feel like you won't ever regret this decision."

Strong Feather

Jimmy looked at the floor and nodded his head, not believing him. He hadn't even left town and was already sorry he said he would go.

"You go home and pack some clothes," Bob said, standing up and smiling. "I'll go get the money your grandparents are sending for your bus ticket. They told me it would take them about an hour to get over to another town where they can send the money. Meet me back here in front of the police station in an hour."

"Yes, sir," Jimmy said, getting up and heading toward the door. He smiled his big smile. "Thanks, Officer Bob."

"That's OK, Jimmy," he replied, walking around the desk and opening the door for him. "See you in an hour."

Jimmy nodded and walked out the door and across the outer office towards the door his mother just went through. Bob stood in his office doorway and smiled as he watched the door close behind Jimmy. "I think I've saved another one," he said to himself. "I sure hope so."

CHAPTER II

Jimmy sat in the alley daydreaming. Shaking his head, his stomach growled as he looked up and down the alley. Nothing moved, and he relaxed. He scratched his head trying to remember why he was there. Then he remembered. Standing up, he walked over to the trash cans. He smiled when he saw his suitcase was where he left it.

Turning around, he walked out of the alley and down the street. He scanned everyone closely. A smile came across his face when he spotted a likely sucker. He walked up to him and asked him for a quarter, but he didn't get any money. He spotted a short fat man in a baggy brown suit and gray hat. He thought about letting him pass, but the hat caught his eye. He turned and looked at him again. The hat looked new, and it matched the man's eyes. The suit and hat didn't match, but that hat made him think twice. He grinned at the sight he saw approaching and decided to try him.

"Hi, Mister," Jimmy said. "Could you spare a little money so I could get something to eat?

The man stopped and looked at him. Jimmy asked again and the man reached into his pocket. Jimmy smiled his big smile knowing he'd found an easy touch. This day wasn't going to be as bad as he thought earlier. With the smile still on his face, he waited.

But instead of money, the man pulled out a badge. He was a cop. "What's the idea of begging on the streets, young man," the officer asked in a gruff voice. "Don't you know it's against the law to beg?"

"No, sir," Jimmy said, knowing he was in trouble again. Why did this have to happen to him, especially, now? He had to get out of this mess, but how? Putting on

26

his sad face, he looked up at the gray eyes under the gray hat.

"What's your name, son?" the officer asked.

"Jimmy Warrior."

"Jimmy Warrior," the officer said slowly. "It seems like I've heard that name before. Have you ever been picked up for begging?"

"No, sir," Jimmy said. He'd been picked up for taking some apples, but not for begging. "I've never been picked up for begging. I just asked you for some money so I could get something to eat. My mom and dad have split and my dad is somewhere in a veterans' hospital in Texas. Sometimes my mom doesn't have any money for food. I just thought maybe you'd give me a little money so I could get me a good meal today."

The officer stood there looking at Jimmy for a few minutes. Then he said, "You know what, Jimmy. I believe your story. My name is Fred Price and I'd like to help. But begging is not the way to get money. You need to work for your money. It makes a man feel better when he earns his own way. Tell you what. You come with me. I know a fellow that can use a young man like you to help him around his place. I was just talking to him this morning about how young people, like yourself, need someone to help them get on their feet."

Jimmy knew there was no way out now. He was stuck. The only thing he could do was go along with the officer. He'd play it out, until he could leave without causing a fuss. The officer put his arm around him as they walked back in the direction the officer came from. It was also the direction he had to go to get to the police station, and away from where he left his suitcase.

The officer did most of the talking as they walked along. He got in a word now and then. Turning a corner, they walked halfway down the block until they came to a small grocery store. Jimmy waited outside while the officer went in and talked to the owner. He had the urge to run but knew he'd better wait. He was hoping the owner was not in.

The officer brought the store owner out to see Jimmy. Jimmy hung his head when he saw him. The owner looked at Jimmy and shook his head.

The officer looked puzzled. "What's the matter, Bill?" he asked.

"This boy has been taking food from me for about a year," the owner said. "I caught him taking food more than once when I owned my other store. I don't think I can use him. It looks like he hasn't changed since then."

The officer looked at Jimmy, then back at the store owner. "It seems to me if he's been taking food for that long, Bill, there's a real problem here. His parents have separated, and he's had to fend for himself. His taking stuff from you for that long a time proves he really does need some help. What do you say?"

"I'll have to think about it," he said. He looked at Jimmy and shook his head. "You come back tomorrow morning and see me. Bright and early when I open, and we'll see. We'll see." He looked at the officer, shook his head, and went back inside.

The officer smiled at Jimmy. "You show up in the morning, Jimmy, and you've got yourself a job."

"Yes, sir," Jimmy said smiling. He felt a little better knowing it would soon be over.

The officer slapped Jimmy on the back and walked off, leaving him standing there. Turning the corner the officer looked back and waved, and was gone. Jimmy gave a sigh of relief. He needed to get his suitcase and hurry over to the police station as quickly as he could. He sure didn't want Officer Brown looking for him.

Strong Feather

Jimmy ran back and grabbed his suitcase from behind the trash cans. With suitcase in hand, he ran towards the police station. He was out of breath before he got there and slowed down to a fast walk, then to a walk.

When he turned the corner next to the police station, there was Officer Brown standing on the steps of the police station, waiting for him. They waved at each other. Bob was standing there with a big smile on his face when Jimmy walked up.

"I'd almost given you up, Jimmy," Bob said. "Everything is in good shape. Your bus leaves in about twenty minutes. We have plenty of time to get there. My car's parked right over there, and I'll drive you to the bus station."

Walking over to his car, he took Jimmy's suitcase and put it on the back seat. They got in front and Bob started the car. He was about to pull out into the street when he had to stop and wait for a car to pass. He pulled out into the traffic and drove off down the street. As they rode along Bob waved at a man walking along the sidewalk.

Rolling his window down he yelled, "Fred! I'll be back in about half hour!"

The man yelled back, "OK, Bob!" then stopped and stared at the two of them. It was the cop who'd gotten Jimmy the job. Jimmy slid down in the seat as they drove on, leaving Fred standing there with his mouth open.

Bob didn't see his partner's face, so he drove on. He told Jimmy about all the good things that could happen to him if he would give it a chance. A second chance, he called it. Jimmy listened the best he could, but his mind wandered. Things happened too fast for him. Bob saw the look in his eyes and laughed.

"You're a daydreamer aren't you, Jimmy?" he asked.

Strong Feather

Jimmy slowly nodded his head. He wasn't sure how the officer felt about people who daydreamed. His teachers in school didn't like daydreamers at all.

Bob laughed. "I'm a daydreamer too, Jimmy. Don't ever quit daydreaming. Just make sure you know that it's a daydream. Don't get it mixed up with the real world. Some of the most important people in this world we live in are daydreamers. That's how many of the things we use everyday were invented. Men thinking about this and that, and how it would work if it was done this way, or that way. Daydreaming is a very important part of our world, so don't ever quit daydreaming. Just do it when you have time. Realize it's a daydream and nothing more. You do that, Jimmy, and you'll go far. You try it and see if I'm not right."

Jimmy listened to every word Bob said. He was told more than once that daydreamers never get anything done, and they spend most of their lives on foolishness. What Officer Brown said made a lot of sense. He felt a little better about himself. Maybe he could daydream at his grandparents. Looking up at Officer Brown, he grinned. Bob grinned back at him, then looked back at the street as he guided the car through the traffic.

When they neared the bus station Bob reached into his shirt pocket, took out a five dollar bill, and gave it to Jimmy. "Here, Jimmy," he said. You're going to need some money on your trip. I can't give you much, but this should help."

Jimmy took the money and looked at it. "Thanks, Officer Brown," he said.

"You're welcome, Jimmy," he replied. "And the name's Bob. Remember?"

"Thanks, Officer Bob," Jimmy said, smiling.

Strong Feather

Glancing over at him, Bob grinned. "That smile on your face is worth it, Jimmy."

They drove toward the bus station not saying a word, just looking at each other, occasionally. A friendship grew in the short time they'd known each other. Bob turned into a parking spot in front of the bus station.

They got out and Jimmy grabbed his suitcase while Bob went into the bus station to get his ticket. When he returned they sat on a bench and waited for the bus. When it came, they walked over and waited for the people to get off. They shook hands and said their good-byes. Jimmy got on and Bob talked to the driver while he found a seat. Sitting down, he watched them and began wondering what the two of them were talking about. He couldn't hear what they were saying, which bothered him. When they finished talking, he saw Bob hand the bus driver something. Giving Jimmy a short wave he stepped off the bus. The driver closed the door, and the bus started moving. Jimmy wondered what Officer Bob gave the driver. It must have been directions on how he was to get to his grandparents' house. He sat back in his seat and sighed. He wasn't sure if he was really ready for the trip to Colorado to begin.

Bob Brown stood on the platform waving at Jimmy as the bus pulled out of the station. Jimmy waved back through the window and smiled. He watched him walk over to his car and get in. The bus turned a corner, and he no longer saw Officer Bob. Turning around in his seat, he looked up at the front of the bus. He saw the driver looking at him in the large overhead mirror. He smiled, then quickly looked away.

Jimmy watched the large buildings pass by. It was familiar to him. He saw two friends he talked to earlier. He waved at them as the bus passed, but all they did was stare back at him. The looks on their faces made him laugh.

Strong Feather

He saw them about an hour earlier on the street. Now he was on a bus leaving town. They stood there looking at the bus go by as if they couldn't believe what they were seeing.

The bus passed through the city to the outskirts of Newark. He didn't know any of the places now. Everything he now saw was new to him. He was excited and scared at the same time. Then they were in the country. The city passed out of sight behind them. As mile after mile sped by, new things popped up everywhere he looked. His stomach growled. He felt for the money Officer Bob gave him. He forgot just how hungry he was. When the bus stopped and the driver told everyone it was a rest stop, Jimmy made his way to the front of the bus.

"How long will it take us to get to Colorado?" he asked the driver.

"Three days," the driver said. "There's a lot of stops between here and there, and you'll have to change buses once. That means you'll be on a bus the rest of today, all of tomorrow, and get there the morning of the next day."

Jimmy couldn't believe what he heard. He walked back to his seat and sat down. He could only get off when he really got hungry. Or maybe he could get someone to buy him a meal. Then he remembered what Officer Bob told him. "Nope," he thought, "no more of that kind of stuff." If I'm going to make this thing work, I've got to start now. Sitting back in his seat, he looked out the window at the people going into the restaurant to eat, and his stomach growled. He closed his eyes tight so he couldn't see them.

Then he felt someone touch him on his shoulder, and he opened his eyes. The bus driver stood next to him.

"Hi," he said. "I'm George Simms, Jimmy. That officer in Newark that put you on the bus is a friend of mine. He asked me to take care of you on this trip, and see that you get at least one good meal a day. Have you eaten today?"

"They gave me breakfast this morning," Jimmy answered.

"Okay," George said. "Let's make a deal. I'll buy your supper today, lunch tomorrow, and I'll see to it you get a good breakfast the next morning. Is it a deal?"

"Yes sir!" Jimmy said with a big smile. His luck and charm still worked, he thought. He'd keep it up and see how far it would take him. If it didn't work out like he wanted, he could always get off the bus. Maybe go down to Texas and see his dad. The idea just popped into his head, as he looked up at the driver. He quickly decided it wasn't too good of an idea.

He followed the bus driver into the restaurant. As they ate they talked, and soon became good friends. When Jimmy told George where his grandparents lived, George told him the bus would be going right through the town where they lived. He told him the bus usually didn't stop there, but he'd talk to the next driver and make sure he stopped and let Jimmy off. That would save his grandparents the trouble of having to drive about twenty miles to the next town to pick him up. "Everything was working out great," Jimmy thought, as he sat there eating. He relaxed a little, knowing things were starting to go his way. It was about time. Jimmy slept good that night as the bus sped along to Colorado.

The next day was a long one for him. The bus he was on was not an express bus. It stopped at every small town it came to. Jimmy spent some of the five dollars Officer Bob gave him for candy. The candy was his breakfast. "I need to make my money last another day," he thought. At one stop, he sat in his seat jingling what was left of his money in his pocket. George saw to it that he had a good lunch. Not realizing it, Jimmy started to enjoy his trip, even though his money was running out. As he thought about his situation, it bothered him. A strong urge came over him to get off the bus and ask someone for money, while they were stopped. Before he knew what he was doing, he was off the bus and inside the station.

Inside, he looked around to see if there was a soft touch in the place. He saw George talking to the ticket agent behind a long desk. His back was to Jimmy and he didn't see him come in. As he looked the place over, the side door opened and a well-dressed man came in. When he saw Jimmy looking at him, he stopped and smiled. Jimmy smiled back and walked over to where the man was standing.

"Could you spare some money so I could get a meal, Mister," Jimmy asked. "I've been riding that bus out there almost two days, and I'd sure like to eat. I'm being sent to live with my grandparents, and they only sent enough money for the ticket for me to get to Colorado."

It was all true and Jimmy knew that it showed in his eyes. The man didn't have a chance, and he knew it. Reaching into his pocket he pulled out a bunch of crumpled up bills. Jimmy saw they were all twenty-dollar bills. Looking over at the ticket counter he saw that George was done talking, and was getting ready to leave. When he looked back, the man was standing real close to him and smiling.

"I've got to go to the restroom first," the man said, "but I'll be right back and get one of these twenties changed. Then I'll give you enough money for a couple of meals, Sonny."

Jimmy flinched when he called him Sonny, but he kept on smiling. "I'll go with you," Jimmy said, leading the way. Opening the door, Jimmy looked over and saw

Strong Feather

George going out the front door while the man walked past him and into the rest room. Before he let the door close he heard the bus start, then drive off, and he closed the door behind him. Turning, he was surprised to find the man standing very close to him again.

"How would you like to have one of these twenties, Sonny?" the man asked, holding one of them out to Jimmy.

Jimmy grabbed it from his hand. "Thanks," Jimmy said, as he turned and ran out of the restroom and through the lobby. He didn't stop. The man started to run after him, but stopped after a few steps. He wanted to yell at him, but didn't, as he watched Jimmy run out the front door. He looked over at the ticket counter and saw the man looking at him. He shrugged his shoulders, and went back into the restroom. The man at the ticket booth watched as Jimmy ran down the road in the direction the bus went. He watched until he disappeared around a corner.

Jimmy stopped when he realized the man wasn't chasing him. Breathing hard, he put the twenty-dollar bill in his right front pants pocket and smiled. As he walked along, he patted it to make sure it was still there. "I can go a long ways on twenty dollars," he thought. When it was gone he'd get another one just like he got this one. He felt good about himself and how he outsmarted that man at the bus station.

Stopping at a gas station near the edge of town he got a U. S. map. He didn't open it until he was at the edge of town. Standing beside the city limits sign, he read out loud, "Weber City Limits." Opening the map he looked and looked, but couldn't find a town by that name. Folding the map up, he didn't know what to do. "Must be a jerk town," he thought "It's not even on the map." He saw another sign further down the highway. He took off running towards it.

Strong Feather

When he reached the sign he was out of breath. He ran more today than he had in a long time. After a couple deep breaths, he looked at the sign. It read, "Springfield 30 miles." Opening the map, he looked for the name of the town on the sign. Then he saw the name and smiled. Springfield was in the state of Illinois. He saw a red line on the map that went from Springfield down to Texas. Looking closer, he found the city of Big Spring in the state of Texas. Smiling, he folded the map and put it in his back pocket. His dad was at the VA Hospital in Big Spring, Texas. Wouldn't he be surprised when his boy walked in and hugged him?

Jimmy walked along the dirt road and he felt good. His thoughts were about how he always came out on top. All he had to do was catch a couple of good rides, and he'd be in Texas. His steps slowed down after a couple of miles. Instead of a smile, there was now a frown on his forehead that wouldn't go away. There were hardly any cars on the road. The few people who passed honked their horns and waved as they sped by. A couple of times he heard them yelling at him to get off the road. He wondered if he ever would get a ride.

Hearing a car approaching, he turned around. Sticking out his thumb, he smiled real big. When he heard the car motor slow and the car began to stop, he knew he had a ride. But when the car pulled up beside him, he saw a police officer sitting inside. There on the side of the car was a big star with words that read "Illinois State Police,"

"Get in the car, Jimmy," the officer said, opening the door for him.

"Yes, sir," he replied, getting in and shutting the door. How did he know his name, he wondered?

"What happened back at the bus station?" the officer asked, as they drove off down the road.

Strong Feather

"I went to the bathroom back there in Weber," Jimmy said, "and the bus drove off and left me."

The officer glanced over at him but didn't say a word. It was a short answer, with no fear, which made it a believable answer. Silence followed as they rode along. It was a good half hour before the Springfield city limits sign came into view. When they passed it the car slowed down. As the police car made its way through the city the officer looked over at Jimmy.

"You gave that bus driver quite a scare, Jimmy," he said. "I'll bet he checks his passengers better from now on."

"Yes, Sir," Jimmy said. With that said the officer's attention returned to his driving. Jimmy didn't say anything else. He'd done it again and only he knew it. They pulled up in front of the bus station and stopped. Jimmy could see his bus sitting inside the bus parking area. George Simms came running out of the bus station when they got out.

"Jimmy," he said. "Boy, am I glad to see you. What happened?"

"You drove off and left the kid in the restroom," the officer said.

"I'm sorry, Officer," George said. "It won't happen again. I'll check each one of my passengers from now on. I'll make sure they're all on the bus before I move that bus one foot."

"You'd better," the officer replied. He got back into his car and started it. Looking at Jimmy he smiled, gave him a short wave/salute, and drove off.

"Let's get on the bus, Jimmy," George said, as they turned and walked over to the bus. "I'm about an hour behind schedule, but I can make it up if we get started right now."

George got on the bus first and closed the door behind Jimmy. The bus moved before he was up the steps.

Strong Feather

Jimmy walked down the aisle and looked at everyone as the bus drove out of the station. Some people spoke to him and told him they were glad he was all right. Others looked and shook their heads. An hour delay makes most people mad. When he sat down, the lady sitting across the aisle reached over and patted him on the arm and smiled at him.

"Don't worry about the sour apples on the bus, Jimmy. We're glad nothing happened to you back there," she said.

"Thanks," Jimmy replied, feeling a little better, but down deep inside he wasn't feeling too good. He hoped he would be on his way to Texas by now, riding along in someone's big car, telling the driver a big story to make him feel sorry for him. Instead, he was back on the bus headed for Colorado. Jimmy wasn't sure he wanted to go to Colorado, but that was where he was headed. He'd have to make his mind up on what to do after he got there. He knew he wouldn't get another chance to leave the bus like he did in Weber. All he could do now was wait and see what happened.

At one of the stops George came back to Jimmy and said, "Well, Jimmy. This is where you get a new driver. His name is Sam Brack. I've talked to him, and he'll see that you get a good breakfast tomorrow morning. He also told me he'd let you off in Mercer, Colorado, where your grandparents live. I want you to know it has been a real pleasure knowing you. I also want you to know that Officer Bob Brown and I will be thinking about you."

"I won't let you down," Jimmy said, sticking out his hand. They shook hands and George winked at him.

"I know you won't, Jimmy," he said, smiling. He walked back down the aisle and started to get off, but stopped. Turning, he gave Jimmy the thumbs up sign, then got off. The new driver came up the steps and sat down. He nodded at Jimmy in the mirror as he put the bus in gear and slowly moved out of the station.

This bus trip was turning out to be quite an adventure for Jimmy. An adventure he didn't dream would happen to him. Through the bus windows he saw places he never knew existed. From large cities with big buildings, to little towns with only a couple of stores. Then the prairies came into view, stretching out as far as he could see. Mile after mile went by with nothing in sight but wheat fields. The wind moved across the large wheat fields like ocean waves. Occasionally, a farmer's house appeared in that ocean of wheat, then quickly disappeared behind them as they passed.

When evening came, the bus driver turned on the lights. Sitting back in his seat, Jimmy's mind flitted from one thing to another. Lots of things happened that day and he was tired. It wasn't long until sleep enfolded him like a warm hug. The purr of the bus' engine lulled him to sleep. The uncertainty of what lay ahead of him slowly faded from his mind.

Jimmy awoke early the next morning. The sun that went down in front of them the night before, now came up behind them. He watched as the shadow of the bus raced along the side of the road outside his window. The scenery changed from the wide-open spaces to farmland. Off to the left side of the bus, he saw mountains rising high above the prairie. On top of the mountains he saw that snow capped the upper parts of the highest peaks.

He had trouble seeing them through the windows across the aisle. Getting up, he found a vacant seat on the other side of the bus. The mountains slowly grew as the bus sped along. Jimmy watched as the clouds moved over the tops of the mountains, slowly covering them in their embrace. He felt a lot better about coming to Colorado. It looked like it might be a real nice place. A lot nicer than he thought before. "It couldn't be all bad," he thought. He was born in Denver.

As the bus purred along, he saw they were coming to a big city. He looked out the window and saw a road sign ahead. He returned to his seat just in time to read it, "Denver City Limits." He returned to the city where he was born. He hadn't thought about it until now. He remembered his mother telling him where he was born. It was strange how he forgot about it until now.

Memories flooded his mind as he looked out the window. His mom was born in Taos, New Mexico, and was a full blood Taos Pueblo Indian. His dad, Tommy, was born in Mercer, Colorado, and he, too, was of the Taos Pueblo Indian tribe. Tommy's parents moved to Mercer not long before Tommy was born. He and Mabel met when Tommy's parents, Tom Sr. and Alice, visited some friends and relatives in Taos one summer. He went along for the ride.

Tommy was sent home from Midway Island at the start of World War II. He was wounded and sent back to Hawaii for recuperation. It was there they found out that he suffered from severe shell shock and was sent home on leave. The Denver VA Hospital doctors decided he should not return to active duty, and he was discharged.

They sent him home to forget about the things that happened during the war. He discovered that his being at home and around loved ones helped him a lot. But he still had bad dreams. It was hard, but he slowly put it out of his mind. Tommy and Mabel met and fell in love in Taos, New Mexico, and were married. A year later Jimmy was born in Denver, where Tommy found work.

Strong Feather

Remembering what his mother told him made him feel good. Denver was his hometown. Now everything outside the window took on a new meaning. He was surprised at how nice and clean Denver looked. The bus continued moving through the downtown area. When they came to the station, the bus pulled in and everyone got off.

Sam Brack took Jimmy inside and bought his breakfast. Sam told him it wasn't much farther to the small town of Mercer where his grandparents lived. The excitement that he held back began to show, and he started fidgeting in his chair.

When they got back on the bus, Jimmy sat up front behind Sam. It wasn't long until the bus moved through the streets of Denver. When they were finally out of town, he read each city limits sign that came into view expecting it to be the one he was looking for. When the Mercer sign finally appeared, he was ready for it. He paid no attention to the size of the town; he was only thinking of seeing his grandma and grandpa.

When the bus finally stopped, Jimmy was standing up waiting for Sam to open the door. When he did, Jimmy ran down the steps and got off. He waited for Sam to get his suitcase out from under the bus.

Sam set the air brakes and headed down the steps after Jimmy. He opened the first large bay door on the side of the bus and got Jimmy's suitcase and handed it to him. They shook hands, and Sam wished him good luck. Sam got back on the bus and closed the door. There was a hiss of air as he took off the brake, the engine roared, and the bus moved past Jimmy. He watched it disappear down the road.

With a big smile on his face he turned to look at where he was. The smile disappeared, his chin dropped, and his mouth fell open. He just stood there not believing

41

his eyes. Looking up the street, he only saw two stores.
Looking closer he saw there was a bank and a drugstore in
between them. On the next block he saw a filling station
and a post office. The other buildings on both sides of the
street were beer joints. Directly across the street was a Red
& White Store, with a hardware store on the corner. He
stood there shaking his head, wondering why he got off the
bus. This was hard to believe.

To top it all, there was no one there to meet him,
and he didn't know where to go. Not wanting to stand there
beside the road all day, he started across the street. He'd
ask someone in one of the beer joints where his
grandparents lived. Everyone in a hick town like this
should know everyone else, he thought.

He walked across the street carrying his suitcase,
when something hit him. A sharp pain shot across his back
and up to his neck to his head. Dropping his suitcase, he
stood there in the middle of the street grabbing at his back.
Looking down he saw a large rock lying on the pavement
beside him.

"Get out of our town, punk!" someone yelled
behind him.

Looking in the direction the yelling came from,
Jimmy ducked as another rock whizzed past his head.
Grabbing his suitcase, he ran across the street and headed
towards the nearest building. There were two guys across
the street throwing rocks at him. He stopped at the door of
the first building he came to and looked back at them. To
his surprise they stopped and shook their fists at him. They
laughed, turned and ran off. To his amazement they both
disappeared down a small gully along the side of the road.
He didn't see the gully when he got off the bus. They took
advantage of it to hide in. "What a couple of nuts," he
thought, shaking his head.

Strong Feather

He plopped down on his suitcase. His back throbbed. He wished he had never seen this stupid place. Who'd want it anyway? He looked up and down the street to make sure there were no more nuts running loose. A guy beat him up for working his turf in the big city. He understood that. But he didn't do anything to these two jerks. He got off the bus in this hick town, and was already in trouble. It didn't make sense.

Thoughts ran through his mind of doing what they yelled at him to do. Maybe it would be best to go on down the road and forget his promise to Officer Bob. Then, for some unknown reason, he had a feeling that something was wrong. He froze where he was sitting. Somehow he knew there was someone standing behind him.

A gruff voice caused chills to run all over him. "What do you want here young man? We don't allow runaways to stay in our town. We put them in jail."

The hair on the back of his neck stood up. He was so close Jimmy could hear him breathing. Slowly he turned around to see who it was behind him. Every time he turned around lately, he was in trouble. A minute ago it was two guys throwing rocks at him, and now it was the law. He wondered why they quit chasing him, and now he knew. He was in this hick town less than five minutes, and they were going to put him in jail. "What kind of a crummy place was this Mercer, Colorado?" he asked himself.

CHAPTER III

There was fear in Jimmy's eyes when he turned around to see who was behind him. To his surprise he saw a man with a kind, elderly face looking at him. He was tall, with wavy gray hair and dark brown eyes. Instead of a scowl on his face, there was a smile. The fear in Jimmy's eyes faded as he realized the man kidded him about putting him in jail.

Jimmy stood up and smiled, then looked at the old man's face again. A big smile appeared. That did it. It was only then that Jimmy realized it was his grandpa, Tom.

"Jimmy," Tom said, grabbing and hugging him.

"Grandpa," Jimmy replied, hugging him back. "Boy, am I glad it's you. I thought I was in big trouble when those guys started throwing rocks and yelling at me."

"I did too, Jimmy," Tom replied. "I was standing inside and saw what happened. I walked out the door and they ran off" He started to release his hold on Jimmy, then hugged him even tighter. "I sure am glad to see you."

Jimmy found it hard to breathe, but he wasn't going to miss this chance of being hugged. It was a long time since anyone hugged him, and it felt good.

Finally, they let go of each other. Stepping back, they looked at one another. Tears appeared in his grandpa's eyes. Jimmy was about to ask him what was wrong, but his eyes started to turn moist also.

"Well, Jimmy," Tom said. "Looks like you caught me working. I was supposed to meet you in Longmont at the bus station, but I've got the job cleaning up all of the beer joints in town. I was hurrying as fast as I could so we'd be able to pick you up on time. It looks like I don't have the speed I once had, doesn't it?" Tom paused as he looked across the road. "That bus driver must have let you off when he went through here a couple of minutes ago. I heard it take off, but didn't think a thing about it."

"He sure did, Grandpa," Jimmy said, as they walked inside. Jimmy sat on a stool and talked as his grandpa finished cleaning up. He told him a few things that happened to him on the trip. When he finished, he looked over at his grandpa and saw him frowning. "What's the matter, Grandpa?" he asked.

"I've never seen those two boys treat anyone like they treated you, Jimmy," he replied, rubbing his chin. "I'm going to have a good long talk with them. They can be kind of mean if they want, Jimmy. Especially, when they decide they don't like someone."

Jimmy flinched as he felt the large welt where he was hit with the rock. If they were the "kind of mean guys" around there, he'd hate to meet the mean ones.

Tom saw the pain on Jimmy's face and started to ask him about it, then changed his mind. "I've got something for you, Jimmy. I was going to give it to you when we picked you up at the bus station, but I'll give it to you now."

He walked over to a nearby table, picked up a paper sack, reached inside and brought out a baseball cap. It was black with large orange letters across the front that read, "Tigers". He handed it to Jimmy. "Here's a small present from me to you. It's a Mercer High baseball cap. Do you like baseball?"

"Yeah. Thanks, Grandpa," Jimmy said, taking the cap and putting it on his head. Pulling it down, he bent the bill a little. "It fits real good."

"Sure am glad of that," Tom replied. He winked at his grandson. "I sure wouldn't want you to have a baseball cap that didn't fit."

Strong Feather

Jimmy was about to agree when a car pulled up to the curb outside. The driver rolled down his window and sat there.

They both walked outside and over to the car. The driver stuck his head out the window. "You ready to go, Tom?"

"Nope," Tom said, looking at him. He then looked at Jimmy and grinned.

"What do you mean, nope?" the man asked, with a strange look on his face. "We're running late as it is. That bus went flying through here a while ago. I heard it go by while I was working in the back of my shop. We'll have to hurry to catch it. It had to run early today."

"Don't get yourself in an uproar, Bill," Tom said. "This is my grandson, Jimmy, standing here. The bus driver stopped and let him off. So we don't have to go to Longmont and pick him up after all." Turning, he looked at Jimmy. "Jimmy, this is my good friend, Bill Wilson."

Bill smiled, pulled his head back inside the car, and stuck his hand out. "I sure am glad to meet you, Jimmy,"

Jimmy stepped up to the car and shook the man's hand. "Thank you, sir," he said. Jimmy looked at his grandpa, then at Mr. Wilson. "This isn't a very large town, is it?"

"No it's not, Jimmy," Bill said, looking at Tom, then at Jimmy. "But it'll grow on you. You'll see. Just give it a chance." He put the car in gear and smiled. "I'll see you two later; I've got work to do." He honked his horn as he drove off. He turned around at the corner and headed back in the direction he came from.

They both waved at him and watched him drive down the street to his filling station. Jimmy looked at his grandpa and asked, "Where's Grandma?"

Strong Feather

"Oh, she's at home waiting for us to bring you back from Longmont. I'd better get someone to go over and tell her you're here. Better still. Why don't you just go on over to the house and surprise her?"

"That a great idea, Grandpa," Jimmy said, his spirits picking up. He needed something after all that happened to him.

Tom told him how to get to the house and assured him he'd be along as soon as he finished. Jimmy hugged his grandpa again. Picking up his suitcase, he walked down the street. As he neared the filling station, he could see that there was no one in the office. The sign across the front of the building read, "Wilson's Service Station." This had to be the place where Mr. Wilson turned in. Hearing a strange pounding noise, he stopped and listened. As he stood there listening, he realized it was someone pounding on something in the back of the shop building next to the station. Then it stopped. A few seconds later Mr. Wilson came walking out of the shop building holding a large hammer in both hands.

"Hello again," Bill said, smiling at Jimmy. Mr. Wilson was not a small man. He was only five feet eight inches tall, but was big all over. His hair was a salt and pepper color, and he had steel-blue eyes. There was a stern look in his eyes that went along with his weathered face.

Jimmy couldn't say a word. He started backing up with his mouth open. He tried to say something, but no words came out. "What's the matter, Jimmy?" Bill asked, watching Jimmy back away from him. Then he realized he was holding his hammer up in front of him as he walked toward Jimmy. With a little laugh the hardness in his eyes left, and a smile appeared on his face. He put the hammer behind his back. "Sorry," he said.

Strong Feather

Jimmy stopped. He too gave a little laugh as he walked over to where Mr. Wilson was standing. Being hit with a rock put him on edge, and he sure didn't want to be hit with a hammer.

"What's the matter, Jimmy?" Bill asked. "You acted as if I was going to hit you with this hammer." He brought the hammer out from behind his back and set it on the floor next to the bench by the door. "Let's sit down here and talk a little, Jimmy. We need to get to know each other."

Jimmy started to sit down, then stopped. He was supposed to be on his way to see his grandma.

"Your grandmother, Alice, can wait a couple of minutes, Jimmy," Bill said, seeming to know his thoughts. "Set your suitcase down and come over here and sit next to me." Bill sat down and gave a big sigh of relief. "It sure feels good to get the weight off my poor old feet. Come on over here and do the same."

"Yes, Sir," Jimmy said, with a grin. "This sure is a strange place," he thought, as he set his suitcase down next to the hammer. He looked over at Mr. Wilson and smiled. He could get to like this place a little more than he did if more people were like him. He could do without those two that greeted him.

Bill listened as Jimmy told him about his experience with the two who hit him in the back with a rock when he got off the bus. "It still hurts, Sir." Jimmy said, rubbing his back.

"The name is Mr. Wilson, Jimmy," Bill said slowly, as he thought about what he just heard.

"Yes, Sir, I mean Mr. Wilson," Jimmy replied. That brought a smile from Bill, which quickly left. He was irritated by what Jimmy just told him.

As they talked, Jimmy looked up and saw the two guys who hit him with the rock. They were on the other

Strong Feather

side of the street. The skinny one saw Jimmy and pointed at him. They both stopped and smiled. Seeing Mr. Wilson sitting with him, they quickly stepped between two buildings and were gone. Jimmy felt uneasy about the place again, especially, with those two troublemakers running around town.

Bill didn't see them, and Jimmy wasn't about to tell him. Jimmy stood up and acted like he had to go, but Bill put his hand on his shoulder and sat him down. Bill smiled at him and stood up. Stepping inside the door of his office, he opened the lid on the pop box and took out two big Nesbitt Orange soft drinks. He opened them on the side of the box, and came back and sat down. Handing one of them to Jimmy, he tipped the other one up and took a big drink.

Jimmy did the same, and was surprised how good it tasted. That was his first taste of a Nesbitt Orange, but one he would look forward to. From that day on, Jimmy saved every penny he got until he had five. He then found some excuse to return to Mr. Wilson's pop box and get himself another Nesbitt Orange drink.

When Jimmy drank the last drop of his soda pop, he thanked Mr. Wilson. "I've got to go, Mr. Wilson. Thanks for the soda pop."

"You're more than welcome, Jimmy," Bill said. "I'll see you later." He took Jimmy's bottle and disappeared through the door.

Jimmy felt a lot better. Picking up his suitcase, he walked down the road. When he reached the last street, he turned right, but kept looking around to see if those two guys were following him. There was no one in sight, so he kept walking. There were no buildings past the last street of Mercer, and the street was dirt. He saw an old-looking house at the end of the street. That had to be the place where his grandparents lived. It was run down and needed painting, but the yard was nice and he could see a small garden on the right side of the house. There were two fruit trees by the garden that were starting to bloom, which made the place look some better.

He looked beyond the house at the end of the street. Behind their house he saw an open field. There were trees off in the distance that followed the wanderings of a small creek. On the far side of the creek the ground gently rose upward to meet nearby rolling hills that stretched off into the distance. His eyes followed the hills on an upward march until they encountered the majesty of the mountains. The Colorado Rocky Mountains Range, rising upward into a deep blue Colorado sky. "They are an awesome sight," he thought. As he neared the house he stopped. Jimmy didn't know that much about mountains, and not knowing things bothered him. While deep in thought, he became aware of someone yelling.

Lowering his eyes, he saw his grandma running down the steps toward him. Her arms were open, and she was yelling, "Jimmy, Jimmy, Jimmy. My beautiful Jimmy! You're here. Oh, my heart jumps for joy within me!" she exclaimed, as tears filled her eyes. "Your Grandpa has already left to go get you, but he'll be back soon. Come in the house and we'll wait for him. I've got cookies and milk for you. I just got through making them and they're still warm." She didn't let Jimmy answer as she stood there hugging him.

"Come in, Jimmy. I'm so glad you've come to live with us. Come on now," she said, as she stood there talking and hugging him. He couldn't move, or say anything if he wanted to. She was kind of plump, and the Indian in her showed. Her long black hair and black eyes left little doubt in people's minds that she was Indian.

Strong Feather

Being Indian caused some problems for the Warrior family when they first moved to Mercer. Some of the people didn't like Indians, and they let the Warriors know they didn't. But now, the majority of the people in Mercer didn't think of them as Indians, just good friends and neighbors.

When Alice finally let go of Jimmy, she grabbed his hand and began pulling him and his suitcase back up the steps she just ran down. Jimmy didn't resist as he followed her. She opened the door, and they went inside and into the kitchen.

She was laughing and singing and having a grand time as she set a big plate of cookies and a glass of milk on the table. "There you are, Jimmy. I hope you still like oatmeal cookies with raisins."

"I sure do, Grandma," Jimmy said, with a big smile. He set his suitcase on the floor next to the table. "They're my favorite. You found my weakness right off."

They laughed as they took turns talking. Jimmy told his grandma that the bus driver stopped and left him off, and how his grandpa surprised him. He met Mr. Wilson and they had a good talk. Jimmy began to relax and liked the feeling. He looked around the house and it was spotless. There was a big difference between the inside and the outside of the house.

Alice watched her grandson look around the house and knew what he thought. "You may have to change some of your habits while you're living here with us, Jimmy," she said. "But I'll try and make it as easy as I can on you. You can see I keep a clean house. I know some dirt will find its way into the house, no one can keep it all out. But if we work at keeping it as clean as we can, the rest will take care of itself. There are a few rules that I will expect you to keep. I've written them down on a piece of paper and put it

Strong Feather

on your desk in your room. You may have a little trouble following them, but we'll work it out. I believe you'll like it a lot better than with no rules at all. You'll see," she said, with a smile.

Jimmy ate almost all of the cookies, and his glass was empty. As he looked at his grandma, he wondered what he was getting himself into. He went along with it for a while, but would have to think about following a bunch of rules.

"I'll do my best, Grandma," he said, knowing that was what she wanted to hear. "Can I have some more milk?"

Alice smiled. Taking both of his hands in hers, she looked him in the eye. "There's one thing that you must know right off, Jimmy. Your grandpa only works three days a week, and only for a few hours. He doesn't make much money. We sent almost all the money we had for you to come stay with us. We know you're at a turning point in your life and need help. We're glad we could do it, and we would do it again, but we have to live within our income. I must ask you to think about that when it comes to food."

Alice paused as she looked at her grandson. "We eat good when your grandpa gets paid, and then we taper off until he gets paid again. I'll put plenty of food on the table for you to eat. It may not be something you're used to, or something you like, but it will be filling and it will be healthy. I can give you a half glass, but we must save the rest for your breakfast."

Jimmy was saddened by what his grandma said. He was in the same situation he was in back home. His mom was right. He wouldn't have much to eat when he got hungry.

"I don't want to be a burden on you and Grandpa," Jimmy said, looking around the kitchen. This food

Strong Feather

problem, plus the problem of the two guys wanting him to leave town, bothered him. He didn't know what to do, and started to stand up.

A gentle, but firm hand on his shoulder stopped him. "You're not a burden," Alice said. "You are the light of our eyes. Our future. You have always been. You carry the proud name, Warrior. You're part of us. Don't ever forget that. Whatever you do, always remember this is your home, just like it was your father's. When the time comes, you may want to stay and finish growing up here. If you do, tell us. You'll have a home here for life. If it's no, then you'll have to go back East to where your mother lives. See with your heart, Jimmy. Always see with your heart. Even when someone breaks it, see with your heart and love them. You'll never go wrong when you do."

Jimmy felt his grandma's love for him, and again his eyes became moist. He decided he wouldn't ever cry like he did in jail. He was through doing that. "Thanks, Grandma," he said. "I'll try my best to like it here."

"You'll find a different kind of life around here, Jimmy. But it's a good life. You'll have to take care of yourself. No one else can do that for you. Your dad loved it here. His going off to that war changed him. He never adjusted to the small town life after that. I'm hoping it will work in reverse for you. I hope that your coming from the big city life to our small town life will be just what you need. Your roots are here, Jimmy, and here they will always be. You can grow into a big, strong tree around here, one that can stand up to the storms of life. Or you can become a weak tree, one where the slightest of winds that blow in your life will uproot you. You must decide. Come, my Jimmy, let me show you your room."

Jimmy picked up his suitcase and followed her down a hallway to the back of the house. There were three doors at the end of the hallway. Alice opened the one on his right. "This is the bathroom," she said. "You can put your toothbrush and things on that shelf by the mirror."

Closing the bathroom door, she opened the one across the hall. "The other door goes outside to the back yard," she said, going into the room. Jimmy followed her, looking around the room. "This room was your dad's, but it's now yours, Jimmy."

Pride showed in his face. "His dad's room," he thought. This was great. Putting his suitcase down, he grabbed his grandma and hugged her, and she hugged him back. Alice brushed a few strands of his hair back on his forehead, and hugged him again.

When they both had a good hug, they let go. They stood in the middle of the room looking around. "The rules I told you about are on your desk there by the window. You can put your clothes in that closet, and your underclothes and socks and things in the chest of drawers against the wall. I'll leave you alone for a while. It'll take some time for you to get that done. You relax a little from your trip. I'll call you when supper is ready."

They hugged each other before she left the room. When she left, Jimmy realized he was kind of light-headed. He was used to living at sea level. This mountain altitude was getting to him. He shook his head to clear it. On each wall in his room were pictures of different kinds of birds. Each picture was labeled. Walking over to one of them he read the label, "Bald Eagle." Another was a falcon hawk, and the rest were pigeons. "They sure are beautiful," he thought, as he looked at them. Then he wondered why there were so many pictures of birds in this room. His grandma said it used to be his dad's.

As his eyes scanned the pictures, he had a hard time trying to figure it out, especially what happened to him.

Strong Feather

Three days ago he walked down the streets in Newark, New Jersey. Now, he was in Mercer, Colorado. His mother's face came to mind. Being away from her was a new experience for him. He felt a strange longing to see her. He started getting homesick. All of the memories and all the good times they had together flooded his mind. He longed to be back home with her. Then he thought about his friends back there, and felt sick at his stomach. They weren't like those two guys he ran into here in Mercer. For some reason they had it in for him. But why? He would leave this place the first chance he got. Then he remembered what Officer Brown told him, and it irritated him. Coming out here was supposed to be the best thing for him, a chance to get his life straightened out. It sure didn't look like it was working out like Officer Bob told him.

He tossed his cap on the chair next to his bed, picked up his suitcase and threw it on the bed. He opened it, took out a handful of clothes, walked over to the chest of drawers and opened the top drawer. He stuffed them into it and closed the drawer. He walked over to the desk and looked at the paper with all the rules on it. This was too much, having to follow a bunch of silly rules. They were just another good reason for him to leave. He picked up the list and read silently:

1. Keep your room neat and clean.
2. Put dirty clothes in clothes hamper on back porch.
3. When you are dirty, take a bath.
4. Chores will be done before you play.
5. Make your bed when you get up each morning.
6. After bed is made, do not lie on it.
7. Hang your clothes in the closet.

Jimmy looked at the paper for a few minutes. "Chores," he thought, "What a drag." He had to make up his bed, and then not lie on it after it was made. Where was he going to lie down if he couldn't lie on his bed?

He picked up his suitcase and placed it on the chair next to the bed. Then he remembered his hat. He found it on the bed and tossed it onto the top of the desk.

He straightened the quilt, then stepped back and looked at it. He couldn't see an imprint where the suitcase had been. Looking closer at the quilt, he noticed all the different colors. To his surprise, he saw it was a picture of a large bird. His grandma probably made the quilt for his dad.

He placed the paper back on the top of his desk. He took the rest of his clothes out of his suitcase, put some in the chest of drawers, and the rest he hurriedly hung in the closet. Closing his suitcase, he shoved it under the bed. He then went to the desk, sat down and looked out the window. All the unrest that boiled up inside him began to leave. Across the field behind the house was a small creek. There were cottonwood trees along its banks. Beyond the creek, hills stretched off into the distance, and there above the hills were the overpowering Rocky Mountains. He saw snow high up on their peaks, which gave them a look of greatness. He wondered how a place like this could make him feel like he did. It was only a few minutes earlier when he hated this place. Now, he had second thoughts about it. This switching back and forth of his emotions bothered him. Looking out the window cleared his mind and he felt good.

The boy inside of him who liked to sit and daydream was emerging. He found the perfect place to sit and let his mind wander. He could imagine all kinds of things looking out that window. Somewhere tucked away in the back of his mind were forgotten childhood memories of the times when he visited his grandparents. His recollection of those days were lost a long time ago. On the bus trip to Colorado he often wondered why his grandparents never moved away from this place. Now he knew. A dreamy look came into his eyes.

Maybe it would happen to him and he would never want to leave either. As his mind raced, it stopped with a jerk when he remembered the two guys who hit him with a rock. The dreamy look in his eyes left. There was nothing to do in this hick town. They didn't have a movie house, or a place where he could play pin ball machines. He'd be bored stiff if he stayed around this place. He found himself wanting to stay, and wanting to go.

All kinds of ideas came to mind as he sat there looking out that window. Getting up, he grabbed his cap, opened his door, and peeked down the hall. His grandma was nowhere in sight. Quietly he closed his door, opened the back door and stepped out onto a screened-in porch. Closing the door behind him, he quickly opened the screen door and down the steps he went. There was no one around, so he took off running towards the trees along the creek. When he got to the creek he stopped and rested. Below he saw a small stream of water. So, down the bank he went on the run. When he reached the bottom, he tried to jump across the narrow stream of water, but lost his balance. Both feet landed in the middle of the creek and the water splashed all over him. Stepping up onto the bank, he was wet up to his arm pits. He made his way up the other bank and onto the grassy hill a ways from where he lay down. He was wet all over, but it felt good. "It was almost like going swimming," he thought, as he wiped his face with his wet sleeve. Then he heard a loud noise. His body jerked, but instead of drying off he was getting wetter. There was another loud noise, which caused him to sit up.

Strong Feather

Jimmy's head slowly cleared, and he realized he was sitting up with his hands full of grass. Water dripped off the end of his nose. The once tall grass that surrounded him was now being bent over by a blowing rain. It must have just started raining, and he was getting wet. He was dreaming again, but it seemed so real. His head cleared as the rain pelted his face. It was only then he knew where he was.

Jimmy saw his grandparents' house on the other side of the creek. He stood up and looked around. A loud clap of thunder behind him was all it took. Jimmy was off and running. He ran down the hill towards the creek. He didn't have any trouble jumping the creek this time, as on he ran. A couple of minutes later he stood inside the screened-in back porch watching it rain. Opening the back door, he peeked in. His grandma was nowhere in sight, so he slipped into his room and closed the door. He looked to see if anything changed. It looked the same as he left it. Taking off his cap, he beat it against his pants to get the water off of it. He put it on top of his chest of drawers to dry, then went over and sat down at the desk. It felt good, sitting there in wet clothes, watching the raindrops pelting the window panes. The gentle tapping sound of rain falling soothed his nerves. It was a long day, especially for this thirteen-year old Indian.

The mood swings he had of staying, or going, were getting to him. In the last three days he was pulled apart on what to do. He had never had to make decisions like these before, and he found it hard to deal with them.

Putting his arms on the desk, he lowered his head onto them. He forgot all about his wet clothes. He would deal with that later. Jimmy's eyes closed again, and was asleep.

CHAPTER IV

A knocking on the door brought Jimmy out of his deep sleep. He sat at the desk and looked around the semi-dark room trying to figure out where he was. Being in a strange place caused his stomach to tighten. Panic quickly rose within. Was he still in jail? Then he relaxed: the bus ride, Mercer, Colorado, his grandparents, the hill, and this room ... once his dad's. As he looked around, he saw his grandma standing in the open door.

"Your grandpa's home, Jimmy," Alice said, "and supper is just about ready. I came in earlier to check on you and you were asleep. Could you come into the kitchen and talk to us? We can talk while I finish getting supper ready. We'd like for you to tell us all about your trip, and your plans about what you want to do while you're here."

Jimmy rubbed his eyes. He was still half asleep as he followed Alice down the hall and into the kitchen. His grandpa was at the table when he came into the kitchen. Tom got up and they hugged again. Stepping back, he looked at his grandson.

"We surely are glad you came to stay with us, Jimmy," he said. "It sure was a nice surprise to see you like that this morning. It not only made it easier on me, it made it easier on Bill Wilson. I stopped by his garage, and he told me you stopped and talked to him on your way over here. Sure am glad you're making friends like that, Jimmy. It shows that you care for people, and people like that. There's not too many people that live here in Mercer, as you noticed when you got off the bus. But the few we have in this town are good people."

"Yes, Sir," Jimmy said, to be nice. But in the back of his mind he remembered the two troublemakers and how they greeted him when he got off the bus.

59

Strong Feather

"Mr. Wilson told me to come by and see him anytime I wanted," Jimmy said. "He said he was glad I got off the bus like I did. We sat around and talked, then he gave me a orange soda pop, then we talked some more. Boy, that was a good soda pop."

"What kind of soda pop did you have?" Tom asked.

"Nesbitt Orange," Jimmy replied. "It was the best I have ever tasted."

"They are good, Jimmy," Tom agreed, "but I think Bill's just about as good as a cold Nesbitt Orange soda pop. Don't you agree, Alice?"

"Most of the time," Alice said, laughing. Tom looked at her and chuckled.

Jimmy smiled. The two of them were kind of funny, plus they liked each other. He liked them, too. Comparing Mr. Wilson to a soda pop, he thought, and he shook his head.

"It's okay being here," Jimmy said, "but I don't know what I'm going to do around here. There's nothing to do."

"You just take it easy, Jimmy," Tom said. "Don't get all excited or upset about what you're going to do around here. It will all work out. You've got to look around a little and see what we have to offer. That takes time. Like I always say, if there's one thing we got plenty of around here, it's time. No one around here is going to get after you. No one except maybe your grandma, if you don't follow her rules." He looked at Alice and smiled, but it didn't work. She shook her head at his remark as she continued getting supper ready.

"We know we don't have all of the things to offer you like the big city. But, it just might surprise you to find out what we do have. We have great beauty around here, Jimmy. Colorado is one of the most beautiful places I know, especially around here. It'll grow on you if you let it. Like I said, it just takes time.'

'You're wound up tight like a spring about ready to break. Get that unrest out of your inner self. Get to know the people around here. They're good people, even those two who gave you a bad time this morning. Be friendly to them, and the others around here, and they'll become your friends. We know how it is not to be liked, Jimmy. Some of the people around here didn't like us when we first moved here, but we liked them, and now we're all friends. It didn't happen overnight, but we worked at it. In showing them that we cared, we made friends with all but a few. There will always be those who don't want to be friends with anybody, " she said.

Tom added, "Your Grandma and I sure are hoping you'll return the love that we give you. But whether you do or you don't, it's up to you. We can't make you love us, Jimmy, but we're sure going to try."

Tom tried to cover up what he'd said, but Alice caught it. Somebody giving Jimmy a bad time. Tom talked on after he'd said it, as if nothing happened, but he didn't fool her. She stopped what she was doing and looked at Tom. "What trouble are you talking about?" she asked.

Tom knew he was caught. He told her what happened that morning. "Oh, Brad Bradley and Joe Crow threw some rocks at Jimmy when he got off the bus this morning. I'll have a good talk with both of them the next time I see them. I'm sure when they know that Jimmy is our grandson, they won't do it again."

"Oh," Alice said, as she went back to her work.

Tom knew he would hear more on this subject later. "One of these days, I will learn to keep my big mouth shut," he thought, as he watched his wife scurry around the kitchen.

Strong Feather

Jimmy felt better as he thought about what his grandpa said. If he could get along with those two guys, he might want to stay. He remembered he only had two dollars left from the twenty dollars he got from that man in Weber, Illinois. He needed to find a place around Mercer where he could get some money. When a guy doesn't have money, he's nothing. He looked at his grandparents, and even though he was almost broke, so were they. It was a big mess. He didn't want to break their hearts like his mother broke his, but he didn't know what to do.

He got up and hugged his grandpa. "Thanks, Grandpa," he said. "I've been worried about those two guys. If you can get them off my back, I sure would appreciate it."

"I'll do just that, Jimmy," Tom replied, enjoying the hug from his grandson. Alice came over and hugged both of them.

It made Jimmy feel good to know that someone really cared for him. It was new to him, but he remembered when his mom and dad used to hug him like this. Just thinking about those times made him feel better. He didn't want to let go of them. Thoughts of running away still nagged at him. His grandparents cared for him, really cared. Maybe he should stick around just to see what might happen.

Mercer wasn't that great, but he didn't want them to know how he felt. Again he fought back the emotions he was feeling and knowing. He was able to handle it. His past experiences of working the Newark streets drained him of showing his affections like he did before. He needed to learn how to control his emotions.

Alice looked at Jimmy and felt there was something wrong. He was her only grandson, and she was

Strong Feather

sure she knew what he was thinking. "Sit down, Jimmy, it's time to eat," she said.

'It won't be long until you'll be a man, Jimmy. You're growing up so fast, just like your dad did. But don't get in too big of a rush to grow up. Take your time. Enjoy your youth, especially your teenage years. You'll be grown before you know it. Your teenage years can be the best years of your life, or your worst. Work at it to make them your best."

She went back to the stove, and when she returned, she had her hands full of dishes. She quickly placed them on the table. Jimmy looked at the stove next to the kitchen wall. It was different from any he'd ever seen. Pulling his chair up to the table, he waited for his grandma to sit down.

"That stove you were looking at, Jimmy, will be one of your chores," Alice said when she sat down. "That wood box behind it will have to be kept full. It will be your job to keep it full. There's plenty of wood out back. You can start cutting it tomorrow. When that wood is gone, you and your grandpa will have to go around the area and find more. Tom usually gets old railroad ties that have been discarded alongside the railroad tracks. It takes a lot of wood to cook our meals.

The stove looked a lot different to him now. It was something that had to be fed just like him . . . not food, but wood. "What next?", he thought as he looked at the table. There wasn't much to eat. There was no meat at all, just things from their garden and brown beans.

Alice went to get the salt and pepper and came back to the table. The food was passed to Jimmy and he didn't know whether he should take some or not, so he did. When he tasted it, he was surprised how good it tasted, so he dug in. He hadn't eaten much that day and he ate real fast. When his plate was clean, he asked for more.

63

Strong Feather

"You can have all you want," Alice said, "but take only as much as you can eat. I want you to eat all you want, Jimmy, but I don't want to have to throw any of it away."

"Yes, Ma'am," Jimmy said, as she gave him more beans and bread.

Alice smiled at his kind words. "I'd like for you to go to church with me this Sunday." Alice said. "I think you'd like that."

"Yes, Ma'am," Jimmy replied, in between bites.

When supper was over, they sat around the table and talked. While Jimmy and his grandpa were talking, Alice got up and went back to Jimmy's room. When she returned, Jimmy excused himself. After a couple more hugs, he went to his room and got ready for bed. It had been quite a day for him and he was tired. He didn't realize how tired he was until his head was on the soft pillow. It felt good lying there between soft sheets. He turned the light off beside his bed and pulled the sheet and blanket up around his neck and closed his eyes.

His mind went over what happened to him in the last few days. The school year ended. He was put in jail. He missed that bus on purpose, and here he was in his dad's bed. Things happened so fast that he wondered what would happen next. He hoped it would slow down a little.

He remembered his grandma getting up from the table and going to his room. He wondered why she did that. Maybe she was looking for something. But he didn't have anything she would want. Then he felt it. It was a slight breeze from somewhere. His grandma opened his window for him. The coolness of the night air was gently surrounding him. It felt so good. The air was crisp with no smell, none of those strange odors that surprised a person in the big city.

Strong Feather

His eyes opened wide when he heard something outside his window. It was the sound of a cricket chirping somewhere out there in the dark. The moon was out. Its light came streaming through his window onto the floor, lighting up his room. Tossing his covers back, he got out of bed and went over to the desk, pulled back the chair, and sat down. Outside his window was the brightest moon he had ever seen. It was so clear he could make out a man's face in the moon.

He was surprised at how bright the stars were. He saw a wide band of stars stretching across the sky. His eyes searched the skies for the big dipper. It wasn't long until he had found it.

He recalled the time when his dad pointed the big dipper out to him when he was small. He remembered the times on the rooftop of their cold-water flat when his dad tested him. They laughed each time Jimmy found the big dipper. He liked to play the big dipper game with his dad. Those were the fun days of his life.

It felt good looking up at all the stars. He now cherished those times when he sat with his dad for hours, just being together and looking at the stars. But those days were gone. Those were childhood memories, not real like things were now. It wasn't long until his eyes drooped, and his head nodded. He made his way back to bed. Pulling just the sheets up under his chin, he smiled. He sure was tired, but it was a good tired.

As he drifted off to sleep, he saw a big beautiful bird flying high in the sky above him. It floated so gently, not moving a feather. Then it circled round and round and round. "What a sight," he thought. What he wouldn't give to be able to do that.

A clicking noise brought him out of his dream. He found himself in a strange place again. He didn't know

65

where he was. A chill ran over him, and again he was back in jail. Sitting up in bed, he saw his door slowly open. A dim light shone in from the hallway. In his mind he was back inside that dimly lit cell in Newark. Shivers ran over his body as he stared at the figure standing in the doorway.

Alice was taken back by the look on her grandson's face. She walked over to his bed and sat down. Taking her grandson in her arms, she gently rocked him back and forth.

The damp jail cell quickly faded from Jimmy's mind when he realized where he was. Reaching around his grandma, he hugged her as hard as he could. He sure was glad it was his grandma sitting next to him, and not that skinny old jail keeper.

"It's all right, Jimmy," Alice said softly, as she lay him back on the bed. "It's all right. Nothing is going to hurt you around here. I won't let it."

A big smile came on his face as Alice looked at him. She rubbed his hands. "I just came in to check on you and see how you were doing," she said, laying his hands down. She looked at him and winked. "Let grandpa do the worrying around here. He's good at it. You get a good night's sleep, and I'll see you in the morning."

"Yes, Grandma," he said, snuggling way down in his warm bed.

Alice tucked him in and walked to the door. She stopped, looked back at him, smiled, and quietly closed the door behind her.

Jimmy tried to forget that cold jail cell back in Newark. He remembered that large bird again. He tried to recall everything about how big and beautiful it was, but it was gone. Closing his eyes, he slowly drifted off to sleep.

The next morning when he awoke there was the strange sound of silence all about him. He couldn't believe

Strong Feather

how quiet it was around there. In the city there was always some kind of noise being made by someone, even during the night. Rolling over in bed, he looked around the room to reassure himself he was at his grandparents'. He squirmed around under the sheets with the beautiful bird quilt on top. He wondered what would happen to him this day. A lot of things happened to him lately. His eyes opened wide as he looked toward the window. "I know what I'll do," he said, out loud. "I'll go down to that creek and do some exploring."

Jumping out of bed, he looked for the clothes he took off the night before. They were gone. In their place was a pair of overalls and a blue plaid shirt. Confused and irritated, he put them on, wondering what he looked like. There was no mirror in his room, so he opened the door and walked into the hall looking for a mirror. There had to be one in the bathroom, so he went in and turned on the light. There was a tall mirror next to the wash basin, so he walked over to it and looked at himself. He didn't like what he saw. He wasn't going to go down to the creek in clothes like these. Standing there, he heard his grandma's voice behind him.

"You look nice, Jimmy," she said, turning him around to get a better look. "You sure do remind me of your dad in those clothes. He, too, was a handsome lad when he was your age, just like you are. Wash up, then come into the kitchen and eat."

Turning, she left the bathroom and walked back down the hall. Jimmy stuck his tongue out at himself in the mirror before he washed up. Then he headed for the kitchen and sat down. Alice was over at the stove. She brought a small pan over to the table. She poured its contents into a bowl and put the pan back.

Strong Feather

The table had just one setting. Jimmy sat there looking at the bowl wondering what was in it. It looked like oatmeal, but he wasn't sure. It was a long time since he'd eaten oatmeal. There were two pieces of toast on his plate, but no butter. A small pitcher of milk sat beside the toast, and the sugar was in a dispenser like he saw in cafes. Jimmy poured sugar and milk into the bowl, grabbed a piece of toast, and started eating. It was oatmeal.

"I must tell you something, Jimmy," his grandma said, as she sat down beside him. "I let you sleep in today since it's your first day here, but tomorrow you'll have to get up earlier and get your chores done. You'll find out that when you do your chores early, you'll feel a lot better. You won't have to worry about me getting onto you to do them. You won't have to wonder about sleeping late from now on either because you now know you've got to get up. Rules are rules. You'll find all of life's like that. Do what you have to do as soon as you can, and get it over. Then you'll be free the rest of the day to do whatever you want to do," she said.

Jimmy looked at her. What she said made sense. "How could anyone be that smart and live way out here in the west?" he wondered. When he was done eating, he looked around the room. "What are the chores I have to do? You said to fill the wood box and keep it full. What are the others?" he asked.

"It's all on that note I left in your room, Jimmy. You must make your bed when you get up. I'll show you how I want you to do that in a few minutes. After that you can go out back and cut me some wood. I wash clothes Monday morning. You'll have to build a fire under the big pot out back. The garbage must be taken out back after supper each night and put in one of the large barrels. When the barrels get full we burn them. When they are too full to burn, your grandpa hauls them off to the dump. Those are the main chores, and of course I'll think of other things for you to do from time to time."

Jimmy got up and looked around the kitchen. "The wood's out back?" he asked.

Alice nodded and pointed down the hall towards the back door. "First things first, Jimmy. Your bed must be made. Come, I'll show you how. Tomorrow you can do it yourself. After we're finished with the bed, we'll go out back."

It didn't take Alice long to show Jimmy how she wanted him to make his bed. While she straightened up his room, he put his cap on. He didn't want her to know it had been wet. She might start asking him questions on how it got that way. When she finished, they went onto the back porch. It was a nice size porch, all screened-in. Jimmy followed her not saying a word about his knowing about the porch and everything out back. She opened the screened door and they went down the steps together. There was a large shed on their left. It was the first time Jimmy took a good look at it. It was a strange looking shed. It had screen all around the front and two sides. The back of the shed was made up of boards. "What kind of a shed is that, Grandma?" Jimmy asked.

"That's where your dad once kept his homing pigeons, Jimmy. Your dad was one of the best homing pigeon trainers around these parts," she said with pride in her voice. "He won all kinds of prizes with them, and people would come from all the towns around here to look at his pigeons. Some even bought them, which helped us make ends meet in those days. But, the market for homing pigeons is not like it used to be. Tommy sold all his birds a long time ago."

Strong Feather

Alice smiled, remembering those days. "Your dad was one of the best bird trainers around these parts," she repeated, "and he made your grandpa and me so proud of him."

Jimmy looked at the pens. "The wood is over here," she said, bringing him out of his trance. She pointed at a good-size stack of old railroad ties. "Your grandpa goes out and gets these old ties off the sides of the railroad tracks around here. He brings them home so we'll have wood all year long. That's where he has gone this morning. One of the men who works on the railroad told him that they had pulled out a lot of old railroad ties north of town. It's only a couple of miles from here, so he's gone to check and see what they look like. Sometimes they're not worth the effort to bring them back. Let's hope he brings a bunch of them back with him."

Jimmy looked at the pile of wood in front of him. Each tie was about six feet long. "How am I going to cut them up to fit in the stove?" he asked.

"There's a saw hanging on that pigeon pen post over there," she said, pointing. "All you have to do is place one of those ties on that sawhorse over here. You will then saw them into one-foot long pieces. After that, you split the wood with that ax sticking in that block next to the sawhorse," and she pointed at the ax. "Cut them into pieces small enough to fit into my stove. I'll want some big pieces and some skinny pieces. The skinny ones help me start the fire in the morning. You'll have to keep the wood box full. Whenever you come into the kitchen and see it's low, I want you to come out here and cut enough wood to fill it up, no matter what time of the day it is."

Jimmy couldn't believe what he heard. This was too much.

Strong Feather

"It would be a good idea if you cut up a large pile of wood first. Stack it in the shed behind the pigeon pen over there. Then, when I need wood, you won't have to run out here and cut it. How you do it is up to you, but the wood box is low right now. So, you might as well start learning how to saw the ties, and cut the wood. Don't get in a hurry. Just take your time. But don't take too much time," she said wagging her finger at him, then laughed.

She walked back up the steps and into the house, leaving Jimmy standing at the pile of wood. There was no doubt in his mind about how much he disliked this place. He'd never had to do hard work like this in the city. Every time work showed its face, he went in the other direction. He thought about doing that right now. "Just walk on down the road and forget all about Mercer, Colorado," he thought. He walked over and sat down on the sawhorse. He thought about the mess he was in. Then a strange noise came from the front of the house.

He ran over to the corner of the house and peeked around to see what it was. To his surprise, he saw his grandpa coming down the road in an old red Ford pickup truck. "What a sad looking truck," he thought, watching it move along. The back right fender was hanging loose, which made the strange sound. The fender banged up against the truck each time the truck hit a bump in the road, and that was often. Whaap! Whaap! Whaap! it went.

There was a large pile of wood on the back of the pickup. Along with the sound of the fender was the sound of the motor straining under the load of wood. It sounded like it would never make it into the yard. Slowly the truck made its way down the road and up their lane, and finally around the house. Pulling up next to where the other ties were stacked, it stopped and he turned the truck off.

71

Strong Feather

The truck door opened and Tom got out. "I sure am glad to see you here, Jimmy," he said. "I had to load those ties all by myself, and it kinda got to me. I sure could use a hand." He stopped and looked at the load on the truck. "After I sit down for a few minutes, that is," and they both laughed.

"I see your grandma's already got you out here to cut wood. I sure am glad. She's had me doing it ever since your dad left. Kinda glad you're here to help me out, Jimmy. I'm not as young as I used to be, you know, and I get kinda tired if I work too long. You don't mind helping me out do you, Jimmy?"

"No, Grandpa," Jimmy said, looking at him. Again he found himself saying words he really didn't mean. "The problem is, I have never done anything like this before, Grandpa. I don't know what to do, or how to do it."

"It's got you wondering what kind of deal you've gotten yourself into, hasn't it, Jimmy?" his grandpa said, looking at him with a frown. "Are you going to run away and leave us, Jimmy?"

Jimmy was startled by his grandpa's frankness. How in the world did he know what he'd been thinking? "I don't know," he said, looking at the ground.

"It's going to be hard for you around here at first, Jimmy," Tom said, looking at his grandson. "You can't expect to come out here from a big city and not be scared a little. But if you'll only give it a couple of weeks, I think you'll know better what you should do. We understand your problems, Jimmy, but there are rules by which we must live. If you wish to stay with us, then you must follow our rules. They're not that hard, but they are different from those you've been used to. We would also like to help you change some of the values you've been living by, and plant some new ones within you. We think they'll help you grow up to be a fine man. That's what you want, too, isn't it?"

"Yes, Grandpa. I sure do," he replied. "I'll give it a try for a couple of weeks."

"That's my boy," Tom said. "At the end of a couple weeks we'll talk again." He got up off the sawhorse and walked over to the truck. "Give me a hand with these railroad ties, Jimmy, and I'll help you saw and cut some wood for the wood box. Is it a deal?"

"Yes Sir!" Jimmy said, pulling his cap down to shade his eyes. Getting up, he went over and helped his grandpa unload the railroad ties.

CHAPTER V

The first three days Jimmy spent at his grandparent's house were not his best. He learned how to do his chores and got used to his new life. He tried hard, but it slipped from an irritation to a deep dislike.

For Jimmy, a free spirit who did almost anything he wanted to do for years, this reminded him of jail. Some of his despair faded away when he looked at the hills and mountains in the distance. It relaxed him and helped him put up with all his grandma asked him to do around the house. Running away crossed his mind each day. He tried to forget it, when he thought about all his grandparents did for him.

One afternoon while in the back yard cutting railroad ties, Alice opened the back door and yelled, "Jimmy, come in here. I've got something I want to show you."

He laid the saw on top of the tie he was cutting, and went towards the porch. His body was there, but his mind thought of the soft grasses on the hills across the creek. He ran through them like a deer. It was his favorite place. He wanted to be on the side of the hill. It called to him each time he came into the backyard to cut wood. He explored the creek the day before, and stayed there until Tom called him for supper. He saw, felt and smelled it, as he looked towards the creek.

The cool creek water felt good on his hot feet. Instead of walking up the steps, he thought about walking along the creek's sandy bottom looking for minnows that scattered with each step he took. That which lay beyond the backyard was calling to him like a lovely song. He discovered every time he tried to get away, he always wound up in the backyard sawing the ties, or doing his

Strong Feather

chores. There were always chores to be done. He recalled who did the chores before he came along, and started wishing his grandpa would take them back.

"I have something here, Jimmy, I think you might like to read," Alice said, standing at the top of the steps.

Jimmy went up the steps and onto the porch. Alice smiled, and went back into the house. She sat at the table as Jimmy sat beside her. Picking up an envelope off the table, she said, "It's a letter from your father, Jimmy." She opened the envelope and took out a sheet of paper. "I haven't written to your dad since Christmas," she said, "and he very seldom ever writes back. But I wrote him the other day and told him you are staying with us. Let's see what he has to say."

It was only one page. Jimmy saw there wasn't much writing on it. Alice read it to herself, then turned to Jimmy. "Your dad writes that he's glad you're here with us, and that he misses you very much. He wants to know how big you are, and if you're taller than he is. He writes that he would like to come see us, but he's had some problems, and he won't be able to come. But, he writes, he will come see us the first chance he gets."

"Is he still in the Veterans Hospital in Big Spring, Texas, Grandma?" Jimmy asked. Alice turned the envelope over and looked at the return address. "Yes, he is still there," she replied. "He seems to like Texas better than he did Buffalo, New York. Do you have his address in Big Spring, Jimmy?"

"No, not the mailing address," Jimmy answered. Alice wrote the address on a piece of paper and handed it to Jimmy. "Just in case you want to write to him," she said, smiling.

Jimmy thought about doing something different than writing his dad. He knew where he was. He saw it on a map, and now his dad wrote that he wanted to see him. That settled it in his mind. He would leave the first chance he got and go see him. Jimmy was sure his dad would never come back to Mercer, Colorado, so he would go to him.

He listened as his grandma talked about his dad for over an hour. When she finished, she patted him on the hand, got up, and started supper. Tom came in and read his son's letter. When he finished, he thought about his son. It was now his turn to tell Jimmy stories about his dad. Some of the stories Tom told made Jimmy so proud of his dad.

After his dad left him and his mom, he'd heard nothing but bad things about him from his mother. He felt a lot better about his dad after hearing some good things. After supper, Jimmy excused himself and went to his room. It wasn't long until he was in his bed. Before he fell asleep, he spent a long time wondering how he could get to Texas to see his dad.

The next morning Jimmy got up early. He made his bed and cleaned his room like his grandma's rules told him he should. When he finished, he went into the kitchen where Alice was fixing breakfast. He saw the wood box needed wood. He brought in two loads, which filled it up. While he ate, he slipped some biscuits and bacon into a handkerchief he placed on his lap. When he finished eating, he folded his handkerchief, put it in his pants pocket, and excused himself.

In his room, he pulled his suitcase out from under the bed, and placed it on the chair. He put some clothes inside, closed it and placed it on the desk. Putting his baseball cap on, he opened the window, dropped the suitcase on the ground outside, then crawled out after it.

Jimmy made a wide half circle around the house making sure no one saw him. When the house was out of

Strong Feather

sight, he headed towards the highway. Upon reaching it, he headed away from town. He saw the city limits sign up ahead. He recalled how excited he was when he first saw that sign on the bus. Now he walked past it on his way out of town. His lips curled up as he thought about all the rules he followed. If he could get a couple of good rides, it wouldn't take long to get to Texas.

He thought about seeing his father. The sound of an approaching car brought him halfway out of his daydreams, but he was too deep in his thoughts to pay much attention to it. When a horn honked a few feet behind him, he jumped into the ditch along side the road. Looking back, he was surprised to see Mr. Wilson in his garage tow truck.

Pulling up alongside Jimmy, Bill looked at him. Opening the passenger side door of his truck he asked, "What's the matter, Jimmy?"

Jimmy didn't say anything. He just stood there in the ditch. "It can't be that bad," Bill said, taking a closer look. "Do your grandparents know what you are doing, Jimmy?"

"No, Sir," he replied, not raising his head. "There's just nothing to do around this place, and I'm bored."

Bill thought about what Jimmy said. "I tell you what, Jimmy. Let's just pretend this never happened, and you come with me. I'll find something for you to do around my garage. I can't promise you a full-time job, but whenever I need something done I think you can do, I'll let you do it. We'll talk about wages later. What we need right now is to get your mind off leaving town. You'll find the longer you stay around Mercer, the more you'll like it. Just give it a chance, Jimmy. You'll see."

"Yes, Sir," Jimmy said slowly, not meaning it. Stepping up out of the ditch, he stood next to the truck and thought about telling Mr. Wilson where he was headed, but decided not to. "I think I'd like helping you out," Jimmy said. "If I could do that, I might not get so bored."

Tossing his suitcase into the back of Mr. Wilson's truck, he climbed in and shut the door. Bill turned the truck around and headed back to his garage. He parked the truck and they got out and walked over to the office.

"Jimmy," Bill said, sitting there looking at him. "I'm glad I ran into you like I did. I had to close my office, which I don't like to do. I was headed out to Chuck Miller's farm to start his old truck for him. With you here, I can keep the office open, and maybe you'll sell something while I'm gone. I'd like for you to clean up this dirty old office for me, and if you get finished before I get back, there are a bunch of empty oil cans out back that need to be put in the trash barrel. If I'm not back when lunch time rolls around, just lock the place up and go home for lunch. I'll see you when I get back."

He took a key off his key chain and laid it on the desk top. Jimmy asked, "What about my suitcase in the back of your truck?"

"I'll drive over and tell your grandparents that you're helping me out today," Bill replied. "I'll put your suitcase in the garage when they're not looking. I left a couple of things over at your grandpa's last week that I've been meaning to go by and get. I'll stop by there and get them on my way over to Chuck's farm."

He waved as he went out to his truck and drove off. Jimmy strolled around the office looking at the things on the shelves. "I was trying to run away from doing chores and cleaning up," he thought, "and here I am with more chores and cleanup to do than I had at home. I'm in worse shape than when I started."

Thinking about it upset him. Grabbing the broom in the corner, he swept the floor. When he finished, he went

Strong Feather

out back and picked up oil cans and put them in a large barrel. He was about done when he heard a horn honk out front. He went out the front door to see who was honking. As he came out of the front door, he almost ran into the side of a car. It was big and red, with a dude all dressed up sitting behind the wheel.

"Do you want some gas?" Jimmy asked, looking at the man.

"No, Sonny," the man said. "Which way is Longmont from here?"

"Why did city slickers like this guy have to call him 'Sonny,'" he thought. It made him mad, so he pulled the brim of his cap down and looked at the man. He pointed down the road in the opposite direction from Longmont, then realizing what he was doing, he corrected himself and pointed the right way. He just got this job, and he didn't want any trouble before he got paid.

Not giving the right direction to strangers just came natural to him. In the city, you always gave people the wrong direction. Only chumps gave a sucker the right direction. That's how they taught strangers not to ask stupid questions. He would have to work at not using his old habits. It would have been a lot of fun to see this guy turn around and come back, especially after he called him, "Sonny."

At first, the man didn't say a word as he looked at him. Then he said, "I think you're trying to send me off in the wrong direction, Sonny. Are you?"

"No, Sir." Jimmy replied, trying hard not to laugh. He knew the man could see it in his face.

"That's what I thought," he said, angrily. "You're not fooling me, Sonny. The first direction you gave me was the correct one, wasn't it? You see, Sonny, I'm not as dumb as you think I am."

79

Strong Feather

Putting his car in gear, he squealed his tires and drove off in the wrong direction. Jimmy couldn't hold it in any longer and laughed so hard that he went in the office and sat in Bill's chair trying to catch his breath. Even after he quit laughing, he caught himself snickering each time he thought about what happened. This job wasn't half as bad as he thought it was going to be.

Turning around in the chair, he looked out the front window. Now and then a car drove by, but no one stopped. It was five minutes to twelve when Bill drove up and came inside.

"You can go eat, Jimmy," Bill said. "I'll take over."

"Okay," he said. Outside, he took off running and ran down to the dirt road by the edge of town. He smiled when he saw his grandparents' house at the end of the road. He was out of breath, so he walked towards their house. He felt a lot better about himself. He picked up a handful of rocks beside the road and threw them at the telephone poles along the side the road. When he hit one he laughed and yelled, "gotcha!"

Then from out of nowhere, a rock sailed past the side of his head, and he heard someone yell, "gotcha!"

Ducking his head, he heard someone else yell, "Take off that Mercer High baseball cap, kid! You're not wanted around here, especially on our baseball team!"

Jimmy didn't see who yelled at him. He knew who it was and he took off running again. He jumped over everything between him and his grandparents' house. When he stood on the porch, he looked back to see if his two attackers were still there. Sure enough, there they were. They stood in the middle of the road laughing and making gestures of Jimmy jumping over things. They turned and walked down the alley, laughing and patting

Strong Feather

each other on the back. "Those two guys are nuts," he thought.

Jimmy was really upset. He opened the screen door, stepped inside, and thought about what happened. "What a pair those two made," he thought, shaking his head.

He heard his grandma moving around in the kitchen fixing lunch, and for no reason at all, a picture of the man at the station driving off in the wrong direction popped into his mind. He laughed out loud.

"Is that you, Jimmy?" Alice asked, from the kitchen.

"Yes, Grandma," he replied, closing the screen door. He felt better when he walked into the kitchen. Why those two guys made him think of that man he didn't know. Maybe it was because all three of them were weird. Sitting down at the table, he found it hard not to laugh. Instead of laughing, he had a big grin on his face looking at his grandma.

A big chicken salad sandwich and a glass of milk were in front of him and he ate. He found it very hard not to tell his grandma what happened, both the good and the bad. So instead of going into all the details, he told her some of the things he did at Mr. Wilson's garage.

"I think it will be a good experience for you. Someday you might need it," she said. When Jimmy glanced at the clock he saw he spent almost an hour at home. Kissing his grandma on the cheek, he headed for the front door, leaving his baseball cap sitting on the table. Lunch took more time than he thought it would. Jimmy ran all the way back to the garage.

When he walked into the office, he found Mr. Wilson laughing. When he saw Jimmy, he slapped his leg and laughed even harder. When he finally regained his composure, he looked at Jimmy. "Did you give some directions to a man in a new car on how to get to Longmont?" Bill asked.

"Yes, Sir," he said, a little afraid of what happened.

"Well, he just left here mad as could be," Bill said. "He started off by telling me that your directions were all mixed up and he thought you were trying to be smart. Then he told me you gave him the wrong directions first and then the right directions. He said he drove twenty miles the wrong way before he stopped to find out where he was. It was only then that he knew you told him the right directions, so he turned around and came back.'

'I tell you, Jimmy, he had me so mixed up I didn't know what he was talking about. I stood there and almost laughed in his face. He kept telling me over and over until I realized that he thought he was outsmarting you and he only outsmarted himself. I'm proud of you not lying to that man, Jimmy. Looks to me like you're working out some of those problems you thought you had around here."

Bill told everyone that came in that afternoon what happened. They each had a good laugh and were glad to meet Jimmy. In a small town like Mercer, it wasn't long until everyone knew Jimmy and what he did. A couple of people stopped him the next day and talked to him about the wrong-way driver. They sure thought it was funny. They told him how glad they were he was helping Bill around his station.

He liked the recognition, but it didn't fill the void he had deep inside. A couple of days later, the longing to see his dad got the best of him again, and once more he made plans to go see him. Only this time he would leave at night, not during the day when someone might see him. He didn't want anyone stopping him like they did last time.

Strong Feather

That night when his grandparents were asleep, he left a note telling them that he'd come back and see them some day, and for them not to worry about him. He was big enough to take care of himself. He'd been doing it for years, and he could do it now.

He left his suitcase under the bed and put some socks and a pair of pants on one of his shirts. He put his handkerchief with two biscuits and bacon in with his clothes. Folding his shirt up, he wrapped the arms around his clothes and tied them tight. It made a nice bundle. He crawled out of the window, walked around the house and down to the highway. The night air was cool and the moon was out. At the highway, he looked around but saw no one. He walked down the highway, and was soon out of Mercer. "It would be a long time before it got light," he thought. Jimmy doubted anyone would give him a ride at night, but with each step he took he was closer to his dad.

He heard a strange noise up ahead. He stopped and listened. Off in the distance he heard a train. As he listened, he knew it was moving back and forth not far up ahead. He ran down the road until he saw the train; it was switching railroad cars off the train and onto a siding. As he watched, he could tell they were about through and were ready to hook up to the train and leave.

He wondered what he should do. He saw the train was headed in the direction of Denver. All he had to do was jump on one of those box cars and catch a ride to Denver. From there he could catch another train down to Texas. That would be a lot easier than trying to get rides in cars. You never know who's going to pick you up. He remembered the highway patrolman stopping and picking him up. He sure didn't want that to happen again.

He walked down the road towards the train. When he got close, he knelt down in the tall grass by the side of the road. He watched as the train was finally hooked up. He jumped when the train whistle blew. There was a loud banging sound that started up at the front of the train and worked its way past him to the end of the train. The train started to move. Slowly at first, then it picked up speed. Jumping up, he ran alongside one of the open box cars. He first tossed his pack roll through the open door, then reached up, grabbed the handle on the door, and pulled himself up and into the box car.

He looked out the door as the train picked up speed. "Why didn't I think of this before?" he wondered. This was great. Why hitch hike, or ride a bus, when you can go free on a train? He walked around the box car and was relieved to find it empty. Placing his bundle in one of the corners, he lay down. The rocking of the box car and the clickity clack of the wheels on the rails soon lulled him to sleep.

The stopping and starting of the train caused Jimmy to stir a little, but not enough for him to wake up and realize what was happening. When the box car he was in was put on a siding in Denver, Jimmy slept on.

The early morning mist over the Denver railroad yard slowly lifted when the sun came up. Trains were being put together by the yard switch engines. When they were complete, groups of three or four large engines would back up to them. When they were hooked up, the engineers pushed the controls forward, and the long trains slowly headed out of Denver.

The closing of his box car door caused him to stir a little, but that was all. But the squeaking of the latch, as it was put over the hasp, woke him. When the pin on the end of a short chain was dropped through the hasp, Jimmy opened his eyes wide. There was somebody outside. He lay there listening. When he heard someone walking outside

Strong Feather

the box car, he stopped breathing. The footsteps faded and silence returned. That was a close call, he thought. He wondered who it might have been. It was dark inside the box car, which led him to believe it was still night.

He looked around. It was then he saw the slit of light under the door. He ran over to the door. With a sinking feeling he realized it was not night. Someone had shut the door on him, and it was light outside. Grabbing hold of the door the best he could, he tried to shove it open, but the large door wouldn't move. He was locked in and couldn't get out. Fear took over his body. He began kicking and beating on the door, as he screamed as loud as he could. He had to get out of there.

There was a big bang and the car lunged backward, throwing him to the floor. He had no idea what happened. Then the box car jerked forward a couple of times as it started moving. Jumping to his feet he started yelling again, but the noise the box car made as it moved along on the rails, drowned out his cries. He was locked in a box car going somewhere, but where he didn't know. "Why do things like this always have to happen to me!" he shouted. He continued to beat on the door until he slumped to the floor. With his face up against the vibrating door, he caught his breath. "All I wanted to do was go see my dad in Texas," he said, against the box car door. Fear now replaced his thoughts with anger.

He went to where he left his bundle and brought it back. He sat down by the slit of light under the door. He was going to stay there, and the first time someone walked by outside he would yell for them to let him out. He placed the bundle of clothes under his head. He listened to the box car wheels rolling over the cracks in the tracks, only this time he didn't go to sleep.

Strong Feather

His stomach growled, which reminded him that he hadn't eaten. He unwrapped his pack and felt around inside until he found the biscuit and bacon sandwiches. He ate one and put the other back. It tasted good. He wished he had some milk to wash it down. It was only then he thought about how he had gotten them, and he wished he'd brought more. Then he thought about his grandparents and that they would probably miss him. But they'd gotten along without him before he came to Mercer, and he'd be back as soon as he saw his dad. A slight smile flickered across his face. Maybe this train is going to Texas. Even if it was, he'd have to wait until someone opened this door. When they did, he would wait until they weren't looking, then sneak off without them ever knowing he had been on the train. "Boy, wouldn't that be great?" he thought.

Jimmy stayed awake as long as he could, but after a couple hours his eyes closed again and he fell asleep. Again the stopping and starting of the train brought him halfway out of his sleep. A loud pop, then a hissing sound, caused Jimmy's eyes to open wide. He heard the train sounds moving off in the distance, but his box car wasn't moving. They must have put it onto a siding somewhere and the train was leaving. Again fear and anger raged within him.

He started kicking and beating the door again. He yelled as loud as he could. When he stopped, all he heard was silence. His ears strained to hear the slightest sound, but there was none. He would die in this box car if someone didn't come get him out. Tears filled his eyes and ran down his cheeks as he looked at the crack of light at the bottom of the box car door. His yelling and kicking the door drained his strength. Collapsing on the floor, he didn't move. Placing his head up against the door, he cried as if his heart would break and fell asleep sitting there.

Strong Feather

When he woke, the crack of light was gone. Off in the distance he heard a train moving back and forth. Occasionally, he heard a short blast of a whistle. He felt some better knowing someone was out there, but they were too far away. Grabbing his pack roll, he lay down and tried to sleep. Sleep came and went throughout the night. When he awoke the next morning, he saw that the slit of light was back. It was then that he realized this was his second day to be locked in this box car. He had to get out, but how?

That day was a long, hot one for Jimmy in that box car. The night was even longer. He still heard a train moving back and forth not too far away. Once it got real close, but no one came to his rescue when he yelled. Jimmy tried hard not to go to sleep that night. He wanted to be awake, just in case someone walked by. Slowly, sleep overtook him. It was a restless night as he tossed and turned. When morning finally arrived, he was worn out. He was half asleep and didn't hear the steady plodding of footsteps outside. There was the raking noise of the pin as it was pulled out of the hasp, the loud grinding noise as the hasp moved and fell against the door. His eyes opened wide. The door slid open, and a man looked in.

The brightness caused Jimmy to squint his eyes as he tried to see who opened the door. Then he made out a big man standing there looking at him. He had on a suit and a short-brimmed felt hat. He looked mad.

"Get up, you bum!" the man said harshly, "I'm the railyard cop, and you're under arrest. Get out here before I come in and drag you out."

When Jimmy got to his feet, the officer got a good look at him. "Why, you're only a boy," he said. "What are you doing hitching a ride at your age? Do you know you would have probably died in there if I hadn't checked this car?"

Strong Feather

For once Jimmy was at a loss for words. He usually could talk his way out of anything that came his way. This time he'd not been awake long enough to think up a good story. His mind was still all fuzzed up from everything that happened to him.

The officer looked at him. "You're running away from home, aren't you?" he asked. "I can see it in your face. You'd better get your things and come along with me, lad. We've got to let your parents know where you are."

Jimmy got his bundle together and climbed out of the box car. He stumbled along after the man as they crossed a bunch of tracks. They slowly made their way to the other side of the railyard and a small office. Inside, Jimmy was put in one of the empty offices, while the officer reported he'd found a runaway.

It wasn't long until a police car drove up, and a tall police officer got out and came inside. The two officers talked a while before the police officer came into the office where Jimmy was waiting. Smiling at him, he sat down on the desk and looked at Jimmy.

"My name is Fred Smith. What's yours?"

"Jimmy Warrior," he answered, looking at him with scared eyes. He was in trouble with the law again. "Why me?" he thought, "Why is it always me?"

"OK, Jimmy," Fred said, handing him a sandwich. "I'd like for you to tell me what happened."

Jimmy took a big bite of it. "It would be best to tell him the whole story," he thought. When he finished, Officer Smith stepped out of the office and called his grandparents. He made another call before he came back into the office. "I'll be sending you back to Denver, Jimmy," Fred said. "Your grandparents will pick you up there. One of the other officers at our station has to make a run to Denver today, and you'll go along with him."

Strong Feather

"Where am I?" Jimmy asked, looking at the officer.

"Colorado Springs," Fred replied, shaking his head. "You are very lucky, Jimmy. You could have been in that box car for months. You really don't know where you are, do you?"

"No, Sir," Jimmy answered. "I know where I want to be. Home."

Fred nodded his head, but didn't say a word. "That box car really put a scare into the boy," Fred thought. "It was probably the best thing that could have ever happened to him."

Another police car drove up and Fred took Jimmy outside. Fred shook hands with him and opened the back door. Jimmy got in and Fred closed the door. "So long, Jimmy," Fred yelled, as they drove off, leaving him standing there waving.

The officer in the front seat didn't say a word to Jimmy all the way to Denver. Jimmy liked that arrangement because he didn't want to talk about what happened to him. He dozed off a couple of times, only to wake and discover they were not there yet. It was after noon when they finally pulled into the parking lot at the police station in Denver. The officer took him inside and told him to sit in the waiting room. A few minutes later he came back and took him up the stairs to the juvenile office on the second floor. Another officer opened the door for him and he went in. The door closed behind him, and he found himself standing in front of a big desk.

"Your grandparents will come and get you tomorrow morning," the red-headed officer behind the desk said. He looked at Jimmy. "You gave them quite a scare, young man. You'll have to spend the night in the juvenile detention center upstairs. You won't have a record from this episode of yours, Jimmy. Your grandparents wanted to make sure of that, but you came close."

He rang a bell on his desk. Another door opened behind Jimmy. He was taken upstairs and turned over to another officer. He was put in a cell with six other guys about his age. He felt strange when the officer went back to his desk and sat down. Being in a jail cell again brought back bad memories.

The eighteen hours Jimmy spent upstairs in that juvenile detention center turned out to be the longest he'd ever spent. At first, he thought his stay wouldn't be too bad. As the afternoon passed, he discovered the other guys were hardened offenders. It wasn't long until he was in trouble. His roommates seemed to enjoy knocking him around. Once when he tried to fight back, he was thrown onto the floor. Four of them held his arms and legs, while the other two stood next to their bunk watching. They didn't want to miss what was about to happen. Only the yelling of the guard outside the cell saved him. Getting up, he went over and lay down on his bunk.

He was a quick learner and quit fighting back when they knocked him around. He took it and didn't say a word. Once he found himself sitting on his bunk with his ribs hurting so bad he had trouble breathing. This waiting was getting to him. He waited for someone to get him out of that box car, and now he waited for someone to get him out of this place. The thought of his grandparents coming to get him made him feel a lot better. He vowed he would never get himself in a fix like this again. Never!

The next morning when the officer got him out of the cell, Jimmy was one happy guy. His grandparents arrived and waited for him downstairs. When the door to the juvenile office was opened, he could see his grandparents and Mr. Wilson inside. Smiling, he stepped through the door, then stopped. The memory of what happened when he saw his mother flashed through his mind. He took a couple steps backwards when they came towards him. Instead of a slap, he got hugs from each of them. They asked him to forgive them. He couldn't believe his ears. They were asking him to forgive them, when he was the one who should be asking their forgiveness.

He started to tell them that, but Alice put her fingers up to his lips and stopped him. He looked at her, then his grandpa. He then knew what true love was. Tears ran down all of their faces as he hugged them.

Bill Wilson stood next to Jimmy and gave him a couple of pats on the back. "Don't run away from us, Jimmy," he said. "We all love you, and we can always find a way to work out your problems. I thought you understood that the other day when I talked to you. But maybe you didn't believe me."

Jimmy turned loose of his grandparents and looked at Bill Wilson. "I believed you, Mr. Wilson," he said, "but there were other things on my mind at the time."

The four of them made their way down the stairs and outside to where Bill's car was parked. Alice and Tom got into the back seat and Bill and Jimmy got in the front.

"Jimmy," Tom said, before Bill started the car. "I want you to promise us that you will never run away again. There is no need for you to do that. If you want to go somewhere, we'll get the money."

Jimmy said. "I'll never run away again, I promise."

Bill started the car and it wasn't long until they were headed towards the mountains. Fifteen minutes later they passed the Denver City Limits sign, and were now riding along through green farmland. Hay that had recently been cut was now being bailed in some of the fields. The green wheat was starting to turn golden here and there. Corn

Strong Feather

stood straight and tall, row after row, as they drove by. It wouldn't be long until the green beans would need picking. Tomatoes were still green, and the oats and barley were starting to head in some of the fields. It was the growing time of the year. Jimmy, too, grew a bit the last two weeks. A little on the outside, but most of it had been on the inside, where it counted.

CHAPTER VI

It didn't take Jimmy long to change his attitude about his grandparents and the small town of Mercer, Colorado. He didn't mind working around the house. He sawed and cut a lot of wood, and it wasn't long until the pile of wood behind the pigeon shed got bigger and bigger. With his chores done, he had lots of free time on his hands. He knew almost every nook and cranny on his favorite hillside. Only when the stack of wood got low did he work all day at cutting wood.

He walked around the town of Mercer and talked to everyone he met. There were about seven hundred people in the town and surrounding area, most of them elderly like his grandparents. It didn't take him long to find out there were not many kids around there his age. His grandpa told him most of the kids his age visited relatives for the summer. There were quite a few that worked on the farms around town. Very seldom did they get home early enough to do much around town.

Those in town that worked on the farms got up early each morning, except Sunday, and caught trucks the farmers sent to town to pick them up. The same trucks brought them back in the late afternoon. Some of the older people worked in the fields also. There were beans to pick, tomatoes, corn, peas or whatever the farmers needed picking. There was a canning factory over in Longmont that bought most of what they canned from the local farmers. When it was picking time, the farmers needed a lot of hands to pick the crops when they got ripe.

Jimmy noticed there were only a couple of girls his age. It was a strange town, but he was starting to like it. Every so often, he got lonely and wished there were some guys he could hang around with. Hanging around the town

Strong Feather

by himself was no big deal, but it was something to do. He liked to talk with Mr. Wilson, but that got old. So, he spent more and more of his time around the house. He didn't see the two troublemakers around town, which made him feel some better. Just thinking about them bothered him.

One afternoon when he was at his desk looking at some pictures of pigeons, his grandma came in to do some dusting. She looked to see what he was doing, smiled, then left the room. When she returned a few minutes later, she had a stack of books, which she placed on his desk.

"These were your dad's books on birds," she said, flipping through a few pages of the top book. "I thought you might want to read them. I find them very interesting. They're easy to read, and the pictures are so beautiful. You seem to like birds, don't you?"

"I don't know, Grandma," Jimmy said, looking at her. "I like to watch those big birds when they soar high up in the sky. I surely like that. I don't know much about pigeons though."

"That's all right, Jimmy," she said. "Fortunately, not everyone in the world likes the same thing. The things you like are what makes you the way you are. Just make the most of what you like." She patted him on the back and went back to her dusting. It wasn't long until she was done and left.

Jimmy wondered about his dad's books. He opened the top one and thumbed through it looking at all the pictures of the different kinds of birds. Time passed quickly that afternoon. Before he knew it, his grandma called him to come to supper. That afternoon flew by for him, and he discovered he really enjoyed his dad's books. He found it hard to close the book he was reading. His grandma was right. They were easy to read, plus interesting.

Strong Feather

At the table, he saw that his grandpa wasn't feeling too well. When the food was passed, there was no meat. Disappointment showed on Jimmy's face as he ate.

Alice saw the look and felt it was time to remind Jimmy why she hadn't served meat since he came to stay with them.

"Jimmy, I would like to explain why we haven't had any meat at our meals. We just don't have the money to buy it right now. It's just that plain. We plan on getting caught up on our bills in a few weeks, and then we'll have meat, but for now we'll have to make do with what we got."

Jimmy nodded, knowing the real reason. They'd spent all of the money they had to pay his way out here, then more when he ran off. Now they had to scrape by on what they had until there was enough money to buy meat. Lowering his head, Jimmy sat there, not eating. He made up his mind he was going to do something to help out around here. He didn't know what, but he would do his best. Maybe Mr. Wilson needed something done around the garage.

"Your grandpa's not feeling well today," Alice continued, looking at Tom, then back at him. "I was wondering, Jimmy, if you'd mind going with him and helping him clean up this weekend?"

"I'd like that, Grandma," Jimmy said, with a big grin. His grandma gave him the opportunity to help that he wanted. As he now ate, he had a hard time believing what he thought about happened so soon.

The next three days Jimmy enjoyed helping his grandpa clean all the beer joints in town. He found that each day was a full one. In fact, he hurried each morning to get his chores done before going to work with his grandpa. Jimmy sure was glad when Monday came. He wouldn't have to worry about those places again until Friday. That gave him plenty of time to read a few more of the bird books that his grandma gave him. But even though Jimmy helped his grandpa do some of the work, it didn't help much. When they sat down to eat each night, he could tell that his grandpa still didn't feel good.

After chores were over the next morning, he went to his room to do some reading. He only read for a few minutes when his grandma came into his room and sat down on the chair next to his bed. Looking up from his book, Jimmy frowned when he saw her looking at the floor.

"Jimmy," she said slowly. "Your grandpa and I are getting old, and it looks like we're starting to show our age. Your grandpa is not feeling well. I believe it's because of what we have to eat. He got paid today, and I'd like for you to walk over to Mr. Miller's farm with me in the morning and get a chicken. Would you like to do that?"

"I sure would, Grandma. We could do it right after my chores," he said. They looked at each other, then laughed. He sure had changed, and it showed.

The next morning Jimmy hurried through his chores and finished them all by nine o'clock. It was another beautiful Colorado morning, with a coolness in the air that made one feel good to be alive. Alice and Jimmy were both excited, knowing they would be doing something together. A closeness between grandma and grandson grew each day. For Jimmy, it was having someone that really cared about him. It was starting to change his outlook on life. For Alice, it was the thrill of having her grandson around to love.

Their walk out to the Miller farm that morning turned out to be what both of them needed. It was the opportunity to do something together. It was a time for bonding. Some grandmas and grandsons never find that time. It is a time they so desperately needed, just to be together. It shows in their later life when they don't have it.

Strong Feather

As they walked towards the Miller farm, they passed a small pond beside the road. Next to the edge of the pond were quite a few reeds growing up out of the water. Alice motioned for Jimmy to stop. She went over and gathered a bunch of the hard pods from the tops of the reeds. When she had gathered a big arm full, she laid them down beside the road.

"We'll pick these up on our way back," Alice said.

"Okay," he replied. Picking up a rock, he threw it out into the middle of the pond.

They continued on their way to the Miller farm. It wouldn't be long until they would have their large plump chicken. Jackie Miller caught it for them, and told them that her husband, Chuck, was out in the fields plowing. Alice paid her for the chicken, and they started back. Nearing the pond, they stopped.

"I'd like for you to carry those pussy willows for me," Alice said.

"The what?" he asked.

"The pussy willows, Jimmy," she said laughing. "That's what I picked off those reeds by the pond. I'm going to make you a pillow from the soft down that comes from their pods when they dry. They make the softest pillows."

Jimmy went over and picked up the pile of pussy willows. With both arms full, he smiled as he walked along beside his grandma. They talked and laughed all the way back to the house. It was a grand day for the two of them.

Alice cooked the chicken that afternoon for supper. Tom seemed to perk up a little after supper, and the next day he was like his old self again. The three of them laughed and had a good time enjoying each other. What a difference one chicken made.

As the days passed, Jimmy found himself spending more and more of his time reading the books his grandma gave him. Even though he liked the time he spent reading, sometimes he stopped and looked out his window to daydream. One of those days, he remembered the promise he'd made himself to explore that creek out there. He also longed to return to his favorite spot on the side of the hill where he fell asleep the first day he came to Mercer.

"Today would be the perfect day to do that," he thought. He would see if there were any birds around there that he read about in his dad's books.

He went out onto the back porch, opened the porch screen door and listened to the sounds around him. They seemed to call him to come out and play. Down the steps he went as fast as he could, then across the open field to the banks of the creek and stopped. He looked at the small stream of water below him. Slowly, he made his way down the creek's bank and up to the edge of the creek. There were only a few inches of water in the creek, but enough for it to capture his desire to explore its unknown areas. Jimmy slowly walked along the creek bed, not letting anything escape his view. He stopped when a small flock of birds flew overhead and landed in a nearby tree. Looking closer, he saw that they were redwing blackbirds. He remembered their pictures in one of the books. They sat in their tree and watched him. Making a quick arm movement in their direction, they made a lot of noise as they all flew off.

This was a new and exciting experience for him, and he liked it. In the water he saw a group of small minnows. Their silver sides flashed when they were scared. A closer look in the water brought a smile. There on the sandy bottom of the creek was a crawdad looking up at him. Jimmy picked up a stick and poked at him to see what would happen. It backed up so fast that it made the water all muddy. It left him mystified as to where it went. He waited until the water cleared before he found it hiding under a stick. "They were something else", he thought.

Jumping across the creek, he climbed up the other bank. He looked at the green rolling hills in front of him and smiled. He ran and didn't stop until he was on top of his favorite hill. He was breathing hard and looking at his grandparents' house. "Nothing has changed," he thought. Sitting down, he again felt the coolness of grass under him. He noticed that the grass was not as tall at the top of the hill. Lying back, he looked up at the deep blue sky and wished he had brought his baseball cap. Shading his eyes with his hands, he enjoyed the beauty all around him. It was a peaceful spring afternoon.

He was pleasantly surprised to see a large bird soaring on the air currents high above him. The bird looked as if it stood still at times, and then at other times, it moved quickly from one part of the sky to another. He looked around to make sure he wasn't dreaming. When he was sure, he lay back down. He smiled when he saw the bird was still there.

He decided it was some kind of a large hawk. In the back of his mind he vaguely remembered seeing all of this before. As he tried to remember, his eyelids started getting heavy. He fought it the best he could, but they slowly closed. "What was it about that bird he wanted to remember?", he kept asking himself. With that question on his mind, he soon fell asleep.

About an hour later he awoke and to his surprise the large bird was still flying around high above him. The recollection of all that happened to him the last month now flowed through his mind. Then he remembered the times when a large bird was in his dreams. Once while he was in jail, and again in his room. "But why a big bird?", he wondered. To be free like this large bird above him was probably what it meant when he was in jail, and to soar on the wind away from Mercer was what he had wanted to do that night in bed. But what did it mean here on the side of this hill?

Jimmy sat up and watched the large bird as it folded its wings and went into a steep dive, diving almost straight down. Nearing the ground it opened its wings and soared a few feet above the ground and landed on a large rabbit. It then fluttered across the ground about ten feet before the powerful strokes of its wings caused it to rise into the air and fly off with its catch.

Jimmy followed every move the hawk made. What he saw amazed him. "What a powerful bird," he thought. It had to be the Samson of the bird world. As he watched the hawk fly off, he remembered reading in one of his dad's books that hawks could be taught to hunt. If that was true, that would be a way to get some fresh meat for his grandpa. But he'd have to catch a hawk and train it to hunt. He didn't know anything about training a hawk, let alone how to catch one. It was a good idea at first, but it didn't look too hot now. But it was a good idea.

He ran down to the creek, jumped across it, and ran back to the house. Going straight to his room, he looked through his books until he found the one on hawks. He opened it and read it with great interest. The book told about some of the different hawks that were used in hunting. There were pictures of different size hawks. It showed some of the different types of hoods that were used to cover the hawk's head. When their eyes are covered they don't flutter around. Everything he read about hawks interested him. He found himself wanting to find out as much as he could about hawks and how to train them. The book whetted his appetite.

Strong Feather

When he finished reading the book, he wondered where he could get more information about hawks. On his walks around Mercer he hadn't seen a library. He would find out where the nearest library was located, then see if they had any books on hawks. Hawk falconry, his book called it.

That night at supper he asked his grandma if there was a library in Mercer. She told him the nearest library was in Longmont twelve miles away. That didn't help much. He needed to find a way to go over to Longmont, or have someone pick up the books for him.

He wondered who he knew that could take him over to Longmont or pick them up for him. He thought of Mr. Wilson. He recalled Mr. Wilson telling him to come see him whenever he had something he wanted to talk about or find out. He told him more than once to come see him whenever he needed help. Jimmy decided he would go over and talk to him about falconry the next day.

When his chores were done the next morning, Jimmy hurried over to Mr. Wilson's filling station. They talked for over an hour about what Jimmy wanted to do. Bill told him he would pick up some books on falconry the next time he went to Longmont.

"When will that be?" Jimmy asked.

"Tomorrow," he replied. "I've got to get some parts tomorrow."

"Great," Jimmy said, knowing he'd have the books the next day.

A car drove up and Bill got up and went outside. He was putting gas into the car when Jimmy walked by.

"Thanks, Mr. Wilson," he said. "I'll see you tomorrow."

"Okay," Bill said, watching the numbers roll by on the gas pump.

Strong Feather

Jimmy walked off down the street thinking about hawks. When he turned the corner, he looked at the hills behind his grandparents' house. What a sight, he thought. What a place to daydream.

That night he lay awake for hours thinking of all the things he was going to do when he learned to train hawks to hunt. It wasn't until the wee hours of the morning that he fell asleep.

It was after nine o'clock the next morning before he finished his chores and was sitting in his room. He reread the book on hawks, and when he was done, he looked at the hills. He almost heard them calling to him. With a sigh, he gave in and headed for the back door. He was soon lying on his favorite spot, looking up into the sky.

There high above him in the deep blue Colorado sky, he could see the hawk circling around and round. He watched it make large circles high overhead. Just the sight of the hawk caused chill bumps to run all over him. The hawk's wings fluttered, then folded up against its body. Again it dove, arcing up at the last moment and catching the largest rabbit he had ever seen. There was a lot of commotion on the ground as the hawk fluttered along, trying to rise into the air with its catch. Time after time, the hawk struggled to get airborne, but couldn't. Then with one mighty downward thrust of its wings, it rose into the air. Slowly it gained altitude as its large wings beat the air with powerful strokes. The trees on each bank of the creek now blocked the path of the hawk. But its large wings kept stroking, and it rose higher and higher until finally it cleared the trees.

Then from out of nowhere, another hawk swooped downward at it, trying to take its catch from its grasp. With a loud screech, it let go of its prize and veered to the left, barely getting out of the path of the other hawk. In so doing, its right wing struck a large tree limb. The hawk's wing was bent backwards and it fluttered to the ground. Jimmy was on his feet now and watched the injured hawk as it started hopping around on the ground with its right wing dragging along on the ground.

He couldn't believe what he just saw. "What a sad thing to happen to such a beautiful bird," he thought. Then he realized exactly what had happened. He ran down the hill and over to where the hawk was flopping around on the ground. As he came up to it, the hawk fluttered at him, which caused him to back up in a hurry. It surprised him to see such a big hawk on the ground. When the hawk stopped, he stopped. Taking off his shirt, he slowly moved towards the hawk. The next time the hawk fluttered at him, he threw his shirt over its head. The hawk immediately stopped hopping around and quieted down. "Now what?" he thought, looking at the clump moving around under his shirt.

Looking around for a good size stick, he saw one off to his right, picked it up, and lifted one corner of his shirt just enough to see what the hawk was doing. He then placed the stick near the hawk's feet, and it hopped up onto it. Picking the stick up with both hands, he made sure his shirt stayed over the hawk's head all the time. When his prize catch was at eye level, he made his way over to the creek. It was slow going as he made his way down one bank and up the other, always holding the stick out in front of him. His arms grew tired, but he kept going. Step by step, he crossed the open field until he stood next to his dad's pigeon pen.

Putting one end of the stick through one of the holes in the chicken wire, he opened the door into the pen. He then carried his prize into the pen. There was no place to put the hawk, so he walked over to one of the corners of the pen, placing one end of the stick through the chicken wire on one side of the pen and the other end through a hole on the other side. With the stick across the corner of the pen, it made a good perch for the hawk.

Stepping back, he breathed a sigh of relief as he rubbed his arms and shoulders, relieving the tension. "Everything went real well," he thought. But he had to get his shirt off of the hawk and get out of the pen. He didn't want to get hurt or cause any harm to the hawk. A quick pull on his shirt, and he ran out of the pen, closing the door behind him.

Picking up a small stick, he put it through the latch on the pen. He looked through the chicken wire at the hawk inside. He sure was glad that was over. The hawk just sat there, looking back at him with its right wing hanging down by its side. He forgot all about its wing being hurt. If it was broken, he didn't know how he'd get it fixed. Every time he thought he got one thing solved, there seemed to be an unanswerable question facing him. He looked at the hawk and shook his head.

The squeaking of the back screen door opening caused him to turn just in time to see his grandma coming down the steps.

"What do you have there, Jimmy?" Alice asked, walking up to the pen.

Jimmy was about to say something but was interrupted.

"Oh, it's a Grand Hawk with a broken wing," she said, answering her own question.

"A Grand Hawk?" Jimmy asked.

"That's what the Indians call large hawks like that one, Jimmy. Where did you find it?"

He told her what happened and how he caught it. He went on to tell her that he wanted to learn how to train

Strong Feather

hawks to hunt. They talked for quite some time about the hawk inside the pen. Jimmy told her that he asked Mr. Wilson to get him some books from the library on how to train hawks.

"We'll have to make a hood for it before I can put a splint on that wing," Alice said. "I've fixed a lot of broken wings on chickens and ducks. I'm sure it won't be different for hawks. By the way, what are you going to call it?"

"Samson," Jimmy said, smiling. "Today I saw him pick up the largest rabbit I have ever seen. I'd say he's the strongest bird around these parts of the country. I'll go get the book on hawks so we can see how to make a hood for him. Thanks for helping me, Grandma." he said, as he headed for the house.

"You're welcome," Alice replied. When he was inside, she turned and looked at the hawk sitting inside the pigeon pen. "You may be just the thing my grandson needs, Samson," she said. "I've been hoping you would come our way. I didn't know it would be you, of course, but I knew it would be something, or somebody. If you can help me mend the many dents that have been put in my grandson's mind, I'll be eternally grateful to you. It won't be an easy job for you, or for me. But I want to see him grow straight and tall like an oak. I can mend that wing of yours if it's broken, but it only looks sprained to me. I'll be glad to help you get strong again, so you can help my grandson get strong, too."

Alice walked around the outside of the pen where Samson was perched. Looking at the hawk sitting on the stick, she recalled another day when she stood in the same spot and said almost the same words to a pigeon about her son. She felt good inside, just knowing that what she asked for was perched inside the pen. The pigeons that were once in the pen were gone, and this hawk took their place. "It

105

Strong Feather

was strange how things worked out," she thought. A pigeon's worst enemy was the hawk, but there it sat in her son's pigeon pen. She turned and went back into the house.

Jimmy was not thinking about it that way. He liked all kinds of birds, especially the large falcon hawk he just caught. He decided to work hard at becoming as good a trainer of hawks as his father was of pigeons. It would be a challenge, but he wanted to give it a try.

Looking through his books, he found a small book on falconry. It didn't take him long to realize that he would have to get a lot of things before he could even start training his hawk. As he leafed through the pages, he stopped. There before his eyes was a beautiful colored picture of a falcon hawk on the gloved fist of a trainer. It was the most beautiful picture he ever saw.

In his mind he saw himself standing in the picture with Samson on his gloved fist. "They would make a good looking pair," he thought. Deep inside, he had the strangest feeling. It was a feeling he had not had before. It was the desire to learn all he could about hawks. Whatever it took, he would do it. For the first time in his life, he had something he could call his own. He was given toys when he was young, but never something alive. He placed the book on his desk, looked out his window at the mountains rising high into the sky, and sighed.

The sun started its downward trek from its zenith, which made the snow on the tops of the mountains glisten. Small white dots above the mountains grew and grew until they were soft, fluffy clouds. Slowly they made their way across the royal blue sky, heading for the wide-open plains. Now and then one of the clouds grew large enough to block out some of the sun's dazzling display. When they did, a golden ring surrounded the outer parts of the darker clouds. He watched as golden rays streamed through a large hole in

Strong Feather

the cloud. A golden halo now made its way across the bottom of the cloud, turning it a bright violet.

It was an awesome sight to watch. His eyes flickered back and forth across the sky as he watched the clouds grow smaller on their way across the plains until they were no more. His eyes focused in on a small black spot. There, high above the earth, he saw the large bird circling round and round. It had to be the hawk that swooped down on Samson.

"Thank you, Mr. Hawk," he said out loud. "Thank you for sending Samson my way.

CHAPTER VII

The idea of having his own hawk made Jimmy feel good each time he thought about it. He looked up from the book he was reading when Alice came in the back door. He opened his door.

"Grandma," he said. "I've looked at all the different types of hoods in the books you gave me the other day. There are a few pictures that show how to make different kinds of hoods. I put one of the books on the table in the kitchen. We'll need a Rufter hood so he can eat easily, and an Indian hood the rest of the time. The book I'm reading says hawks have to be fed meat, so I thought I'd go back and get the rabbit he dropped out there by that tree."

"That's a good idea, Jimmy," Alice said, walking past him and down the hall towards the kitchen. "I'll look at that book while you're gone."

Jimmy grabbed his baseball hat and headed for the back door. Once outside, he ran towards the tree where the hawk dropped the rabbit. He slowed down a little as he crossed the creek, then ran over to the tree where he caught Samson.

Looking around the base of the tree, he spotted the rabbit. It was lying in some tall grass about ten feet from the tree. He sure was glad the other hawk didn't find it.

He looked up and high above him, he saw the other hawk circling. Once again he was fascinated by the sight of another large bird high above him. He then realized it was dropping lower and lower. Then it dove almost straight down, swooping up at the last moment as it caught a large field mouse. It didn't stop, its wings beating the air as it flew off. He watched as it landed in the top of an old dead tree nearby. Jimmy picked the rabbit up and ran over to the tree. He stood there looking up at the top of the tree, trying to see the hawk, but it disappeared. He listened, but couldn't hear a thing. Walking over next to the tree, he put his right ear up against it. To his surprise he heard chirping.

Stepping back, Jimmy looked up at the top of the tree again. There was something up there besides that hawk. There were baby hawks up there, too. He wondered if they were Samson's. "That would be something," he thought. A hawk's nest right here on the creek where he could watch them grow. It was more than he expected to find, and he was so excited he let out a yell. There was the sound of flapping wings above him as the hawk took off.

He ran back to the creek with the rabbit. Down one bank and up the other he ran with the rabbit swinging back and forth. It was a big rabbit, so it slowed him down a little. When he came to the pigeon pen, he stopped to see what his hawk was doing.

Samson sat perched on the limb with both wings folded back along its body. He was about to run past the pen when he stopped and looked again. His wing must not have been broken like he thought. He walked around the pen to get a better look. It was then he saw something on each of Samson's legs. It looked like small pieces of leather thongs. Both thongs were real short, but were probably much longer at one time. He would have to find out what they were. He ran up the steps and into the house with the rabbit.

When he entered the kitchen with the rabbit he forgot about the thongs. His grandma smiled when she saw the rabbit.

"My, my," Alice said. "That is a large rabbit. Are you going to give it all to your hawk?"

He looked at her. "Do you think there might be enough for him and us too, Grandma?"

Strong Feather

She nodded her head and said, "It sure looks like it, Jimmy."

"I've never eaten rabbit," he said, with a puzzled look on his face. "What does it taste like?"

"They say it tastes a lot like chicken, Jimmy," she said. "But I think it tastes much better than chicken."

His face lit up when she said that. "If it tastes better than chicken, then Grandpa will love it," he said. "Grandpa sure likes chicken."

"He likes rabbit too, Jimmy," she said, nodding her head.

Jimmy placed the rabbit on the drain board next to the sink. Alice put her hand on his shoulder. "I've been checking around the house, Jimmy, and I think I've got all we're going to need for the two hoods you wanted. I found an old pair of your grandpa's lace-up boots out in the garage and cut the tongues out of them. I'll have to have some soft material though. Mrs. Wendell had a small piece of velvet when I was in her store the other day. I'd like to sew it on the inside of the hoods. If you'll run down to the store and get it, I'll be able to finish the hoods today.

"Yes, Ma'am," he said. "I'll be glad to run down and get it."

"There's something else you need to know," Alice said. "I believe you're going to have to change the name of your hawk."

Jimmy was headed for the door when she said that. He was ready to make a fast dash to Mrs. Wendell's store, when he realized what she said. He stopped and looked at her. "Why?" he asked.

"I believe you'll find that the female is larger than the male in the hawk world. I'd say you have a female hawk, not a male."

Strong Feather

"I'll have to think about that, Grandma," Jimmy said, turning and walking out the door. "How could that be?" he thought as he walked towards town. Males are always larger than females. If what his grandma said was true, there had to be a good reason for it. But what could he call her now? She was a Samson no matter how he looked at it. He'd have to give this a lot of thought before he gave her a new name. He sure hoped he could come up with a female name that fit her.

Jimmy waved at Mr. Wilson as he walked by his station. He waved back. He saw someone in the office with him, but didn't pay much attention to who it was. He was in a hurry to get the velvet. He'd stop on his way back and tell him all about his hawk. It was only then that he realized he was walking instead of running, so he ran.

Jimmy stopped when he neared the stores on Main Street. He saw there was a car parked in front of Mrs. Wendell's. Walking up to her store, he looked through the large plate glass window. Mrs. Wendell had a lady customer inside. So he decided he wouldn't go in because he didn't know the lady in the store. Walking on past the store, he stopped by the light pole. He waited until she left before he went in.

Time passed slowly for him out there on the street. He leaned against the light pole. Every so often a car drove by, and he waved at those inside the car. They stared back at him as they drove past. Most of them didn't wave, but some did, which made him feel good. He was having a good time.

Hanging onto the light pole with one hand, he'd swing himself around and around the pole. He'd go one way for a while, stop, change hands, then go in the opposite direction. Tiring of that game, he sat down on the curb with his back up against the pole. It sure was taking that lady a long time to buy what she wanted.

Finally the door opened behind him, and the lady came out with a large bag of groceries.

"Hello," she said, as she walked past Jimmy. She walked around her car and opened the front door.

"Hello," Jimmy replied, getting up from the curb. The lady gave him a little wave, got into her car, and drove off.

Walking over to the door he went inside. "Hello, Mrs. Wendell," he said, walking up to the counter. "Do you have some velvet? My grandma said you had some the other day."

"Hello there, Jimmy," Mrs. Wendell said, with a wink. "Velvet, you say". She thought a minute, then smiled. She'd remembered where it was and went right to it. Pulling it out of a drawer, she showed it to Jimmy. It was only a foot square, but it was the most beautiful blue he had ever seen.

"Yes, Ma'am," Jimmy said. "I'm sure that's what my grandma wants. It sure is pretty."

"It is, isn't it," she replied, looking at it. "Since you like it so much, you can have it. It's all that's left of a larger piece I had, and no one would buy a scrap like this. You go ahead and take it."

"Thanks, Mrs. Wendell," he said, grinning his best grin. Picking the piece of velvet up, he rubbed it against his face. It felt so soft and fuzzy. He was sure Samson would like it too. Jimmy headed towards the door, then stopped, turned and waved at Mrs. Wendell. "Thanks again."

"You're welcome, Jimmy." she said. "Tell your grandmother hello for me."

"Yes, Ma'am," he replied, "I'll do that."

Strong Feather

It made him feel good knowing nice people like Mrs. Wendell. He put the velvet up to his face again. It sure was nice and fuzzy.

The feel of velvet started him thinking about being a great falcon hawk trainer. He was so caught up in his thoughts that he walked right past the filling station. Someone yelling brought him out of his daydream. Looking over his shoulder, he saw it was Mr. Wilson who yelled at him. He headed back to where Mr. Wilson was and showed him the blue piece of velvet.

"Look at what Mrs. Wendell gave me," Jimmy said.

"What are you going to do with a piece of blue velvet, Jimmy?" Bill asked, with a strange look on his face.

Jimmy was about to tell him when he remembered the books. "I've caught a big hawk that I'm going to teach to hunt, Mr. Wilson. Did you get those books I...?"

His words trailed off when he saw a blond-headed girl come walking out the door behind Mr. Wilson. She had blue eyes and seemed to be about 5' 5" tall, maybe a little more. He wondered who she was, and where she came from.

Bill wondered why Jimmy stopped talking. He was about to answer his question about the books when he realized what happened.

"Jimmy, this is Mary, my daughter," he said. "She's been visiting her grandma in Denver ever since school was out.

"Hello, Jimmy," Mary said, smiling at him.

"Hi," he replied.

"I had to go over to Longmont and pick her up today. They wouldn't let her off the bus like they did you." He looked at Jimmy, then at his daughter. The two of them just stood there looking at each other. He had to touch Jimmy on the shoulder to get his attention.

Strong Feather

Mr. Wilson continued, "I picked up the books you were about to ask me about. I didn't know you were going to capture a hawk this soon though. How in the world did you do it? Did you set a snare with some bait?"

Jimmy looked at Mary a couple of seconds before he realized Mr. Wilson asked him a question. With a big smile he told him all that happened, and that his grandma sent him to Mrs. Wendell's to get the velvet so she could make a couple of hoods. Jimmy got more and more excited as he told them the story, which caused Bill and Mary to get excited also.

"I read a couple of those books I picked up for you this morning," Bill said, pointing at a half dozen books on his desk. "You're going to have to make a lot of things before you'll be ready to start training hawks. I'd say you should be able to make all of the things you'll need, but you're going to have to have someone to help you train it. Your grandparents will be able to help some, but they have their work. I'd say you'll probably need to get someone else to help you. You'll also need a dog to flush the quarry out into the open when you do get the hawk trained."

Jimmy thought about what Mr. Wilson said. Those were a lot of obstacles in his path. He hadn't given much thought to things like that. "How was he going to be able to do all those things?" he thought.

"Jimmy," Bill said smiling. "I have a Cocker Spaniel named Goldie. I've trained her to hunt. She can flush just about anything you'd want to hunt around these parts. After you get that hawk of yours trained, you're more than welcome to work with my dog, Goldie."

"That would be great," Jimmy said, relaxing a little as he glanced at Mary, then at Mr. Wilson. "I'd like to thank you for the use of your dog. I have to catch some kind of food for the hawk to eat. That rabbit it caught won't last too long."

"There are a lot of wild pigeons over at the Miller barn." Mary said. "Mr. Miller is always shooting them. I'd say he'd be glad to have you go over to his barn and catch some of them."

He smiled at her. She broke the ice, and he knew they were going to be good friends. "That's a great idea, Mary," he said. "Thanks."

He started to leave, then stopped. Hurrying inside the office, he picked up the books Mr. Wilson got for him. So many things happened that he had to stop and think about what he was doing.

"When do I have to return the books, Mr. Wilson?" Jimmy asked.

"Two weeks, Jimmy," Bill replied. "I'll take them back for you."

"Thanks again," he said, heading out the door.

"Could I go see his hawk, Daddy?" Mary asked, looking at her father.

Bill looked at her and nodded his approval. "If it's all right with Jimmy."

"Sure," Jimmy said, with pride in his voice. "Let's go. My grandma is waiting for me to get this velvet home so she can make the hoods. The hawk's wing looks a lot better. I don't know if it's broken or not. I'm sure hoping it's OK. I saw a couple thongs tied around its legs that I hadn't seen before. I'll have to read all these books so I'll know what they are."

Stopping to catch his breath, Jimmy said, "Let's go, Mary," and he hurried out the door.

Mary followed him a short ways, turned and waved at her father, then off she ran after Jimmy.

Strong Feather

Bill waved back. Leaning up against the door, he shook his head. "It looks like those two are going to get along just fine," he thought. He turned and went back to his desk. He continued shaking his head as he looked at the mess of bills on his desk.

Jimmy opened the screen door for Mary. They hurried through the front room and into the kitchen. Jimmy placed the books on the table. Alice stood with her back towards them when they came in. She was getting supper started. Tom would be home in an hour and she was busy getting everything ready. When she did turn to ask Jimmy about the velvet, she smiled.

"Well, hello there, Mary," she said. "I'd say that my grandson has told you about his hawk and you couldn't wait to see it.

"That's true," Mary replied, smiling at Jimmy.

Jimmy handed his grandma the velvet Mrs. Wendell had given him. "Isn't it the best looking piece of velvet you ever saw, Grandma?" he exclaimed, bubbling over with excitement.

"I'd say it is the prettiest blue velvet I've ever seen, Jimmy," she said, his excitement rubbing off on her. "I'll take care of the velvet Jimmy, while you take Mary out back and show her your hawk."

"Okay," he said.

The two of them ran down the hall and out the back door. When they reached the pen they both stopped and looked at the hawk inside the pen. Neither of them knew much about hawks.

"What kind of a hawk is it, Jimmy?" Mary finally asked, looking at him.

"My grandma said it's a Grand Hawk," he replied. "I don't know much about hawks, but I plan to find out. I've read all the books my dad had on pigeons. But all they had in them about hawks was how to keep them out of the pigeon pens. Two of the books had a few things about hawks and how to train them. But I need to know a lot more. I'm hoping the books your dad got for me will help."

Mary looked at the hawk. "I'd sure like to help you. That way we both could learn how to train her." she said.

"How do you know it's a her?" Jimmy asked.

"I don't know. She just looks like a her to me."

"Grandma told me the larger hawks are female," he continued, scratching his head. "I always thought that the bigger birds would be male birds. That's the way it is with most things. I called her Samson when I saw what a large catch she could carry. But if she's a female, I'll have to rename her."

"Maybe not," Mary said. "She could be the Lady Samson of the hawks. I think it would be a good name for her."

"Lady Samson," Jimmy said softly to himself. He thought about the name as he looked at his hawk. "Why not? We'll train her and ourselves at the same time. I hope she and your dog can work together, especially with Goldie being a bird dog."

They both frowned, as their thoughts ran on ahead so fast they hardly kept up with them. The more they thought about all of it, the better they felt.

Alice came out onto the porch and looked at them standing by the pen. "Don't forget your chores, Jimmy," she said. "The wood box needs filling. Your grandpa will be home soon and you need to get ready for supper. Will you stay for supper, Mary?"

"No, Mrs. Warrior," Mary said. "Thank you, but I have to go home." She turned to Jimmy. "Let me borrow a couple of those books you brought home so I can read up on hawks tonight. I'll come over early tomorrow morning and we'll get started."

They went back inside and Jimmy let her pick out the books she wanted. "I've got to go do my chores, Mary. I'll see you in the morning."

"OK," she said. "I'll see you then."

Jimmy hurried out back and started chopping wood for the wood box. When he returned with an armload of wood, Mary was gone, but his grandpa was there instead.

Tom sat at the table watching Jimmy fill the wood box. He was tired and didn't say anything until Jimmy came back with another load of wood. "Jimmy," he said slowly, his voice reflecting how tired he was, "we had a good talk awhile back about your checking things out. It's been almost a month now, and I was wondering if you've made any decision you might want to talk to us about?"

Jimmy brushed himself off over the wood box before he walked over to the table where his grandpa was sitting. "Yes, I have, Grandpa," he said. "I've decided to stay here the six months. I don't know how I'll feel then, but if it's okay with you and grandma, I'll stay for now."

"You know it's okay with us, Jimmy. We just don't want to force you to stay with us. As you've already found out, your grandma is a rough character. She'll get after you and make you work real hard at times, but we feel it's for your own good."

Alice came over to the table and set a large plate of rabbit in the center of the table. Tom stopped talking and his eyes got wide when he saw the rabbit. "Where did the rabbit come from, Alice?" he asked, looking up at her.

Alice saw the chance where she could have a little fun with her husband. She winked at Jimmy and said, "Jimmy went out and got it for you today."

Strong Feather

"You got it, Jimmy?" Tom asked, looking at his grandson with pride. "Rabbit is one of my favorite dishes. How did you get it? Did you set a snare? I used to be able to set a good snare for rabbit, but not lately. The rabbits seem to be getting smarter, or maybe it's me. Whatever. Tell me all about how you got it, Jimmy."

Jimmy looked at his grandma and they giggled. Tom looked at both of them and snickered. It wasn't long until the three of them were laughing so hard tears were running down their faces. Alice finally had to sit down at the table and wipe her eyes. When she caught her breath, she looked at Tom.

"Jimmy caught a hawk today, Tom." she said. "The hawk caught this rabbit, but was attacked in midair by another hawk, which made it drop its catch."

Tom sat with his mouth open. Alice started to giggle, but caught herself and looked away. She then told him everything that happened that day. She finished by saying, "The hawk's out back in the pigeon pen. Jimmy went back and got the rabbit for meat to feed his hawk. When he brought it in I could see there would be enough left over for us."

Alice looked at Jimmy. "You haven't fed your hawk, Jimmy. After supper you'll have to feed it. I've got plenty of scraps left. You look in those books you got and find out how you're suppose to feed her. I think that only one of us should feed her. She needs to get used to you, and you need to get used to her. I'm sure that will help when you want to work with her."

"This is great," Tom said, as he ate some of the rabbit. "Your grandma is right about your feeding her, Jimmy. I don't know much about falconry, but I do know they are a one-man bird." Tom then got busy eating rabbit.

Strong Feather

Alice and Jimmy tasted the rabbit and found it was delicious. There was not much said around the table that night as they enjoyed the rabbit.

When supper was over, Tom leaned back in his chair. "I'm proud of you, Jimmy," he said looking at him, then his wife, and then at the empty plate. "That is the best rabbit I've ever eaten," and he laughed.

The Warriors ate well that night while the hawk that caught their meal waited outside to be fed. It, too, would soon be fed.

The wonder of it all lay ahead; a hawk and an Indian boy were about to start on a great journey.

Strong Feather

CHAPTER VIII

Jimmy awoke with a start. He drug himself out of bed after staying up reading most of the night and falling asleep in bed. The books Mr. Wilson got him on falconry were very informative. He picked the books up and put them on his desk before he made his bed. He straightened up the room, and then remembered he had to feed his hawk. He ran out the back door and over to the pigeon pen.

Lady Samson sat on her limb perch watching every move he made. Her eyes didn't blink as she watched him. Her head bobbed up and down a couple of times like she expected him to do something. He knew exactly what she wanted as if she were talking to him. He turned and ran back into the house and into the kitchen.

"Grandma, I've got to have something to feed Lady Samson," he said, out of breath.

"That's a good idea, Jimmy," Alice replied, looking at him. "So it's Lady Samson now? I like that name. I have her rabbit all ready for her in the refrigerator." Opening the door she took out a package and laid it on the table.

"By the way," Alice said. "You were not the only one reading last night. I was reading where you'll have to find a good heavy glove. You'll need it so you can hold her when you teach her to eat from your hand. You need a good size board right now, to tie the rabbit down on, so she can learn to eat from it. There are quite a few things you're going to have to make. But one thing you won't have to make are the hoods. I've got them ready."

Reaching up on one of the shelves over the sink, she picked up the hoods she made for the hawk. "How do you like them, Jimmy?" she asked, handing them to him.

His eyes lit up as he looked at the hoods. One was a plain Rufter hood with two leather laces hanging from each

Strong Feather

side. The lace was used to tie the hood onto the bird's head. The other one was an Indian hood, with the lace interwoven through the leather with the ends hanging loosely off the back. Alice painted both of the hoods with bright colors. There was an Indian arrowhead pattern on both sides of the Indian hood. She also placed two short white feathers that stuck out of the top notch part of the hood.

"They're great, Grandma, Jimmy said. "Those in the book don't look half as good as these."

Jimmy sat at the table and looked at one, then the other. Alice fixed his breakfast for him and put it on the table. He ate, not really knowing what he was eating. Even after the dishes were cleared from the table, he looked at the hoods again. His mind pictured all kinds of things. There was a sharp knock on the door. Looking up, he saw Mary come in.

"Hello there," Mary said, walking into the kitchen. She had a large bundle under her arm. She hurried over to the table, pulled a large paper sack out from under her arm and placed it on the table. She then saw the two hoods on the table in front of Jimmy.

"Oh, Jimmy. Those are beautiful!" she exclaimed. "That blue velvet sure does set them off, doesn't it?"

"It sure does," he said, picking up the Indian hood and looking at it.

"I've brought some things with me that my daddy and I worked on last night, and this morning. We made a nice lure for Lady Samson. We also cut two long pieces of leather thongs that we can tie the lure to. Daddy had some brass swivels down at the garage. I stopped there on my way over here and picked up two of them. He also gave us two old welding gloves that he fixed up for us. We'll need the gloves if we're both going to train Lady Samson."

Strong Feather

Jimmy didn't know what to say. He wanted all the things she had brought, but he had second thoughts about letting her get involved. He wanted to do all of the training. It seemed to him as if she was butting in. He didn't say a word.

Alice sensed what was going on in her grandson's mind as she watched the two of them. "You know, Jimmy," she said, "it sure is a blessing that Mary wants to help you out like this. You know what? Someone is going to have to help you do all those things that have to be done to train that hawk out back. It will have to learn to fly to the lure. Then there are a lot of other things you'll want it to do, and someone will have to help you. There's a lot of things the two of you will have to do before that beautiful hawk out there will be ready to hunt."

"You're very lucky, Jimmy. In fact, both of you are. You're both going to learn how to train a wild creature so it will do your bidding. That's a major job for anyone. It rarely happens to people these days. They expect someone else to do it for them. You two are blessed with the opportunity to learn together. I think that is just great."

Jimmy thought about what his grandma said. "It is, isn't it, Grandma?" he said. Then his face turned sad. "You know something. I think Lady Samson may belong to someone else."

"Why do you say that?" Mary asked.

"Well," he said. "I told you I saw a couple of small pieces of leather hanging from Lady Samson's legs yesterday. I read last night that when you capture a hawk the first thing you should do is get two pieces of leather strips and tie them onto the legs of the hawk. They're called 'jesses'. I think that is what Lady Samson has on each of her legs."

Strong Feather

"Let's go out back, Jimmy, and take a good look at her legs," Mary said, as she headed for the back door with the paper sack she'd brought.

"I'll take the hoods and Lady Samson's food with me, Grandma," he said, getting up. He picked up the two hoods, a package of rabbit scraps, and followed Mary out the back door.

He walked over to where Mary stood, next to the pigeon pen. She opened her sack and took out one of the gloves and gave it to him. He handed the rabbit scraps to her, and put the glove on his left hand. He tied the Indian hood to one of the small iron posts outside the pigeon pen. Placing one end of the Rufter hood's leather laces in his mouth, he walked over to the gate. The hood swung back and forth under his chin as he walked. Removing the stick from the hasp on the gate, he looked at Mary. She nodded her approval. Opening the gate he stepped inside, and quickly closed it behind him.

Lady Samson's neck was now bowed as her whole body became tense. Two unblinking yellow eyes now looked at him suspiciously. Slowly he made his way over to where she sat on her stick perch. He was as tense as his hawk was, but he didn't want her to know it. Slowly he raised his gloved hand until it was only a few inches from her feet. Before he knew what had happened, Lady Samson stepped off her perch and onto his glove. She now sat on his hand looking him right in the eye. She waited for his next move. Her size and weight caused his hand to move slowly downward. Gritting his teeth, he held his arm as steady as he could. His confidence grew and he raised his hand until he thought she was in the right position to put on her hood.

Removing the leather thong from his mouth with his free hand, he tried to remember what the book said on how

Strong Feather

to do it. He fumbled around trying to slip the hood over her head. He gave a sigh when he saw it was over her head. There was now no movement from the hawk. She sat on the glove like a stone statue. "That's what the book said they would do," he recalled.

Reaching behind Lady Samson's head with his free hand, he caught the far end of the other leather thong lace. Leaning forward, he grabbed the free thong in his teeth and pulled on them until they were tight. He then looped one thong over the other and tied a knot, then another. When he finished, he smiled. "It was pretty good for his first time," he thought.

He looked over at Mary. She stood outside the pen, and almost jumped up and down, but her feet never left the ground. He, too, started getting excited as he watched Lady Samson, even though his left arm was getting tired. So he walked over to the corner of the pen where he placed the stick as a perch.

Now he tried to remember how to get a hawk off the glove. Slowly he moved his gloved hand backwards towards the stick, until the back of his hand was barely touching the stick. Lady Samson just sat on his fist, not moving. Next, Jimmy moved his hand under the stick until the back of her feet touched the perch stick. She stepped upward onto the stick as Jimmy's hand passed under it. He remembered reading how to do that last night, but he never thought he would do it so soon.

"We've got to feed her," he said, stepping out of the pen and walking over to the wood pile. He rummaged around until he found the board he wanted. Digging through the garbage barrel, he found a piece of string that his grandma threw out. Tying the rabbit onto the board he went back into the pen. He then placed the board on a small bench his dad used to put things on for his pigeons. Going over to where Lady Samson perched, he looked at her. This time he reversed what he had done earlier. He now placed his gloved hand behind the stick, then brought it slowly over the top of the branch. When his glove touched the back of her legs she stepped up onto his fist. He nodded his head, as he congratulated himself on how good he was doing.

He carried her over to the bench, and with his free hand he helped her step off his glove and onto the bench. Even though the hawk couldn't see, she seemed to know exactly what to do. She hopped onto the scraps and started eating.

He wondered how she could eat with a hood on. "She could really eat if she could see," he thought. The books specifically said to start training new hawks on a meat board with their hoods on. Maybe later on when she was trained, he could take the hood off and let her eat. He'd have to check the books and see if he could do that.

As Lady Samson ate, he bent over and looked at her legs real good. He could see the remains of leather jesses on both of her legs. Lady Samson was trained by someone else. There was no way of telling how long she had been free, but it must have been some time for the jesses to look like they did. "She may have picked at them," he thought. She was so wild when he first caught her, but she settled down since then. It saddened him some to know that his hawk belonged to someone else.

Mary came into the pen and looked at the leather jesses on Lady Samson's legs. "There's no way of knowing how long she has been free, Jimmy," she said. "We can ask around and see if she belongs to anyone around here. If not, then we'll keep her. Until then we can work at learning how to teach her to hunt. When we've learned that, it will be a lot easier for us to train others hawks."

Strong Feather

Jimmy turned and looked at her. "That's right!" he said, almost shouting. "I bet you can't guess what I saw when I went back to get the rabbit yesterday."

"No," Mary said, getting excited. "What?"

"First I saw the other hawk that caused Lady Samson to drop her rabbit. It was soaring around high above me. I could tell by looking that it was smaller than Lady Samson. As I watched, it dove down and caught a large field mouse. It then flew over to an old dead tree next to the creek. I ran over to the tree and put my ear up against it and listened. I could hear little noises coming from inside. I'd say it's probably Lady Samson's mate, and they have some babies in the top of that tree!"

"Baby hawks," Mary said, getting more excited.

Lady Samson finished eating, and stood there not moving. Jimmy quickly got her back on his gloved fist, then placed her on her perch and removed her hood. They then stepped outside the pen and he latched the gate.

"Let's run down to the creek and see if there are babies in that old tree," he said. "Last night I read about how you're supposed to catch baby hawks. It said they should have all their down off and putting on feathers, before they can be taken from the nest. It said the nest should be watched. It said one should do that with field glasses. That way they're not disturbed. The book said it would be safer to do it that way, because the hawks get mad at whoever tries to take their babies away from them."

They both giggled as they ran off towards the creek. It wasn't long until they were standing next to the dead tree. They looked up at the top of the tree straining to hear the slightest sound. Now and then they told the other they thought they heard a noise coming from the top of the tree. They weren't sure it was hawk babies though. They put their ears up against the tree and listened, but heard

Strong Feather

nothing. Not knowing if there were baby hawks up there irritated both of them. They'd either have to climb the tree, or find a place around there that was high enough where they could look down on the top of the tree.

"I don't see the other hawk." Mary said, looking up. "I wonder if it is up there in the top of the tree right now. Let's go over to one of those hills and see if they're high enough. Or even better, we could probably see the top of it if we climbed up one of the trees around here." Looking around she pointed. "That tree over there looks high enough."

"Let's make sure he's not flying around above us," Jimmy said.

"Okay," Mary agreed.

They walked over to a large opening near the creek. They scanned the sky above them trying to spot the other hawk.

"There he is," Jimmy said, pointing.

Sure enough, high above them Mary saw a small black speck in the sky. "How do you know it's him?" Mary asked, with her hands cupped over her eyes, blocking out the sun.

"Well," he said. "That hawk is smaller than Lady Samson, and like I told you before, the female hawk is supposed to be larger than the male. If that's true, that's the male, and the noises I heard from that dead tree had to come from Lady Samson's babies."

"Wouldn't that be great, Jimmy," Mary said. "Just think. We couldn't ask for better hawk babies than hers. Let's go over to that tall tree and see if we can climb it. If we can get high enough, we can look down on the top of that old dead tree."

They hurried over to a small group of cottonwood trees. Stopping at the tallest tree they looked up. It looked

Strong Feather

like it was tall enough, but they weren't sure. After they walked around it a couple of times, they looked over at the old dead tree. "I'm sure it's high enough to look down on the top of the dead tree," he said. "But the limbs are too far off the ground. It's going to be a real challenge to climb."

They both walked around it again, looking up at the branches. "You will have to give me a boost," he said. "If I can get ahold of that first limb, I can climb up and get a good look. What do you think?"

"Sure. I can boost you up, Jimmy," Mary said, laughing. "Come on, let's do it."

Mary bent over next to the tree and he stepped up on her back. As he held onto the bark of the tree, she slowly stood up. It was all he needed and he got a good grip on the limb and swung up and onto the limb. He reached down and grabbed Mary's hand and pulled her up until she had a good hold on the limb with her free hand. Letting go of her hand, he grabbed her arm and helped her up onto the limb.

He then climbed on up the tree with Mary close behind. "What kind of a girl was this?", he wondered. She's got more spunk than any girl he'd ever known.

They climbed until they were above the top of the old dead tree, then stopped. Sitting down on a good size limb, they looked down at the top of the old tree. Their faces saddened. Then they both giggled when they saw something move. It was a baby chick. Then another moved, and another. There were three baby hawk chicks about a foot below the top of the tree. They were white fuzzy balls. Jimmy could see no sign of feathers.

The two of them were in a trance watching the three chicks. When they had their fill, they climbed back down, and headed toward the house.

Strong Feather

"I'll bring my father's field glasses next time," Mary said. "We'll be able to get a good close look at them. I can hardly wait until they're grown."

"I'll bring some boards," he said as they walked along. I'll nail them on the side of the tree so we can climb up to that first limb a lot easier."

Jimmy thought about what he wanted to do. "The best part," he thought, "was this daydream was coming true." Daydreaming was a lot of fun, but when it became real, that was even better. He found out that this real-life daydream was the best daydream he ever had, especially when he had a goal. He smiled at Mary.

"We surely have a lot of reading to do," he said, as they neared the house. Stopping, he looked at Mary. "I almost forgot. I've got to find some kind of food for Lady Samson."

"Let's go over to Mr. Miller's and see if we can catch some of his wild pigeons," Mary said. "They make a mess all over his barn, and he's always complaining about them. He even shoots some of them now and then, but they reproduce real fast. He doesn't work that hard at trying to keep their numbers down."

Instead of stopping at the hawk pen, they walked around to the front of the house. "Let me go in and check with my grandma first. I need to see if she has anything for me to do." He ran into the house and returned in a few minutes. "Grandma said we should go by your garage and check with grandpa and your dad. She said they would probably have some good ideas on how to catch pigeons."

When they got to the garage, they found both men trying to straighten out the fenders on a car. They stopped when Jimmy and Mary walked up. They were glad to see them. It gave them an excuse to take a break.

Strong Feather

Bill asked them how the hawk training was coming along. Jimmy told him about the straps on Lady Samson's legs. He then told them about the three baby hawks they saw in the top of an old dead tree, and that they planned on watching them grow. He then asked them if they had any ideas on how to catch some of the wild pigeons in Mr. Miller's barn?

"Tom," Bill said. "What did you do with that pigeon trap your boy used to have?"

"It's somewhere in my garage," Tom replied, getting up. "I'll take them back to the house and get it, Bill. Then we'll go over and talk to Chuck Miller."

"We're going to need your field glasses, daddy," Mary said. "We'll need them to watch those baby hawks. We have to know when they're big enough to be taken from their nest. The field glasses will help us watch them without us bothering them. We climbed up a cottonwood tree near their nest and got a good look at the three of them. The field glasses will help a lot."

"I'll bring them back with me after lunch," Bill said, smiling at his daughter.

The three of them went out and got in Tom's old truck and drove off. Bill watched the truck until it turned the corner. He walked over to the car they'd been working on. "Where else in Colorado could you find kids any happier than those two?", he thought. It was amazing what that bird did in the lives of those youngsters. He wondered what the outcome of it all would be. He shrugged his shoulders and went to work on the car. Soon the ringing of his hammer could be heard all over Mercer, Colorado. He, too, was a happy man.

131

Strong Feather

CHAPTER IX

It was late afternoon when Jimmy and Mary got back to the Warrior house with three pigeons. When they walked around the back of the house, they couldn't believe their eyes. There sat Lady Samson with her hood on. Jimmy couldn't believe that he forgot to take it off. Grabbing up the glove he laid on the top of the railroad ties, he pulled it on.

Mary took the cage with the three pigeons around to the back of the shed and set it on the ground. She returned just as Jimmy opened the pen gate and went inside. He walked over to Lady Samson and untied her hood. As he did, he talked to her in a soft voice to let her know he was there. He read in one of the books that talking to a hawk calmed them. It also helped the hawk come to know the voice of its master, and it wouldn't fear him. Slowly, he slipped the hood off. Lady Samson turned her head and looked up at him as if to say, "It's about time."

Jimmy wanted to do something, but what? Reaching into his shirt pocket he brought out a small stub of a pencil. Gently he stroked her head and neck. She seemed to like it, so he kept it up. There was no doubt in his mind that she was trained by someone who also stroked her. Placing his gloved fist in front of her she hopped on it without any hesitation. He marveled at how well she did things. Jimmy carried her around the pen a couple of times before he stopped and put her back on her perch.

After she came to his fist three times, he left her sitting on the limb perch. He then placed the pencil and Rufter hood in his shirt pocket. Leaving the pen, he closed the gate and picked up the paper bag Mary left by the gate that morning. Taking out the lure she made and examining it, it looked a lot like one of the pigeons they caught.

Strong Feather

Turning the bag upside down he poured all of its contents out onto the ground.

Mary watched as he knelt down and looked at what she brought. There were two swivels and a half-dozen lengths of leather cut to different lengths. They were each cut into half-inch wide strips. "What kind of leather is this?" he asked, holding one of the strips up and looking at it.

"It's goat," Mary said. "My father tanned some goat hides a couple of years ago, and he had these pieces left. We cut most of it up into those two long leashes and still had enough left for whatever else we may need. I'm sure there's enough for at least two falconer's bags. I'll make them tonight after supper."

"It looks like we're going to be in good shape for equipment," he said, looking at the things on the ground. "I sure would like to try this lure out. Let's put the Indian hood on her. I need to learn how to do that. Then we can take her out to the field and see how she comes to the lure. What do you say, Mary?"

"I'm ready, if you're ready," she replied.

Jimmy put everything back into the bag except the short leash, two jesses and a swivel. He handed Mary the sack and untied the Indian hood from the metal post. Mary pulled the Rufter hood out of his shirt pocket and dropped it in the bag. He pulled his glove back on and went back inside the pen. With ease Lady Samson jumped onto his gloved fist and looked at him. He had no trouble placing the Indian hood over her head. He tied it like he did the Rufter hood. Placing her back on the perch, he removed the glove.

Jimmy untied the two small pieces of leather jesses on her legs. He quickly replaced them with two long ones. Next, he tied a swivel to the leather jess on her left leg.

Strong Feather

Then he tied one end of the short leash to the swivel and stepped back to see how it looked. Holding the leash in his right hand, he walked back and forth checking it out. It looked good to him. He saw a big smile on Mary's face, which meant she approved.

"Let's see if it all works," he said, putting his glove back on. Wrapping the leash around his right hand, he placed his gloved hand behind Lady Samson's feet. He talked softly to her as he moved the glove forward until it touched her legs, and she stepped off the perch and up onto his glove. "What a great bird she was," he thought, as he watched her.

Mary opened the gate, and he stepped out. They headed towards the open field behind the house. Once into the field, Mary looked around for a good spot. "This looks like a good place for us to start Lady Samson's training," she said.

"OK," Jimmy replied. "I'll start her off on this short leash. You work the lure for her after I take off the hood, and we'll see what happens."

They looked at each other, wanting to do it, but afraid to try. Mary shrugged her shoulders and walked off about ten yards and started twirling the lure around and around over her head. She wanted to get used to it before Jimmy took off Lady Samson's hood. Around and around the lure went over her head. Then she let go of the leather and the lure seemed to fly for a short distance before it dropped to the ground. It looked good, so she nodded at Jimmy.

Jimmy reached up and removed the hood. Lady Samson perked up when the hood was removed. She was not in the pen. She looked at Jimmy as if she knew exactly what was expected of her.

Strong Feather

Again Mary twirled the lure around and around over her head as Jimmy unwound her leather leash. Then without any warning, she let it go and it sailed off. Before Jimmy knew what happened, his left arm rose about six inches. Lady Samson flew off. She swooped down towards the ground at first, then up she flew and caught the lure in her talons. She fell to ground with the lure in her grasp. Her left wing still drooped a little but it didn't seem to bother her. She stood over the lure and pulled at it with her beak a few times before she looked up at Jimmy.

The two of them were hypnotized, not believing what they saw. Lady Samson broke their trance when she hopped towards Jimmy. They each gave a short laugh of joy at seeing her work. No longer in a trance, Jimmy ran over to her, rolling up the leash. He talked to her as he placed his glove on the ground in front of her. She hopped on and sat there looking up at him. She still had ahold of the lure. He couldn't stop praising her as he reached for the lure. She gave it up easily.

Jimmy handed the lure to Mary. He was so proud of Lady Samson, and it showed in the way he looked at her. He took his pencil out of his shirt pocket and began stroking her head. The way she bobbed her head up and down, it looked like she was growing taller with each stroke of the pencil. Lady Samson was a proud bird, and it showed in the way she held herself. When she turned her head and looked at Jimmy, he saw a twinkle in her eye. The two of them liked each other and it showed.

"She surely knows how to take the lure, doesn't she?" Jimmy asked Mary, looking at Lady Samson.

"I'll say she does," Mary replied, as proud of her as he was.

Jimmy frowned. "Lady Samson needs to be fed, but all of the rabbit is gone."

135

Strong Feather

"We have those pigeons we caught for her," Mary said. "We've got to get over being squeamish about what has to be done. Hawks catch all kinds of things to eat. They catch rats, field mice, gophers, and other small animals. They also catch doves, pigeons and other birds. If you hadn't captured Lady Samson, I'm sure she would have caught some of those pigeons over at Mr. Miller's. Those babies up in that dead tree have to be fed. Let's not think of it as something bad. It's the same thing we do when we want chicken."

He saw her point of view, and felt better about it. If Lady Samson didn't eat, she wouldn't be able to catch things so his grandparents could have meat. "Okay," he said.

Mary ran back to the pen and got the cage with the pigeons in it. When she returned, Jimmy was tying the long leash to the swivel. She quickly took one of the pigeons out of the cage and closed it. Standing up, she could see that Lady Samson had not taken her eyes off of the pigeon. It was time to hunt, and Mary saw it in her eyes.

Lady Samson easily caught the pigeon they had for her, and gave it up to Jimmy just like she did with the lure. He then hooded her, and they walked back to the pen. Taking her inside, he placed her on her perch and removed the Indian hood. Mary placed the other two pigeons behind the pen. When she came around the pen, she saw that Jimmy was talking to his hawk, as he stroked her with his finger. They were growing closer, but they were so much alike. It would take time before the two of them would overcome the distrust each had deep inside. But a lasting friendship always takes time.

Setting her paper sack next to the gate, Mary went into the house. She asked Alice if she would cut up the pigeon so Jimmy could feed Lady Samson. Alice was glad

Strong Feather

to hear that she caught the pigeon. When Mary returned, the pigeon was in four pieces.

Jimmy took one of the pieces in his gloved hand. He then held it out to Lady Samson. She hopped onto his glove and began to eat. When she finished, he put her back on the perch and repeated the feeding method until she ate all of the pigeon. He stepped out of the pen, took off his glove, and placed it on top of the railroad ties.

Mary picked up her paper sack and glove. She and Jimmy watched the hawk. They walked over to the house, stopping at the bottom of the steps, and looked back at Lady Samson one more time before they went inside.

When they told Alice all they did, she said, "It surely has been a full day for you two, hasn't it? But, don't forget your evening chores, Jimmy. Mary, we sure would like for you to stay for supper tonight."

"I can't. Daddy told me to be home for supper tonight," she replied. "Maybe some other time. A lot happened today, and I've got a lot to do tonight, so I'll see both of you tomorrow.

"OK," Jimmy replied.

"Don't forget we want you to eat with us one of these days," Alice said.

"I won't," she said, walking over to the front door. She waved before she went out.

Looking over at the wood box, Jimmy thought it was in good shape, but his grandma wanted it full. Getting up from the table, he went out and got a big armload of wood and filled it up to the top.

As he started to leave the kitchen, Alice stopped him. "You need to fix some place to keep those pigeons you caught, Jimmy, she said. "You sure can't leave them out behind the hawk pen. That cage is too small for them. Your dad had another pen around the other side of the house by the garage. It's not in too good of shape. Tommy used to keep about a dozen pigeons in it. You'll need to check it before you put those pigeons in there."

He recalled seeing something up against the side of the garage but didn't pay any attention to it. "I'll go out and see, Grandma," he said.

"If Lady Samson's as good as you say she is, it won't take long before she'll be strong enough to start hunting for you. Just don't get in too big a hurry, Jimmy, and don't hold her back either. The book I read last night said you can cause a hawk not to want to hunt if you hold them back. You need to read all you can on falconry, and when the time comes for you to let her fly free, you'll surely know it."

"I'll do that, Grandma," he answered, looking at her. "I remember reading that. I don't think it will be much longer."

Alice nodded and went back to fixing supper as he went out the back door. He returned a couple of minutes later with another large armload of wood. He put all of it on the wood box until it overflowed. He went out the front door and around the right side of the house and then stopped. About halfway down that side of the house he saw the remains of a pen. It was small, just like his grandma said. He could see about a dozen pigeon roosts inside. It wouldn't be hard to catch a pigeon in there if he had to.

Opening the gate, he stepped inside and looked around. He saw a couple of places in the chicken wire that needed mending. Looking around, he found a piece of bailing wire he used to mend the holes. The roosts were sturdy enough for the pigeons.

He checked his work to make sure the pigeons couldn't get out. It wasn't the best job, but it would keep them inside the pen. Leaving the gate open, he walked past

Strong Feather

the pen to the back of the house. As he neared the hawk pen, he checked on Lady Samson. She sat inside her cage watching his every move. It made him feel good just knowing she was interested in everything he did. Nothing happened around her pen that she didn't see. "She sure had sharp eyes," Jimmy thought, as he walked past her.

Jimmy walked around the pen to the pile of wood. Stooping over, he looked at the pigeons in the cage. His grandma called it a 'hawk pen' a couple minutes ago. That surely sounded better than a 'pigeon pen' to him. Picking up the cage, he continued on around the far side of the shed. He didn't want Lady Samson to see the pigeons. "She might get worked up and want to catch another pigeon," he thought. He held the cage at his side in such a way that she wouldn't be able to see what was inside.

Past the corner of the house, he raised the cage so he could carry it easier. Stepping through the open gate, he went inside and closed it. He placed the cage on a small bench, then opened the cage door so the pigeons could get out.

Stepping back, he watched as the pigeons came out of the cage. They looked all around, cooed a couple of times, then flew up onto a long board that ran in front of all the roosts. There they started cooing again, as they walked back and forth, stopping now and then to peck each other's beak. This was all new to them. He left the pen, hooked the latch on the gate, and went back into the house.

His grandma gave him two pieces of dry bread, and he took them back to the pigeon pen. He broke them into four pieces and placed them on top of the bench. He found an old rusty pan and filled it with water. When he'd placed it next to the bread, he closed the gate and watched them eat and drink.

Strong Feather

It was then he realized he hadn't gotten his hawk any water. He remembered seeing a large pan on the back porch. Filling it with water, he placed it on the table next to where he placed the rabbit.

Lady Samson fluttered over to the table and began drinking. Jimmy watched as she took water into her beak, raised her head to swallow, then looked at him before she drank again. She acted as if she was scolding him. He had to be more mindful of her needs.

Jimmy soon felt at ease talking to Lady Samson. She listened to everything he said. She might not know what he said, but she listened. What happened was not only good for the hawk, it was good for him, too. He never had anything in his life like her. She may have belonged to someone else before he caught her, but right now she was his.

He began to hope they would never find her other owner. That way she wouldn't have to leave. "That would be great," he thought. "That would be the greatest."

While he watched her, he realized someone was watching him. His grandma was on the screened-in porch looking at him. He didn't know how long she'd been there, but when he saw her, she motioned for him to come to her. He locked the pen and ran over to the porch. She motioned for him to come into the house. Opening the screen door, he followed her down the hall and into the kitchen, where they sat down at the table.

"You know something, Jimmy," she said. "I've been watching you and that bird out there, and I like what I see. As I watched you two it started me to thinking. I'm sure that you've given some thought about Lady Samson belonging to someone else before she came your way. I hear it in your voice when you talk to her. If she's been trained as good as you say she has, I would think that her owner surely wants her back."

"That's what I was thinking about just before you called me," Jimmy answered.

"I want you to do me a big favor," she said. "You take good care of Lady Samson, but try not to get too attached to her. I think that her owner probably lives in one of the nearby towns around here. But, whether they do or don't, we need to know. It's no good keeping something that belongs to someone else, especially when you start getting attached to it. You might not want to give it up when they come to get it."

She stopped and looked at Jimmy. "I think we should advertise in the Longmont paper that you've captured a hawk. If her owner lives in this area, they'll either see or be told about the ad. Then they can get in touch with us. If no one comes for her, you'll know you can keep her. What do you think of that idea, Jimmy?"

He didn't want to think about it. He shook his head from side to side as Alice watched him fight the idea. Placing her hand on his shoulder, she didn't say a word. It wasn't long until his head stopped, and he shrugged his shoulders.

"I guess you're right, Grandma," he said, looking down at the floor. "It sure would be hard to give her up," he thought. Looking up he said, "When do we have to advertise we have her, Grandma?"

"Well, I think we could wait a couple more days," she said. "At least long enough for her to teach the two of you a few things." Getting up from the table, Alice looked at her grandson. His eyes sparkled as they looked at each other. She was so proud of him.

"You're going to have to learn a lot of things from that hawk of yours in a short period of time, Jimmy," she continued. "If someone does come for her, you're going to have to know enough to be able to train those baby hawks. Even if no one comes and gets her, you're going to have to know how to train them later. Let's look on the bright side of all of this. It looks to me like this is going to be a training ground for you and Lady Samson. I'd say she has a real good teacher, and you're going to have to learn as much as you can, as fast as you can."

Jimmy's thinking about Lady Samson began to change. Whoever trained her might not want her, but if they did, by then she would have taught him enough to train her babies.

"That's a great idea, Grandma." he said. "Just give me enough time to learn what I need to know. I could let her go then if I had to."

She placed her hand on his shoulder and said, "I'm proud of you, Jimmy. It will all work out for the best. Just you wait and see."

"I sure hope so," he said, placing his face in his hands.

CHAPTER X

Jimmy and Mary spent every spare moment they could during the next week working with Lady Samson. The days quickly slipped past, and it wasn't long before they gained confidence in themselves. Even though they were excited about working with Lady Samson, there were three other small things on their minds.

After their daily workout with Lady Samson, they headed for the big cottonwood tree near the creek. Up the tree they climbed with the field glasses so they could watch the baby hawks. The three balls of fuzz were watched very closely, and the slightest change in each of the babies was noted. Occasionally they saw the papa hawk soaring high above. The chicks grew, and they knew he took good care of them. It wouldn't be much longer until they would put on feathers and begin to fly.

Each time Jimmy and Mary sat down on that tree branch, their hearts beat a little faster. To watch the chicks in their nest was beyond their wildest dreams. They grew bigger and bigger.

One day as they sat on their branch watching, the male hawk returned to the nest with a large crow it caught. What a commotion there was in the nest. All three of the chicks were now good eaters, and fighters. It was each chick for itself when it came to food. They saw that all three of them would be good hunters when they grew up.

The two of them stayed up in the tree as long as they could. When the time came to leave, they mumbled a little as they climbed down the tree. But once on the ground they ran over to the dead tree, placed their ears up against the trunk, and listened. What a beautiful sight they made. Large green cottonwood trees encircled the dead tree, a deep-blue Colorado sky glittered above their heads, and the softness of the green grass was their footstool. The dead tree was bleached alabaster white by time, and stood majestically in the middle of a large opening. A tanned lad and lassie stood with their ears pressed up against a grand monolith, listening. It was a sight to behold.

Oh, so faintly their ears heard the chirps of the chicks. With those chirps still ringing in their ears, they ran back to the house to tell Alice how the baby chicks were doing, plus all of the plans they had for them.

As each day passed, they spent more and more time down at that old dead tree. Their excitement grew as they watched the chicks changing before their eyes. Seeing the chicks was exciting, but watching Lady Samson's progress was exhilarating. The two of them began to feel a sense of accomplishment as they worked with her, plus the good feeling that goes with success. The time was getting closer for Lady Samson to fly free. A thin ribbon of leather was all that kept her from flying off. They surely didn't want to take the chance of losing her during training, plus they realized they needed her help in their training program. If she decided to fly off during her free flight, they wouldn't have a hawk. There was no way of knowing how long it would be before the babies would be ready to train.

Inwardly they fought the idea of letting her fly free. They knew it was not a good idea to hold back a hawk when it was ready to hunt. Holding one back could stop the hawk's desire to hunt. It would expect to be fed the rest of its life by its trainer. It was something the two of them didn't want to face even though they knew it was coming. Finally, one Saturday, they both knew it was time for Lady Samson to fly free off the leash.

Mary started bringing her dog, Goldie, over to watch the hawk work. She lay by herself and watched the two of them as they trained the hawk. Goldie, being a bird

Strong Feather

dog caused trouble at first. The first day Mary brought her, she chased the lure. After a good talking to, she lay around and watched. Then when Lady Samson took flight, she stood point at the hawk, with an eager look in her eyes. Another good talking to stopped that. Now all she did was lay around with her head on the ground. But her eyes followed every move the lure and hawk made.

A few days earlier, Mary picked Goldie up and carried her over to Jimmy. Lady Samson sat on his glove watching the dog as Mary introduced Goldie to her. That was all it took. The eager look in Goldie's eye was gone. It wasn't long until the dog and hawk seemed to be friends, if that could happen between a bird dog and a bird.

This was the day Lady Samson would fly free. The two of them went out to the hawk pen to look at her. While they were in the pen, Alice came out the back door with something in her hand.

"I've made Lady Samson a leg bell like I saw in one of the books," she said, handing it to Jimmy. "I also made you a willow whistle from a branch off that willow tree down by the creek. You put the bell on her before you take her out, then use the whistle to call her when you want her to return."

"That's great, Grandma," he said, remembering what he read about having a bell and whistle in one of the books. He placed the whistle in his shirt pocket next to the pencil. "I'll put the bell on her."

He placed the Indian hood over Lady Samson's head before he tied the bell to her right leg. It made a noise when he put it on. He released the bell and it jingled. Lady Samson cocked her head when she heard it. She then stood very still. " She probably had a bell on her leg before," he thought. There wasn't much that bothered her. He took the leash swivel off her left jess. She was free to fly when she wanted today. He hoped it would be back to him.

Alice watched as Mary and Jimmy took Lady Samson out of the pen and walked over to the field nearby. Goldie ran on ahead of them smelling everything. Alice watched until they were in the middle of the field before she turned and went back inside.

The only thing different this day was that the leash would be off Lady Samson's leg. But that small difference was causing a lot of nervousness between the two hawk trainers. When they reached the middle of the field, Jimmy placed Lady Samson on Mary's glove. She walked about 100 feet, turned, and waited. Goldie lay down in the shade of a bush. She was ready for the daily show. Jimmy took the lure from his hunting bag and started swinging it around over his head.

"Okay, Mary!" he yelled. "Remove her hood!"

Mary took off her hood and waited. She then raised her hand above her head. When Lady Samson saw the lure sailing around in the air, she took flight. Swooping down, she flapped her wings as she flew towards the lure. Jimmy quickly pulled it back and hid it behind his back. Lady Samson kept flapping her wings as she flew past him. She flew higher and higher until she was soon flying high above him in a large circle. Bringing the lure out from behind his back, he began to swing it around and around over his head again in a large arc. When the lure started upward, he released it. Upward it flew and down Lady Samson dove, catching it at the top of its arc.

Down she came to the ground with the lure in her claws. Jimmy ran over to where she was on the ground and placed his gloved hand close to her feet. She hopped onto his glove, not taking her eyes off of him. He quickly removed the lure from her grasp, talking to her excitedly.

Strong Feather

Mary ran up and handed him her hood. He quickly placed it over her head and gave a sigh of relief. He tied the swivel back on her left jess. The trial was over.

"Wasn't she just perfect?" Mary said, softly stroking Lady Samson's neck and wings with her finger. She looked at Jimmy. "I think she's ready to hunt. I think we've been holding her back too long. She knows a lot more about all of this than we do. What do you say, Jimmy? Will today be the first day we hunt with her?"

"She's only flown once off leash, Mary," he said, frowning as he looked at her. "What if she takes off and we don't see her again?"

"I don't think that will ever happen, Jimmy," she said, looking at him seriously. "She has her babies down there on top of that old dead tree. Even if she decides not to come back to you, she'll go there for sure. If that happened, I'm sure we could call her down with the lure. Let's try it, Jimmy. I know she's ready. Not only that, we don't have any more food for her. We'll either have to go over to Mr. Miller's and catch some more pigeons, or let her hunt for herself."

He didn't like her idea too much, but it made sense. They did need some food for the hawk. Not only that, the books said some hawks wouldn't hunt wild game after they got used to having pigeons given to them. He didn't know what to do, but he felt Mary was probably right.

"Okay, Mary, you win," he said. "I agree, we need to let her hunt." He looked at his hawk. "Where do you think we should take her first?"

"Let's take her over where she caught that big rabbit, Jimmy," she replied, looking across the creek. "One of the books I read last night said that hawks need to have rabbit quite often. So let's go see if we can find her one."

147

Strong Feather

"That's a good idea," he said, looking over at the creek.

Mary looked over at her dog, "Come, Goldie," she said. "Let's go scare up a rabbit or two for your friend, Lady Samson."

So, off they went with Goldie running ahead of them. Goldie liked to run through the tall weeds and grasses. She also loved to run back and forth smelling everything in sight. Her tail wagged so hard that it sometimes looked like it was wagging her. Jimmy recalled the first time he saw her. When she looked up at him, she looked like she was laughing. With that laugh on her face, and the wag of her tail, she let you know that she liked you. There wasn't a person in Mercer that didn't like Goldie.

Mary called her when they neared the creek. She didn't want her wandering off when they got there. It was Mary's plan to let her hunt in the field by the large trees on the other side of the creek. Goldie ran back to her and sat down. Mary pointed across the creek and followed her across the creek.

Once across they headed for the large trees. Nearing them, Mary called Goldie. When she came up to her, Mary patted her right leg. Goldie ran over and sat down beside her right foot. She looked up at Mary with that big smile on her face.

Mary patted her on the head a couple of times, then said, "Hunt!"

Off Goldie ran, smelling every bush and clump of grass, as she ran here and there through the tall grass.

Jimmy untied the swivel from the jess on Lady Samson's leg. He looked at Mary and then at Goldie running back and forth in front of them. He untied Lady Samson's hood and took it off. She looked around to see what was happening. Lifting his gloved hand above his head, she was off.

Downward she swooped towards the tall grass where Goldie ran back and forth. Flapping her powerful wings, she arced upward. The steady beating of her wings caused her to quickly gain altitude, and soon she circled high above their heads. It was a breathtaking sight to see, as they couldn't take their eyes off the hawk. They were so caught up in watching the bird they forgot all about the dog. Goldie came to point.

The silence of Goldie not moving through the weeds caused Mary to look down. She whispered to Jimmy. "Goldie's found something over there in those bushes, Jimmy."

They both ran over to where she was and made enough noise to scare a dozen rabbits from their hiding places. But only one rabbit jumped out from under a small bush and hopped off. They watched as the rabbit vanished in the tall grasses. They looked up and saw Lady Samson diving straight towards the grass where the rabbit disappeared. Spellbound, they watched as she arced upward and then downward into the grass. She had the rabbit before it knew what happened.

They ran over to where Lady Samson was flopping around on the ground. Jimmy placed his gloved hand next to Lady Samson as he talked to her. She hopped onto his gloved hand with one foot, holding onto the rabbit with the other. Mary reached over and she released it to her. He quickly put the hood back on Lady Samson, and they both sighed, Jimmy stroked her neck with his fingers as he talked to her. She was something else.

"It's a nice size rabbit, Jimmy," Mary said, looking at it. Goldie came running up and smelled it. It was her way of letting them know she had done her part. Mary patted her on the head and said, "You're a good girl, Goldie. Let's not stop with one, Jimmy. Let's have rabbit for supper tonight."

Jimmy nodded, and Mary told Goldie to hunt. Off she went, bounding along through the tall grasses. She had as much fun hunting as Mary and Jimmy did. A good working relationship formed between the four of them. The more they worked together, the stronger the bond became.

Removing Lady Samson's hood again, Jimmy raised her over his head. She swooped over Goldie's head, then flew upward into the sky. It didn't take her long to gain the altitude she wanted and began to circle. Again Goldie came to point, and another rabbit was flushed out and Lady Samson caught it. With the second rabbit in their game bag, Jimmy and Mary laughed and jumped up and down. This was exciting, and they enjoyed themselves.

On the next try Lady Samson dove on her own, catching a rabbit that was trying to sneak away from Goldie. The hawk and the dog worked well together.

"One more rabbit should do it," Jimmy said. "We don't want to catch all the rabbits in one day. Plus, we don't want to lose Lady Samson either."

It wasn't long until they had the fourth rabbit. There was a feeling of relief when Jimmy placed the hood back on Lady Samson, and they headed towards the house. Mary had three rabbits in her game bag, and he had one. Lady Samson's wing was drooping as she sat on his right fist. They were four tired hunters returning from the hunt. Each did their part, which made them feel good, especially Goldie as she ran back and forth between Mary and Jimmy.

When Jimmy placed Lady Samson in her pen and removed her hood, he was proud of her. "I'll be back to feed you as soon as I can, my Lady Samson," he said. "Be patient and you'll have a feast tonight." Removing his

Strong Feather

pencil from his shirt pocket, he stroked her head as he talked. When he returned the pencil to his shirt pocket, he felt the whistle. Putting it up to his lips, he gently blew on it. A soft low note came from the whistle. Lady Samson cocked her head and looked at him. It didn't startle her, which meant she probably heard a whistle before.

They hurried into the house carrying their game bags over their shoulders. In the kitchen, Alice was busy with her back towards them. Quietly they placed the rabbits on the table and waited for her to turn around. When she did, she let out a little shout.

"Four rabbits!" she said excitedly. "Sit down and tell me all about it!"

They took turns telling her all about what happened during the hunt. She nodded her head excitedly when they told her how the hawk and dog worked together.

When they finished, she said, "I thought today was only supposed to be a free flight day." She looked at both of them real seriously. "What would you have done if Lady Samson flew off?"

"We talked about that Grandma," Jimmy replied, "and Mary thought that if she decided to fly off, she'd probably only fly over to where her babies are. If she had flown over there, we could have called her down with a lure." He looked at his grandma kind of sheepishly and continued, "I didn't want to do it at first, but what Mary said made sense. So, I decided to let Lady Samson hunt, and hunt she did."

Alice considered what he said, then nodded her head in agreement. What they did was probably the right thing to do. "I'd say Lady Samson deserves a good meal for all she's done today," she said. "How about if I show you two how to cut up a rabbit for your hawk. After I do that, I'll show you how to cut one up to eat. I'm glad we have those books on all of these things we're doing. The books recommend that when you feed a hawk rabbit, you cut it into four large pieces. You don't remove the skin either. That's the way they eat it in the wild, and it's a very essential part of their diet."

"Take these rabbits outside and around the house to that old tree stump, the one I use as a chopping block. I'll get my pan and a bucket of water. Go on," and she motioned for them to leave.

They carried the rabbits out the front door and around the house to the tree stump next to the garden. Alice had set a small table up against the stump. She used it to place her vegetables on before taking them into the house. The tree stump was her chopping block. It was nothing more than the stump of a tree Tom cut down a couple of years earlier. Alice came around the corner carrying a large pan and a bucket of water. Setting the pan down on the ground, she splashed some water on the tabletop and then the tree stump. She then took a stiff bristle brush out of her apron pocket and scrubbed both surfaces real good before she splashed more water on them. Reaching into her apron again, she brought out a large butcher knife and went to work on the first rabbit. Jimmy and Mary were amazed at how fast she cut it into four pieces. Back into the apron pocket went her hand, and this time she brought out a piece of paper. Unfolding it, she placed it on top of the table and placed Lady Samson's four pieces of rabbit on the paper.

"Watch me real close," she said. "There's nothing to cutting up a rabbit. The two of them watched her every move. She soon had three rabbits skinned. She then cut them into smaller pieces. She looked at the large pile of rabbit in front of her.

"There's enough here to make a fine supper for both of our families," she said, looking at them.

152

Strong Feather

Jimmy and Mary were pleased.   That was what they were hoping she would say.

"Mary, I'd like for you to help me get this meat washed real good while Jimmy takes Lady Samson's rabbit into the house. Jimmy, I want you to wrap three of those pieces in the newspaper that's on the kitchen table. When you've done that, take the other piece out and feed your hawk."

"Okay," he said, picking up the four pieces of rabbit. He carried them into the house as they started washing the rabbits she cut up. Inside, he quickly wrapped the three pieces of rabbit and put them in the refrigerator. He took the other piece out back and fed Lady Samson. He watched her eat and realized how hard she worked that day for the meal she was now enjoying.

After she ate, he ran back into the house. Mary and his grandma sat at the table talking. Some of the rabbit was wrapped in waxed paper for Mary to take home. Alice placed it in a paper sack when he came in and sat down. When it was wrapped nice and tight, she put a rubber band around it and sat it in front of Mary.

Looking at her grandson she said, "Mary and I have been talking about your hawk, Jimmy. It looks like you've got a hunter for sure. It also looks like someone trained her real good. I'd say the person who did all of that hard work would like to have her back. Maybe even more than you would like to keep her."

Jimmy didn't say a word as he looked at the paper bag in front of Mary.

"If what I'm saying is true, Jimmy, I think it's time we placed that ad in the Longmont newspaper, the ad we talked about the other day. It could be that Lady Samson is not from around here, and we may never find her owner. It would be nice if that were true. But, if the owner does live around here, he needs to know we have his hawk. I know that you would want someone to do the same thing for you if it were your hawk, wouldn't you?"

"Yes, Grandma, I sure would," he said, with no wavering in his voice. He knew it was time they ran the ad. He dreaded it, but it was time and he knew it. It bothered him the last two days. He wanted to know one way or the other to whom Lady Samson belonged. She needed to be with her owner, whoever it was. It could turn out to be him. He would like that. They grew closer each day, and he had someone that liked him. He liked the look of acceptance in her eyes when he approached her. If he had to let her go, it had to be now. It would hurt, but not as much as it would later.

"Let's put the ad in the paper tomorrow, Grandma," he said. "We can work with her until we find out who she belongs to. How long should we run the ad, Grandma? How long will I have to wait before I'll know for sure she's mine?"

"How about two weeks?" Alice asked, with pride in her eyes as she looked at Jimmy. "I would say that two weeks should be plenty of time for us to find out if someone around here owns your Lady Samson. In the meantime, you two can continue with your training program."

Jimmy and Mary nodded their heads in agreement. "That would be plenty of time," they thought. They still had a lot to learn, especially if they wanted to train those babies of hers.

"I'd advise you two to think about letting Lady Samson hunt for different types of quarry, Alice said, looking out the kitchen window. "The pheasant season is just starting. Those wild pigeons over at Mr. Miller's would also be different. I'm sure there are other types of game she can hunt that we don't know of right now."

Jimmy and Mary agreed. "This is going to be a lot of fun," Mary said.

"When will your father be going to Longmont again, Mary?" Alice asked.

"At supper last night he said he had to go tomorrow. He has to pick up some parts for a truck he's working on," Mary replied.

"OK," Alice said. "I'll write out the ad right now, and you can take it home with you." Alice got a pencil and some paper out of the top drawer of her sink cabinet. She quickly wrote the ad out on a piece of paper. Reaching into her apron pocket, she brought out two dollar bills. She placed the money inside the paper and handed it to Mary. With the ad in her hand, Mary stood up to leave. It was kind of a sad time, especially after they had such a great time that day.

"Don't forget to take your rabbit with you," Alice said, handing her the paper sack.

Mary placed the paper under the rubber band on the paper bag, then walked over to the door. She looked at Jimmy and said, "I'll see you tomorrow, and no matter what happens, I'm glad Lady Samson came our way, even if it's only for a short time."

"I'm glad, too," Jimmy said, looking at her, then at his grandma.

Mary closed the door and was gone. It was a grand day at the Warrior house. Alice started preparing the rabbit for supper. Tom wouldn't believe it when they had rabbit again. They could hardly wait to see the big smile on his face.

CHAPTER XI

The days began to get hot, but the nights had a coolness to them that only Colorado nights have. It was on one of these cool, quiet nights that Jimmy lay on his bed, and thought about all the things that happened that day. There was an excitement about it all, but the unknown, was even more exciting. The unknown no longer scared him like it once did. He looked forward to it, all except the part about losing his hawk. That was the only flaw in his dreams. If only it would go away he'd be the happiest boy in the world. That was the only dark cloud that hung over him, which caused him to frown when he thought about it.

Each day dragged by for Jimmy and Mary. Even though there was lots to do, they couldn't shake the feeling that something awful was about to happen to them. The ad was placed in the Longmont newspaper. It wasn't long until everyone around that area knew about the hawk Jimmy caught. If they were the owner, or if they knew the owner, they were instructed to contact Tom Warrior in Mercer, Colorado.

As the first week came to an end, much was accomplished. They hunted with Lady Samson every day. Day by day she grew stronger. It seemed like the more she caught, the better she performed, and the more she caught, the better she ate. Not only her, but the Warrior and Wilson families soon found their refrigerators full of wild meat.

It wasn't long until the people around Mercer talked about the hawk Jimmy caught. People he knew stopped him on the street and talked to him about his hawk. They wanted to know how his hawk was doing, and what she caught lately. Jimmy had pride in what he did. What he thought now was a lot different than what he thought when he first came to Mercer.

Strong Feather

There were a couple of times when he came back to reality. One was when he saw the two guys that hit him with a rock the first day he arrived in town. They were always standing off in the distance watching him. His grandpa told him he talked to them, but they let him know they didn't care about him or his grandson. He knew from the first day they wanted him to know Mercer wasn't his turf. It was theirs. So, he did his best to stay out of their way. If there was going to be trouble, they'd be the ones who started it.

One day Mary's dog, Goldie, flushed her first pheasant. Lady Samson's job was cut out for her as they watched her miss on her first try. They couldn't believe it when she missed the second pheasant. But Lady Samson and Goldie were a team now, and on her third try she caught a large rooster pheasant. She had that twinkle in her eye when she hopped onto Jimmy's glove. She looked up at him as if to say, "I did it just for you."

Jimmy stopped using his pencil, and was now using the back of his pocket comb to stroke her head and neck. The young boy and his hawk were a sight to behold, the tall, slender Indian lad, with a beautiful hawk perched on his hand. It caused one to catch their breath when they were together. And the love that grew between this lad and his hawk could be felt, as well as seen.

When Mary had the pheasant in her bag, he sent her up again. It wasn't long before the second and the third pheasants were caught. Jimmy proudly placed the Indian hood on Lady Samson, and they headed home. This was definitely a day they would never forget.

The next morning they went over to Mr. Miller's farm. Two days earlier they asked him if it would be all right if they brought Lady Samson over. They wanted to see if she could catch some of his wild pigeons that roosted

Strong Feather

in the top of his barn. Chuck Miller had told them he would have to think about that. He told them he'd heard about Jimmy's hawk being a good hunter, and he sure would like to see it work. He thought about it as he looked at the two of them. Then he said, "There's one thing you've got to promise me. I want you to promise me your hawk won't catch any of my chickens."

"She only catches what we send her up to catch," Jimmy said.

Mary nodded her head in agreement. "You'll see, Mr. Miller," she said.

Chuck agreed to let them come over that weekend. He let them know he would pen up his chickens before they got there. That way, there shouldn't be any trouble with the hawk and his chickens.

They hurried back to Jimmy's house and told Alice what Mr. Miller said. She agreed they'd have to watch Lady Samson real close and make sure she didn't get any of his chickens. The one thing they didn't need was for her to be called a chicken hawk.

When Jimmy went to bed that night he had some doubts about taking Lady Samson over to Mr. Miller's. What if she went after his chickens and not the pigeons? He thought about all of the things she did right, and he felt better. Lady Samson proved to him that she would hunt what he sent her up to hunt. He hoped she wouldn't let him down.

He looked over at the window and the moonlight as it came streaming through his window, falling upon his desk, and then the floor. He wanted to get up and see what it looked like outside, but before he knew it, he was asleep. He had a busy day.

It was a few minutes after noon when Mary and Jimmy arrived at Chuck Miller's farm. Jimmy had Lady

Strong Feather

Samson perched on his fist. On her head was the Indian hood. She was a handsome bird, sitting there in her painted hood, with its two white feathers sticking out the top. Lady Samson was a beautiful reddish brown with a large white area that covered most of her head. With her hood off she looked a lot like a Bald Eagle, except her white feathers didn't extend all the way under her neck.

Chuck Miller looked at Jimmy and his hawk. Chuck had straight, sandy-blonde hair. He stood about an inch shorter than Jimmy, but weighed twice as much as Jimmy. His eyes were a light brown, with blue specks in them. His smile was big and seemed to engulf all it touched.

"I've got my chickens penned up," he said, looking at Jimmy and his hawk. "If she works as good as she looks, she'll be something else. She's sure a beautiful bird."

Jimmy and Mary beamed at the praise he gave Lady Samson. "We don't know too much about hawks, Mr. Miller," Jimmy said. "But if there are other hawks that look better than she does, I'd like to see them."

"Let's see her work, boy. Let's see her work," he said, grinning.

Jimmy removed Lady Samson's hood, and she looked around the strange place. She then looked at Jimmy to see what he wanted her to do. Jimmy lifted his gloved hand and she took off. She swooped downward at first, then with mighty wing strokes she started her climb. Higher and higher she went above her three spectators. Finally, all they could see of her was a black dot up in the sky. She found a good wind current in which she now soared back and forth, high above them.

"She's ready," Jimmy said, looking at Mr. Miller.

"OK," he replied. "Mary, you go into the barn and climb up into the loft and chase some of those pigeons out."

Strong Feather

Mary ran over to the barn and disappeared through the large front doors. They heard her yelling as she climbed up the ladder into the loft. She was up there the day she helped Jimmy catch pigeons for Lady Samson. The only difference this time was that Lady Samson would have to catch her own pigeons. Mary ran around in the loft, yelling and waving her hands. There was a mass evacuation of pigeons from the loft window, as all of the pigeons tried to fly out of the loft at the same time. There were so many pigeons flying around in the loft she could hardly see.

As the pigeons emerged from the loft opening, Jimmy was sure Lady Samson saw them. As he watched her, she tucked her wings along her sides and went into a stoop dive, diving straight down. Opening her wings, she struck one of the pigeons in midair before it knew what happened. As the pigeon fluttered downward, Lady Samson circled and grasped it in mid-air then fluttered to the ground. Jimmy and Chuck ran over to where she was pecking at the pigeon. Jimmy took the pigeon from her grasp and she hopped onto his glove. He then sent her up again and it wasn't long until she had caught four pigeons.

On the next dive, Lady Samson veered away from the pigeons. Chuck's face turned pale when he saw where she headed. Shaking his head, he said, "Looks like she's headed for my chicken pens on the other side of the barn."

They took off running for the other side of the barn as Mary climbed down from the loft. When they rounded the corner of the barn, they were surprised to see Lady Samson hopping around the ground. She held onto a big rat she caught. Chuck let out a big sigh as they walked up to her. He had thoughts of killing her, especially when she headed for his chicken pen. But the sight before him quickly changed his mind. He smiled as he looked at the big rat she caught. He was overjoyed.

Strong Feather

"I've been trying to catch that rat for months, Jimmy," he said, his big smile returning to his face. "That rat has been killing all of my baby chicks, plus eating a lot of my grain. This hawk of yours saved me a lot of work and money. She can hunt over here any time she wants."

Lady Samson definitely won another friend in the town of Mercer. And so it went the second week as they waited for someone to come tell them that Lady Samson belonged to them. Some days Jimmy felt great, but there were others when he felt like he was being torn apart inside. He hoped no one would come by. Some of the earlier joy now left as he went about his chores. Even his working with Lady Samson wasn't as much fun as it was when they first started.

After the first week went by and no one came, they started to feel better. But as the second week slipped past, the tension mounted each day. When it was past, Lady Samson would then be his.

The day after they went over to Mr. Miller's farm, Alice went downtown. She stopped at the store and Mrs. Wendell asked her about her grandson's hawk. They talked for some time, and she marveled at how everyone had come to know her grandson. She was so proud of how he was getting along with all the people in town. When she returned home from the store that afternoon, she went to the back door. She saw Jimmy and Mary out in the hawk pen talking to Lady Samson.

Alice called to them, and motioned for them to come in. She said. "I just came back from the store a couple of minutes ago, and I've been talking to Mrs. Wendell about your hawk, Jimmy."

Jimmy and Mary looked at each other. They were sure she was going to say that Mrs. Wendell knew who their hawk belonged to.

161

Strong Feather

"My, what sad faces," she said. "They should be glad. Mrs. Wendell asked if you'd like to sell her some of your catch, Jimmy. She told me she wouldn't be able to pay you much, but some of the people in town have been talking to her about your hawk. Also, she's heard about the different kinds of game Lady Samson caught. She said that some of the people around town might pay you for them. If you'd like, she will take your catch on consignment and sell it in her store. That way you both would make money. But, like you once said, Jimmy, there's not too many places to spend it here in Mercer. But with a little money in your pockets, you'd at least be able to buy a Nesbitt orange every now and then. You won't have to save every penny you find around here any more. You might even get enough money to buy Mary one."

The sad faces turned to glad ones. They quickly let her know they wanted to try it for a while, just to see how it worked.

"There is one hitch to it," Alice said, and their faces froze. "All of the meat has to be cleaned and cut up." The smiles reappeared. "I can show you how to do that, and I'll help whenever I can. But you two will have to learn how to do it by yourselves. I might not be around to help you. I may take off and go to one of the nearby towns with some of my friends. Wouldn't that be fun?"

"It sure would, Grandma," Jimmy replied.

"Something else," she continued. "There may be a few of the people around here that want your catch without it being dressed out. They could do that themselves and save some money."

Jimmy liked that idea. "That sounds even better," he said. "The only problem is we don't know what we'll be catching each day. We're getting pretty good at knowing where to go for different things to hunt. Like you told us,

Strong Feather

Grandma, we're learning each day we work with Goldie and Lady Samson. It's amazing how much we have learned."

"I know," she said. "And it will amaze you how much more you'll learn. In fact, if you don't know it, that's what this life's all about. Life is a place where we should learn something every day. If we don't, we're not making the most of our life like we should. If we're not learning, we're going backwards."

"Sure hope no one comes around and spoils all of this for us," Mary said, looking at her hands.

"No one has so far," Alice replied, smiling. "Keep your chins up. Don't give in now. We've only a couple more days left and we'll have won this game."

One day slowly turned into another as Jimmy and Mary continued to hunt with her dog and his hawk. A lot of the tension around the Warrior house vanished when Mrs. Wendell started buying some of their catch. Jimmy felt like he was helping pay back a little of the money it cost his grandparents to send for him.

The next afternoon they talked, Jimmy looked at Mary, and said. "Today would be a good day to go down and look at those baby hawks. They should be putting on feathers by now. Let's take that basket Grandma fixed for them. This could be the day we bring them back. If it is, we'll have to get serious about being real falconers."

"We're going to need those baby hawks if someone claims Lady Samson," Mary replied. "The sooner we get them away from that dead tree, the better."

After eating some soup and a sandwich, they went out onto the back porch. They got the basket, the field glasses, some cloth gloves, and a small blanket. Placing everything in the basket they headed for the creek. Capturing baby hawks would be another one of those great learning experiences they talked about, and it should be a lot of fun, too.

When they reached the base of the large cottonwood tree, they set the basket on the ground, Jimmy started up the ladder steps he nailed to the tree. Mary followed as they climbed up to the limb where they looked down on the nest. Sure enough, the three white babies were now brown. Their fuzzy down disappeared, and new feathers began taking the down's place. The time came for them to be taken from their nest before they got too wild.

Back down the tree they climbed. They left the basket at the base of the tree and ran back to the house. A few seconds later they emerged from the garage with a wooden ladder and headed back towards the creek. Getting across the creek with the ladder slowed them down a little, as they had to find rocks to step on so they wouldn't get their feet wet. Then up the other bank they went and over to their climbing tree. Jimmy picked up the basket and carried it and the ladder over to the dead tree.

They now had everything they needed to get the chicks. The only problem would be the papa hawk. Setting everything down next to the trunk of the dead tree, they scanned the skies looking for papa hawk. Then Jimmy saw a slight movement off to his right.

"There he is," he said, pointing to his right. "We'll have to wait until he dives for something. Then, when he is busy, we will have to get the ladder up quickly. I'll go first and you bring the basket. When I get to the top, give me the cloth gloves so the chicks won't be able to peck me when I pick them up. I'll hand the chicks to you, and you put them in the basket. I don't think we should take all three of them. Just two. One for you and one for me. That way we'll both have our own hawk to train."

Strong Feather

"Okay," she replied, getting excited. They waited for the papa hawk to dive.

It was a long wait, but finally he dove and went out of sight behind one of the nearby hills. Hurriedly they placed the ladder up against the dead tree and climbed it as fast as they could. The ladder wobbled back and forth with the two of them on it. With a lot of gasping and holding tight, Jimmy reached the first limb and climbed onto it. Mary stopped at the top of the ladder. It stopped wobbling when Jimmy got off. She opened the basket and handed him the gloves. Sticking them in his back pants pocket, he climbed on up to the top of the tree where the nest was located. Carefully peeking over the top, he saw that everything was okay. He pulled the gloves out of his pocket and put them on.

Reaching into the nest, he picked up the largest baby hawk. He climbed down the tree to where Mary waited. She opened the lid and he placed the baby hawk inside. Releasing it, he pulled his hand out and she closed the lid.

This wasn't hard at all, Jimmy thought, as he climbed back up to the top. Grabbing the next largest baby hawk, he headed back down the tree to where Mary was waiting for him.

Mary opened the lid just enough for him to stick the baby inside, then closed it again. As he removed his hand from the basket he heard Mary gasp. "Here comes the papa hawk," she cried, pointing. She latched the lid on the basket and started down the ladder.

Jimmy swung around the tree just in time as the hawk went sailing by with its talons spread. It made an ear-piercing shrieking sound as it flew by, then swooped upward flapping its wings to gain altitude.

Strong Feather

When Mary reached the ground, she ran over to their climbing tree and stood under it watching the hawk gain altitude.

Jimmy swung back around the tree and scrambled down the ladder. When he reached the bottom, he saw the hawk diving at him again. Pulling the ladder away from the tree, he stepped behind it and ducked down as the hawk came straight at him.

The hawk's claws struck one of the rungs of the ladder above his head, and splinters flew. The hawk was stunned from the impact and fell to the ground a short distance away from the tree. Jimmy stepped out from behind the ladder. He felt badly about the hawk hurting itself, but as he watched, it started hopping along the ground flapping its wings until it was airborne again. Grabbing the ladder in the middle, he carried it over to where Mary was.

They stood next to the tall cottonwood tree and watched as the papa hawk landed on top of the dead tree. They heard him making all kinds of noises up there. He knew that two of his chicks were gone, and it was time for them to get out of there. Jimmy took the basket from Mary. Picking up the ends of the ladder, they walked as fast as they could back to the creek. There were a lot of quick glances over their shoulders before they reached the creek.

The hawk didn't follow them, which was a relief. "I sure hope he's glad we left him one of his babies," Jimmy said, as they made their way across the creek.

"It sure was a good idea not to take all three of them," Mary replied, breathing hard.

When they reached the house, Jimmy sat the basket down beside the hawk pen. They carried the ladder around the house and put it back in the garage. When they returned, they were excited about what they did. "That was kind of close," Jimmy said as they walked up to the basket. "Let's take the basket in and show our prize catch to Grandma. I'm sure she'll want to see them."

Each grabbed a basket handle and ran into the house, laughing and talking about their narrow escape. Alice was peeling apples when they came in. They quickly told her all about what happened. Mary opened the basket and showed Alice the two baby hawks. The size of the baby hawks surprised all three of them. They were too excited to realize how big they were. They wouldn't be babies much longer. In fact, it wouldn't be long until they would be trying to fly.

Alice was happy for them, but the joy she usually had for all they did was gone. Something was wrong. They were so sure she'd be as happy as they were, but instead, her sadness let them know that something was bothering her, and it bothered them.

Gloom now settled down on the three of them. "What's wrong, Grandma?" Jimmy asked. "Has Lady Samson's owner come for her?"

"No. It's nothing that simple, Jimmy," she said, patting his hand. "Your grandpa was brought home awhile ago with a broken leg. He broke it cleaning out one of the places this afternoon. They told me he stepped out the back door onto a rotten step and it gave way under him. He broke his right leg."

Jimmy and Mary looked at each other, then at Alice. "He'll be out of work for about a month. That means there won't be any money coming in."

"Lady Samson and I will fill the gap for Grandpa," Jimmy said. "We can hunt more than we've been hunting. That should bring in more money from Mrs. Wendell, plus we'll have meat to eat."

Strong Feather

Alice smiled at her grandson. "That's right, Jimmy," she said. "We're not going to let this get us down. All of us working together can overcome this problem. Mrs. Wendell told me a couple of people asked her if they could buy rabbits and pheasants directly from us. That will help."

Alice looked at her grandson. "I sure am glad you came our way, Jimmy. You are the joy of my heart." Jimmy got up and hugged his grandma. Alice held her free hand out to Mary, and she came over and hugged her, too. The three of them started dancing around the kitchen. Soon, laughter bubbled forth as round and round they went in the center of the kitchen.

When Alice turned loose, they sat down at the kitchen table out of breath. It was only then that they heard Tom's voice come booming from the bedroom. "What's going on out there?" he roared. "Are you three happy that I broke my leg?"

"No, Tom," Alice replied. "We're just happy being together."

"Oh," Tom said, and there was silence. "I'm glad someone's happy around this place."

They looked at each other and snickered. Mary stood up and looked at Jimmy. "I have to go home, Jimmy," she said. "It's been a great day. Do you need me to help you put up the baby hawks, Jimmy?"

"No," he replied, standing up. "You go home and tell your mom and dad what we did today."

Mary giggled as she looked at them. "I will," she said. "They'll be as happy as I am about the baby hawks. I'll come over early tomorrow morning."

"Great," he replied. "See you then."

Mary waved as she hurried out the front door and the screen door slammed shut behind her.

Strong Feather

"You know what, Jimmy," Alice said. "You and Mary make a good team."

He thought about what his grandma said. Nodding his head in agreement, he said, "I think that Lady Samson, Goldie, and the three of us make an unbeatable team, Grandma."

"I have to agree," she said, grabbing Jimmy's hand across the table and squeezing it. "I have to agree."

CHAPTER XII

Jimmy got up early the next morning and began working in the hawk pen. He divided it into two pens, so the baby hawks had a place of their own. He worked on a new gate at the other end of the pen until it looked pretty good for an amateur carpenter.

The two baby hawks accepted the basket as their nest, so he decided to leave them in it for the time being. They'd soon leave it as they began trying their wings out. When that happened, they wouldn't need a nest. But the basket was the security they needed now in their new surroundings.

When Mary came by, Jimmy was outside the pen talking to Lady Samson about her babies. The closeness of her babies upset her, and she paced back and forth on her perch. Her motherly instincts showed, and Jimmy had his hands full trying to calm her down.

Mary talked to her while Jimmy went into the house to get the three of them something to eat. Lady Samson calmed down until one of the chicks made some noise, then she resumed her pacing.

When Jimmy returned, Lady Samson saw something in his hand and stopped pacing to watch him. She knew it was feeding time.

Strong Feather

They both quickly discovered that feeding time was going to be a fun event today. Lady Samson didn't pay any attention to her chicks when she ate. The two young hawks liked to fight over every scrap they were fed. Just watching them eat was funny. Jimmy and Mary looked forward to each time they fed the chicks, even though the majority of their time was spent with Lady Samson.

Hunting with her each day was great fun. It was also a way of earning money. They both felt good knowing they helped out, but what excited them even more, was the end of the second week was almost there. The three of them sat around the kitchen table after a day's hunt and talked. As the last day drew close, they started feeling a lot better. It wasn't over, but it was close. No one around Mercer had any idea who the hawk belonged to. It looked like Jimmy wouldn't have to give her up.

They went over to Mr. Miller's farm every chance they got, sometimes two or three times a day. Some of the people around Mercer liked pigeon. They called them squab, which was just a fancy name for pigeon. What amazed Jimmy was how the number of pigeons never seemed to decrease, even though they were catching a lot of pigeons. Each time Mary chased them out of the loft, it looked like there were at least a hundred pigeons flying out of that window.

Once when they went over to Chuck Miller's, Lady Samson caught two more rats. They weren't as large as the first one, but Chuck sure was glad. "Looks like she caught these two before they had their babies," he said. "If they'd been born, I'd have had rats eating everything I've got around here. Probably most of the feed I've got stored in my barn for the winter. It sure was a lucky day for me when your hawk came my way, Jimmy."

170

Strong Feather

"It looks like Lady Samson is earning her keep, Mr. Miller," he replied.

"She's done that and a lot more," Chuck replied. "My wife told me about your grandpa breaking his leg, Jimmy. Since your hawk has saved me a lot of chickens, I'd like to give you a couple of fat hens to take home to him. I know Tom loves fried chicken, and I believe your grandma does, too."

"They sure do, Mr. Miller," he beamed. Lady Samson did it again.

They headed home with Mary carrying the pigeons, and Jimmy carrying Lady Samson and the chickens. It was a good day, and he beamed when he handed the two chickens to his grandma. She was overjoyed with the surprise they brought her. Earlier, Alice put a teakettle of water on the stove to heat. She wanted it good and hot when Jimmy came home with some pigeons. The water just came to a boil when they walked in. Picking up the teakettle, she said, "You two go clean up," taking the chickens from Jimmy.

The two of them went to the bathroom to clean up as Alice headed for the front door. They returned to the kitchen and waited. It wasn't long until she returned with the chickens and pigeons. They were now plucked clean of all their feathers. Placing them in the sink, she poured the rest of the teakettle's boiling water on them. She picked the pin feathers off the two chickens when they heard the bedroom door open.

Tom came hopping into the kitchen. The banging of doors and people running around in the house, woke him up. He quickly learned how to get around the house on a pair of borrowed crutches. Not as spry as he once was, it was a chore for him just to get up and come into the kitchen.

Strong Feather

"Well, Jimmy," he said, sitting down. "Tomorrow is the end of the two weeks. If we don't hear from someone by tomorrow, I'd say you have yourself a hawk. I guess that will kinda make you happy. It sure will make the two of us happy. I was thinking earlier this morning how that hawk of yours has been a blessing in more ways than one around this place. I feel like it's brought each of us closer together. It's helped you acquire a new outlook on life, for which I will be eternally grateful." He looked at Mary, then back at Jimmy. "It's helped you find a close friend here in Mercer. That's a lot for one bird to do, wouldn't you say?"

"It sure is, Grandpa," Jimmy replied. He was right, and each one of them knew it, but it took his grandpa saying it for him to realize just how true it was.

The next day when Jimmy and Mary were in the pen working with the baby hawks, Chuck Miller came hurrying around the corner of the house, and walked up to the pen. Their hearts sank when they saw him. This was the last day for the ad to run, and they were sure he had bad news for them.

"Hello there, you two," Chuck said, grinning. "Why so sad? You really shouldn't be, you know. I think I know something the two of you just might like to know."

Their looks turned to surprise, as they waited for him to continue. "I read in yesterday's paper that they're going to have a falcon contest at Colorado Springs, at the Air Force Academy, this Saturday. You may not know it, but the Air Force's mascot is a falcon. It looks like they decided to have a contest to see who has the best falcon around these parts. As far as I've been able to find out, your hawk fits one of their two categories. One is for hawks like yours with long wings. The other is for short-winged hawks."

Strong Feather

Smiles appeared on both of their faces as they waited to hear more. "That is much better," Chuck said, continuing. "That contest is this weekend, you two. I planned on going down near Colorado Springs next week, but if you two want to go see what Lady Samson can do in that contest, I'll be glad to go a week early. We'll just take in that contest on our way down to my friend's farm."

"That sounds great, Mr. Miller," Jimmy said. "But I've got to stay around here and do some hunting with Lady Samson.

Mary's face saddened. She remembered Jimmy's promise to his grandma, and he was right. They couldn't go off right now, even though it sounded exciting.

Chuck knew what happened to Tom and he realized they were in a bind. "Oh," he continued. "I forgot to tell you about the prize for first place, Jimmy. There's a prize of $100.00 for first place, and $25.00 for second. I would say you should not have any trouble taking second place, and with any luck at all, you'll take first. That hawk of yours is one of the best-looking falcon hawks I've ever seen. I'm no expert you know, but I do know she's one of the good ones."

"Wow!" Mary said. "You sure could do a lot with $100.00, Jimmy."

"I could also do a lot with $25.00," he replied, thinking about what Mr. Miller told them. Biting his lip, he said, "OK. We'll do it, Mr. Miller. I think Lady Samson is as fit as she's been since we got her. She overcame the problem she had with her sore wing, and she's eating good. Is there anything you know of we need to do, Mr. Miller, to get her ready?"

Chuck thought about Jimmy's question, then replied. "Nope. I think you two have done just about as good a job as anyone could have in training her. Even if you don't win, it'll be good experience. It will give you a chance to get to know some of the other falconers around Colorado that are in the sport. I'd say most of them would be glad to tell you some of the things they do with their hawks. I'd say getting known in the falconry world would be a very important step for anyone wanting to train hawks. You can never tell what might happen. Just keep on doing what you're doing, and you can't go wrong."

Jimmy hoped he was right. Then he realized that Lady Samson's owner might be at the show. "What if that happened?" he thought. He put the thought out of his mind, not wanting to be bothered by it now. It was settled. They'd go see what Lady Samson could do in a falcon contest.

Later that day he made a padded block perch for Lady Samson. He saw a picture of one in a book. The article said it would keep the hawk from hurting itself during transportation. He sure didn't want her to get hurt on their trip to Colorado Springs. He put plenty of padding under the rug so she would have a comfortable trip. When he finished, he checked his perch with the one in the book. His looked just like it. He was ready for Colorado Springs.

Jimmy got up early the next morning. An orange ball of a sun turned everything a rosy color when he loaded Lady Samson into the back of Chuck's pickup. It was an old green Chevy pickup with a camper shell on the back. When he was satisfied she was alright, they climbed into the truck cab and closed the door. The air was cool and crisp that early Colorado morning. There sure was a lot of electricity in the air from two excited kids and a farmer.

The orange ball popped up above the horizon and started to turn white when Chuck placed his key into the truck's ignition. But before he started his truck, he looked at Jimmy. "Your grandpa told me a couple of minutes ago that your two-week ad ran out yesterday, Jimmy," he said, smiling. "Looks like you've got yourself a hawk. There's no one around here that can say you didn't try your best to find her owner. Even if someone shows up later, or there is someone at the show, they can't accuse you of not trying to find them."

Jimmy's heart sank. and he hung his head. All of a sudden he didn't want to go. As for Mary, she sat beside him bubbling over with excitement. Before he knew it, some of her excitement rubbed off onto him. They did exactly what Mr. Miller said, and there was no reason for feeling sad. "Maybe no one at the show would know Lady Samson," he thought, as he watched the sun's rays burn the dew off the truck's hood.

Chuck started the truck, and they talked and laughed when they drove down the lane and out onto the road. It wasn't long until they were headed towards Denver. Every so often Jimmy turned around and looked into the back of the camper shell. He saw Lady Samson sitting there without a care, as if she had done this before. He put the Indian hood on her before they left. Now she sat there on her perch gently moving with the swaying of the truck. The padded block perch he made was working real well.

It wasn't long until they passed through Denver. Another half hour, and they drove past Castle Rock. "It won't be much longer now," Chuck said, "and we'll see the chapel at the Air Force Academy. It has a lot of long spike-like arches on top of the building which can be seen from the highway. It'll be on the right side of the road up near those mountains over on our right."

They drove for another twenty minutes before Chuck pointed. "There it is," he said. Jimmy and Mary looked as hard as they could, but couldn't see a thing. Then off in the distance they barely made out the spikes on the top of the church. They began seeing small airplanes flying over one of the large fields they passed.

Pointing at one of the planes, Chuck said, "That's some of the Air Force cadets up there learning how to fly." Jimmy and Mary stretched their necks to follow each plane. It wasn't long until Chuck turned off the highway and drove up to the entrance gate to the Air Force Academy. He turned in at the information center building. He went inside and returned a few minutes later with a big smile on his face.

"This is the place, and today is the day," he said. He placed their car pass on the dashboard of the truck and started the truck. "I'm glad they didn't change their minds. Matt Nickels, a friend of mine, told me last night that he thought the date had been changed." He drove down the main street until they came to the football stadium.

Jimmy and Mary were relieved to know the date hadn't changed, but didn't say anything about it as they looked at all the men in uniforms.

"That building over there is where they're having the contest," he continued, pointing at the stadium building. "It looks like there's quite a few people here already. I'll go in and find out what we have to do to enter the contest." Getting out of the truck, he said, "Both of you stay here with Lady Samson, and I'll be back as soon I can."

They sat in the truck about ten minutes before they saw Chuck come out of the building and head their way. "I've already registered Lady Samson for you, Jimmy," he said, opening the truck's door. "You can get her out and take her inside that building I just came from."

Jimmy jumped out, and opened the back of the camper shell. Taking a paper sack out of his back pocket, he took out a few pieces of dried meat. He took off Lady Samson's hood and placed the meat on her perch and watched her eat it. When she finished, she looked at him. He replaced her hood and put his glove on. Placing his hand behind her legs, he touched them and she stepped off her perch and up onto his fist. Mary picked up the two bags of the equipment they brought, and closed the camper shell door.

They were surprised when they entered the building and saw how many contestants there were. Everywhere they looked, there were hawks. All of the hawks were placed around an open arena on the same types of perches. Chuck walked over to a big tall man nearby, and talked to him for a couple minutes. Chuck brought the man over and introduced him to Mary and Jimmy.

"This is Mr. Archer," he said. "Mr. Archer. This is Mary Wilson and Jimmy Warrior, of Mercer, Colorado.

"I'm glad to meet both of you," Mr. Archer said, tipping his white cowboy hat back on his head and showing his brown curly hair. He shook Mary's hand first, then Jimmy's.

"We're glad to know you, Sir," Jimmy said, shaking his hand.

"We sure are," Mary said, excitedly stepping up beside Jimmy.

"You can put your hawk on that block perch over there, Jimmy," Mr. Archer said, pointing. "I believe she'll like it over there. That's the area where the long-winged falcon hawks are located." He stopped and took a good look at Lady Samson. "You sure have a beautiful falcon hawk, Jimmy. I'll see both of you later."

Before Jimmy could reply, he tipped his hat and walked off to take care of some other people who walked up to his desk.

"He's one of the judges," Chuck said, winking at them.

Strong Feather

Jimmy walked to the perch Mr. Archer pointed to, placed Lady Samson onto it, and took off her hood. There were at least two dozen other long-winged falcon hawks on their perches close by. Every one of them really looked good to him. "I wonder if we'll win anything," he thought, looking around. Then looking at Lady Samson, he felt a lot better. She was truly a beautiful hawk, just like Mr. Archer said she was.

Jimmy talked to Lady Samson softly as he stroked her with his comb. She was a little nervous, but soon settled down. It wasn't long until she perked up and seemed to be enjoying it all. Chuck talked to some of the people there. It wasn't long until he knew all that was going on, and what the judges would look for. When he came back, he smiled.

"Just about everyone I've talked to are talking about your hawk, Jimmy," he said, smiling. "They all told me how they like the way she looks and holds herself. I let them know how much we appreciated their comments, especially since this is her first showing. It looks like you have a good chance of winning."

What Mr. Miller said made Jimmy want to jump for joy, but he still felt uneasy about it all. He wondered if Lady Samson's owner was at the show. Anyone that walked by could be her owner. He would be glad when this contest was over.

"A couple of people told me there's one long-winged hawk that hasn't showed up yet. They also told me it always wins its class. Let's hope it doesn't show today so we can win that $100.00 prize. Wouldn't the people back in Mercer get excited if you were to win, Jimmy?" he said, patting him on the back.

Jimmy nodded in agreement. He wanted that to happen, but he was a little afraid to think about it. The time for the judging was about to start. Chuck told them it would start in ten minutes. As they looked around the arena, a small skinny man walked up behind them and placed his hawk on the block perch next to Lady Samson. The man cleared his throat, causing the three of them to turn around. What they saw caused them to shake their heads. This had to be the hawk they told Chuck about. She was a beauty, and she sat on her perch just as proud as Lady Samson.

"Hello there, Sonny," the man said, looking at Jimmy through the hair hanging down in his eyes. Running his fingers through his straight black hair, he looked at Mary, then at Jimmy. His hair fell back into his eyes and he smiled, showing tobacco-stained teeth. "I'm John Crow," he said, "and this is my falcon hawk, Miss Beautiful. Ain't she a beauty?"

Jimmy didn't answer. He looked at the man who irritated him. "Why do people have to call me, 'Sonny' ", he thought. Looking from the man and then at his hawk, her beauty melted all of his irritated feelings.

"She's a very beautiful hawk, Mr. Crow," he answered.

John stood there smiling at the three of them. "She's won every show all over this state for two years running. You'll have to admit that's a hard record to beat, ain't it?" he asked. Not waiting for an answer, he walked off, leaving his hawk sitting on her perch. Miss Beautiful sat there watching as her master disappeared in the crowd. She started raising herself on one foot, then the other. Back and forth she went. Jimmy and Mary walked over to her perch and started talking to her. The calmness in their voices began to calm her down. They were not paying any attention to what went on about them, but some people came over and watched them as they talked to the hawk. They cared for the hawk and it showed. Even if the hawk hadn't needed calming down, it was easy to talk to such a beautiful hawk. Then someone blew a whistle and everyone turned to see what was happening.

"It's time for the judging to begin," a short chubby man said. "We have two groups of judges here today. One group will judge the long-winged falcon hawks, and the other group of judges will judge the short-winged falcon hawks. Please keep your hawks under control at all times. They will be judged according to how they act, look, are handled, and by size. This is not a hunting contest. It's more of a beauty contest."

Everyone laughed as the man joined two of the men who judged the short-winged falcon hawks. The other group of three men came over and started looking at the long-winged falcon hawks where Lady Samson was perched. They began at the other end away from Lady Samson, leaving Miss Beautiful last in line to be judged.

Two hawks quickly disqualified themselves by not letting the judges handle them. "They have a lot to learn," Jimmy thought, standing next to Lady Samson. He watched the judges make their way towards him and hoped Lady Samson wouldn't give them any trouble. The judges were in no hurry as they moved from hawk to hawk. But finally they were in front of Lady Samson. They began checking her over very carefully. He was proud of the way she sat there watching him and not moving. After a final check, they moved on to Miss Beautiful. Taking their time, they went over her as closely as they had Lady Samson.

Then back they came to Lady Samson and checked her again, then back to Miss Beautiful. Jimmy looked at Mary and Mr. Miller, who stood a few feet away smiling. They, too, watched each move the judges made. Jimmy started to feel like they might have a chance in winning this contest.

Strong Feather

The three judges walked back down the line of hawks, checking a hawk here and there as they went. When they finished, they went off by themselves and talked for some time. They came back to where Lady Samson and Miss Beautiful were perched. Again the three men went over the two hawks.

As Jimmy watched, one judge took out a tape measure. He then went over to Lady Samson and measured her wing span. Then he measured Miss Beautiful's wing span. Miss Beautiful's wing span was almost an inch longer than Lady Samson's. He walked over to where the two other men stood and told them the results. Mr. Archer walked past Jimmy and placed his hand on the back of Miss Beautiful. The other judges walked up beside the hawk and spread her wings out as far as they would go. They stood there holding them so everyone could see why she was the winner.

"The winner of the long-winged falcon hawk division is Miss Beautiful," Mr. Archer said, looking around for its owner. But he was nowhere in sight. Then there was a commotion behind everyone as John Crow pushed his way through the crowd.

"She sure makes a beautiful picture with her wings spread out like that," Jimmy said. Mary and Chuck, who stood beside him, nodded their heads in agreement. The three of them smiled as they watched, but there was sadness in their hearts. They came close, just an inch short of winning first place.

Taking it all in, Jimmy heard one of the judges say something to Mr. Archer. The other judge dropped the wing he was holding and the three men gathered around Miss Beautiful. They were checking the tip end of her left wing when John walked up.

Strong Feather

"You've sewn two wing tip feathers onto your hawk's left wing," Mr. Archer said, looking sternly at John.

"She pulled them out last week, he said, getting mad. "All I did was put them back. They're her feathers. I didn't use another hawk's feathers. If she hadn't pulled the stupid things out, she'd still have them. It's no big deal."

"You and your hawk, Miss Beautiful. are disqualified," Mr. Archer said, irritated at him and what he did. "You're barred from this event, and any other event we ever have. You won't be allowed to enter any other hawk contest in Colorado for the remainder of this year, or next year."

John stood there dumbfounded. He was so mad he couldn't speak.

Mr. Archer walked over and placed his hand on Lady Samson's back. "You have a winner, Jimmy," he said, pushing his cowboy hat back on his head and smiling at him. The other judges came over and now held Lady Samson's wings out, showing her in all her beauty. "I told you she was a beauty, and that she is. You can pick up your check from that man over there at that table when you're ready to leave," he said.

"I'll ask that you don't leave right away, Jimmy. Not until everyone's had a chance to talk to you and take a few pictures of Lady Samson. "There's also a reporter here from The Denver Post, and I'm sure he will want to take both of your pictures, so he can put it in his paper."

"That's great," Jimmy said, shaking Mr. Archer's hand. "Thanks a lot."

"Don't thank me for what your hawk's done, Jimmy," he said. "She's a beauty, and she's not full grown yet. She'll be bigger than Miss Beautiful the next time you meet up with her and John Crow."

182

Strong Feather

With another hearty hand shake, Mr. Archer went over and placed his hand on the second place winner. Jimmy watched him but didn't see a thing that happened. He thought about what Mr. Archer said. It was hard to believe that all of this happened. He went back to where Chuck and Mary were. Mary clapped her hands for joy when he walked up. When he told them Lady Samson's picture was going to be in The Denver Post, she couldn't hold it back.

"Everyone's going to know how great she is!" Mary shouted. Realizing what she did, she placed her hands over her mouth. Some people standing nearby started laughing. One judge came over and asked her to calm down. The winner of the short-winged falcon hawks was about to be announced.

They hurried over and watched a judge announce the other first place winner. It was a beautiful Peregrine falcon hawk that won. Second place went to a hawk that looked just as beautiful. "Those judges must have had a hard time reaching a verdict on those two," Jimmy thought. It was as close as the one he just won.

The afternoon quickly flew by. After Lady Samson's picture was taken dozens of times, they loaded everything back into the pickup. Chuck drove out the main gate, over to his friend's farm, and then back home. Happiness and joy, with lots of laughter, filled Chuck's truck as they sped along on their way back to Mercer. It was a great day for all of them.

When they drove up the lane to Jimmy's grandparents' house, they were still in high spirits. The moon came up where the sun came up earlier that day. Jimmy took Lady Samson out of the camper shell and placed her in her pen. Mary and Mr. Miller went into the

Strong Feather

house to tell Tom and Alice that Lady Samson won the first contest she entered.

Standing next to the hawk pen, Jimmy watched as the moon slowly rose into the deep blue sky. The stars blinked, letting the world know they hadn't forgotten it. He recalled the time he looked up at the stars when he first came to his grandparents' house. He smiled, remembering how he sat and watched the stars that night. He searched the sky for the Big Dipper. He recalled how his heart ached to see his dad that night. The ache remained, but he slowly covered it over by keeping busy. Then the day when Lady Samson came into his life, everything changed.

A slight movement inside the pen brought him back to the present. He no longer had that lonely empty place deep inside. It was gone. Inside the pen was the reason for its leaving. "Just a silly old bird," he thought. But it was true. Lady Samson took his hurt away, and replaced it with a good feeling. A smile crossed his face when he looked up and saw the Milky Way stretching across the sky. There was the Big Dipper. The stars were still there. It felt good to know some things never change. Some leaves alongside the house rustled, as he heard the approach of a gentle breeze. It quickly slipped around the corner of the house and caressed him for a moment, then was gone.

The calling of his grandma from inside the house let him know he was wanted. "I'll see you in the morning, Lady Samson," he said. "You sure made me proud of you today."

There was now pride in his voice and a spring in his step, as he headed for the back porch. Upon entering the kitchen, he went over to the stove and looked at the wood box and saw it was low. He started to go back out and get some wood, but his grandpa stopped him.

Strong Feather

"Let it go for tonight, Jimmy." Tom said, motioning for him to come over and sit down. "Come over here and tell us all about the contest. We're so proud of you and your hawk."

He went over to his grandpa and got a big hug. Then Alice gave him another one. With pride showing on his face, he sat down and told his part of the story. When he finished, he reached inside his shirt pocket, pulled out the check and handed it to his grandma. Tears came to Alice's eyes as she looked at the check.

Looking over at his grandpa, he said, "Now we can pay off those bills that you've been worrying about, Grandpa."

Everyone's eyes got misty as they looked at each other.

"Thank you, Jimmy," Tom said. "Thanks a lot."

CHAPTER XIII

The next morning when the first hint of dawn appeared in the east, two brown eyes were open wide. How long he was awake he didn't know, but as he watched the first faint glow of light appear on his wall, his mind danced from one event to another. The day before was filled to the brim. While others might still be asleep, not him. He slept the sleep of a marathon runner: one who runs during the day when awake, then runs all night in his sleep.

Over and over that night he dreamed of winning the falcon contest. But what woke him was Mr. John Crow. In each of his dreams, he came up after the contest and took the check and Lady Samson from Jimmy. He told him she was his, and that Mr. Miller and Mary went somewhere to get their pictures taken, and left Jimmy there by himself. When he tried to follow Mr. Crow, his feet turned to lead, and he could barely walk. Slowly, he made his way through the crowd until he reached the door and went outside. Looking around, he saw Mr. Crow standing next to his truck. When he opened the door to his hawk cage, it sprung open, knocking Lady Samson off his hand. Falling to the ground, she started fluttering all over the place, not knowing what happened. People gathered around to watch this man chasing his hawk that flopped around on the ground.

Mr. Crow tried to catch Lady Samson, but people got in his way. Then one spectator grabbed at her and pulled off her hood. With her hood off, she was let go, and they all watched as Lady Samson took flight. Jimmy watched as she quickly disappeared over a nearby hill and was gone. Mr. Crow then got into his truck and drove off laughing. Jimmy's feet lost their heaviness and he ran after the truck, yelling for Mr. Crow to stop. It was at this point

Strong Feather

in the dream where he always awoke with a start. Realizing where he was, he relaxed, relieved to know it was just a dream.

His eyes were wide open as he watched his room turn from black, to dark gray, to light gray, then to orange. His eyes flitted from one thing to another; he saw his baseball cap sitting on his dresser. My, how things changed for him since that first day when he arrived in Mercer. He went from disliking Mercer, to liking it. For years he considered himself a toughie, not letting things get to him. Now, he cared about others, especially his grandparents.

A lot happened, that's true, but the best of all was Lady Samson. Jumping out of bed, he dressed and went out back to make sure his dream hadn't been real. It hadn't. Lady Samson greeted him with a nod. He knew that nod meant more than hello. It also meant she wanted to be fed. So he went back into the house and returned shortly with some rabbit for her to eat.

It wasn't long until he was the topic of discussion around Mercer. To his amazement, he discovered that those who lived in and around Mercer, Colorado were not only proud of their small town, but everything that happened in it. Whenever somebody they knew deserved praise, they didn't hesitate giving it. He thanked each one of them, but let them know it was his hawk, Lady Samson, that did it all. They agreed, but let him know she wouldn't have done it without him. That answer made him stop and think. It wasn't long until he came to the conclusion they were right. He helped, and so did Mary. He felt good about himself, which he hadn't done for a long time. Surprisingly, the two bullies said "hi" to him one day.

Praise was a rare occurrence in his life, especially as he grew into his teenage years. He'd be fourteen in a month and a half, and it meant a lot for him to know that other people liked him. His grandparents didn't hold back their love for him, but that was different. They were family.

As he visited with Mr. Wilson, Mrs. Wendell, and others in town, he found it easier to talk to them about his future. Now when he was asked about his future plans, he told them he was planning on staying with his grandparents as long as they wanted him. He found it easy to say, and it felt good.

He said lots of things in his life just to make others feel good, especially when he wanted something. Now it was different. He talked differently, thought differently, and felt differently. With this new feeling inside and out, he realized he wouldn't be going back to Newark. He might go back to visit his mother, but that would be it. He had the home he always wanted, and with it came friends who cared. Mercer was nothing like the big city where no one cared what happened to him. Then he remembered Officer Brown. "Well, almost no one," he thought.

The Denver Post newspaper printed the picture of Jimmy standing next to Lady Samson on the second page of the sports section. At first he wondered why they printed it there. Then he realized falconry was considered a sport. Below their picture was the story about how they won first place at the Air Force Academy in Colorado Springs. The next week four reporters from towns around Mercer came by and talked to Jimmy and his grandparents. To his delight more stories with pictures appeared in the local newspapers. His grandma cut them out, and even bought an album to put them in.

One evening after supper, Alice told Jimmy that she put together an album of all his newspaper clippings that she would show his dad the next time he came to visit. He smiled when she told him that when she got older, she would sit in her rocking chair and smile as she looked through this album she put together of him and Lady Samson. She would enjoy looking at the pictures, and recalling the things they did together. She also told him he did a lot of things that made her proud of him since he came to live with them.

He got up and hugged his grandma. They became real good friends, which was very important to both of them. Like all boys, he needed a grandma and grandpa to love him, but especially a grandma's love.

Early one afternoon, he took Lady Samson out to hunt by himself. When he returned, he couldn't find his grandma anywhere in the house. She was always there when he came home, and it disturbed him a little for her not to be there. Going over to the front door, he checked the front yard, but no luck. "Maybe she was out in the garden," he thought. As he was about to open the screen door, a movement caught his eye. Up the street by the highway he saw her turn the corner and head down the street at a fast walk. Her short legs were moving so fast she almost ran. She came hurrying up their driveway and onto the front porch. Opening the screen door, he waited for her to come into the house.

"Jimmy!" Alice said, out of breath. "I meant to be here when you came in from hunting. I'm sorry, but I had to go do something."

"That's okay, Grandma," he replied. "I just came in the back door a couple minutes ago."

Putting her arm around his shoulder, she smiled. "I went downtown to use the phone," she said, softly. He looked at her a little puzzled. "I want you to know what I did, Jimmy. I went down to Bill Wilson's garage and called your mother. I just had to call her Jimmy, and tell her all about the wonderful things you've done since you came to stay with us. I felt your mother needed to know, Jimmy, and you know what? She told me she misses you, and it thrilled her heart when I told her how you took hold, and how well you've done. We talked awhile, and then I told her about the hawk you caught and all the work you did training it to hunt. I saved the best for last, and let her know that you won first place at the show in Colorado Springs."

Jimmy's thoughts quickly returned to the last time he saw his Mother. He remembered her slapping him. It bothered him ever since. But what was etched in his mind was her walking up to the door in the police station outer office. He saw her start to open the door, stop, look at him as if to say she didn't want him to go, then step through the door and close it behind her. He vaguely remembered her asleep on her bed when he got his suitcase and left. It was all of the unsaid words that came to mind as he listened to his grandma.

He was glad his grandma told her everything he did since he came to Mercer. Listening to her, he felt a pain in his chest. The love for his mother appeared in his eyes as tears. He no longer had the dislike for her he had when he left Newark. His moist eyes soon caused streaks to appear on his tan cheeks. Just knowing that his mother still loved him, and cared about what he did, made him feel good.

"I'm glad to see you still care about your mother, Jimmy," Alice said. Taking a handkerchief from her apron pocket she wiped the tears from his face, "and she's proud of you. She wanted to talk to you, so I told her to call back in a half hour and I'd come home and get you."

"That's great, Grandma," he said, as he grabbed her hand. "Let's go."

There was no holding him back, and Alice was half pulled, half dragged, back to the Wilson service station. Bill and Mary were waiting for them when they arrived.

Strong Feather

The four of them sat around and talked about how Lady Samson and her babies were doing. Alice and Bill agreed that Mary and Jimmy were probably learning as much as the hawks were. Jimmy was about to say he agreed when the phone rang.

Bill answered it and handed it to Jimmy. Taking it, he looked at it for a couple seconds, then put it to his ear.

"Hi, Mom," he said, with a lump in his throat.

"Hello, Jimmy," he heard his mom say. "I sure am proud of you, Son! Your grandmother told me all of the wonderful things that you've done. It thrills me to hear about them."

They told each other how good it was to hear the other's voice. Then Jimmy told his mom he decided to stay in Mercer.

"I understand," Mabel said, after a pause. "I think you made the right decision, Jimmy. I'm sorry about the way things turned out, and I thought you would never want to talk to me again."

"I love you, Mom," he said softly.

"Oh, Jimmy," she said, "I love you, too." Then there was a pause. "Jimmy, I want you to know I have been going to night school, and I have a job as a secretary for the Rainbow Bakery Company here in town. I work straight days now, and I'm doing a lot better since I got off that night shift. I sure am glad I don't have to work in bars any more."

"I'm glad, too, Mom," he exclaimed, wiping away his tears.

There was a pause, then Mabel said, "I don't know when I'll be able to come out there and see you, Jimmy," she said. "But the first chance I get, I will."

"That would be great, Mom!" he said, getting excited.

191

Strong Feather

"I can't promise anything, Son," Mabel said, " But I'll try. I've got to go now."

Good-byes were said, and Jimmy handed the phone back to Mr. Wilson and he hung it up. Jimmy looked at his grandma. "Mom told me she has a new job as a secretary for the Rainbow Bakery Company in Newark, Grandma. She told me the first chance she gets, she'll come out and see me."

"That's wonderful news, Jimmy," Alice said, giving him a hug. "Now you really have something to look forward to."

The four of them talked a while, then Jimmy and Alice excused themselves and headed for home. They both felt good as they walked along not saying a word. Evening arrived in Mercer, and with it came a slight coolness in the air. As they walked, the sun began to set behind the mountains. High white clouds made a magical transformation from white to gold. Turning off the main street of Mercer, they walked down the dirt road. A small black fleck high in the sky caught Jimmy's attention. His eyes were taking in all of the beauty that lay all about him. It was the papa hawk soaring on the evening breezes. Nothing could top this beautiful sight and the peaceful feeling he had. Winning first place was great, but having just talked to his mother, and hearing her tell him she loved him, was greater.

Alice and Jimmy walked along with one arm around the other's back. Words were not needed. When Jimmy opened the screen door for his grandma, he heard a beautiful whistle come from inside the house. Stopping to listen, his grandma pushed by him and ran into the house yelling.

"Tommy! Tommy!" she cried, "You've come home!"

Strong Feather

Surprised by his grandma's actions, Jimmy followed her into the kitchen and came face to face with his dad. He stood next to the table being hugged by his mother. She hugged him so hard his face started turning red, but he didn't say a word. Looking up, he saw his boy standing there and held his hand out. "Hello, Jimmy," he said. "How are you, Son?"

Jimmy was speechless. He just got off the phone with his mom, and here in front of him stood his dad. Running up to him, he grabbed his hand and shook it. Alice let go of her son, and Tommy pulled Jimmy to him and gave him a big hug. The three of them stood there hugging each other when Tom came walking into the room smiling.

"Where's my hug?" he asked, looking at Alice and Jimmy. "I'm the one who sneaked him in here. Don't I get anything for doing that?"

They all laughed and let Tom in on the hugging. When everyone got their share, they sat down at the table.

"Tell us your plans, Tommy," Alice said.

"They gave me a week's leave, Mother," he said, looking at her. "I'm sorry that's all I have, but it's better than nothing. They've been letting me stay a night or two at different places around Big Spring, Texas. I've been doing real good, so they let me come home to see my parents, and my boy."

Looking over at Jimmy he said, "I saw your picture in this week's *Time* magazine, Son. I couldn't believe my eyes."

"Wow!" Jimmy replied, looking at him, "That's great, Dad."

Tommy continued, "I had an appointment to see my doctor two days ago, and I showed him your picture. I asked him if he would give me some time off so I could go home and see my boy. He told me he'd check and see what he could do. The hospital board met that afternoon, and they approved a week's leave for me. That picture of yours is what did it, Son. Even the bus driver, Sam Brack, from Denver to Ft. Collins, told me he knew you."

"You've got a boy you can be proud of, Tommy," Alice said, looking at Jimmy. "We had a few shaky days around here when he first arrived, but ever since he caught that hawk, there's been no stopping him. Most of his doubts about us are now gone. He's become a true Warrior."

Tommy looked at him. "Well, Son," he said. "If your grandma says so, it must be true. There's only one thing I can't understand."

"What's that?" Jimmy asked, with a puzzled look on his face.

"Hawks. I could understand it if you liked pigeons, but hawks?" Tommy said, turning his nose up.

He looked around at his grandparents for support, but found none. When he looked back at his dad, he saw the smile start. It got larger and larger, and then he laughed.

"I'm only teasing, Son," he said. "I'll be the pigeon man around here, and you be the hawk man."

"OK, Dad," he said, smiling. "Grandma told me you were one of the best homing pigeon trainers around these parts."

"That's right, Son," he replied. "I was good at it." Stopping, he thought a moment. "I tell you what, Jimmy. While I'm here this week, I'll teach you as much as I can about homing pigeons, and you teach me as much as you can about hawks. That way we'll both learn something new. Is it a deal?"

"That would be great!" Jimmy replied, jumping up and giving his dad another hug. "I'd surely like to learn something about homing pigeons, but I don't know too

Strong Feather

much about hawks, Dad. I'll do the best I can. It'll be a lot of fun though, won't it?"

"It certainly will, Son," Tommy replied.

The conversation around the table soon turned to other matters. Tommy told them how he called Bill Wilson's garage and was glad his dad was there. Then how Chuck Miller and his dad picked him up in Longmont. How they'd driven past the garage while they were inside talking on the phone. Then finally, how he enjoyed the sight of his mother brushing Jimmy aside as she ran past him and into the kitchen.

Time passed so quickly that evening. While the men were talking, Alice got up and fixed supper. She joined in occasionally with a story of her own. After supper they talked some more. Jimmy enjoyed sitting there and listening to all of the stories, especially the ones about his dad. Most of the stories were about the good things he did, but now and then there was one that was not so good. Before they realized what time it was, it was time for bed. It was past midnight when he and his dad walked down the hall towards their bedroom. Opening the door, his dad stepped inside.

Turning on the light, Tommy stood in the middle of the room and looked around. "Nothing has changed, Jimmy," he said, with a sigh. "It looks the same as when I was growing up. Some of my homing pigeons' pictures are still on the walls. And my bird quilt is still on the bed. Your grandma made that for me, Son. It sure feels good to be back home where things don't change. Away from here things change too fast, but here in Mercer, life kinda slows down. No one can stop change, I know that, but your grandma sure has tried."

Strong Feather

The two of them were soon lying in bed with the light out. As they lay there thinking, Tommy asked, "How's your mother doing, Jimmy?"

This was what Jimmy wanted to do for a long time. His heart ached to be alone with his dad, just to talk with him again, like they used to when he was small. He told him what he and his mother had talked about earlier that evening.

"I'm glad to hear she's doing all right, Jimmy," Tommy said.

"Me, too," Jimmy replied.

Once again silence reigned. Before he could say more, the sound of snoring reached his ears. He thought about all of the things that happened that day. He recalled how he thought nothing could top his talking to his mother. But that was before his dad showed up. What a day. And best of all, his dad was home for a week. No matter how the rest of the week turned out, this day was the greatest. The peace of the dark called to him, and he, too, was soon asleep.

Jimmy awoke with a start, and sat up. There was someone yelling next to him. Turning the light on beside his bed, he realized it was his dad who yelled. He was yelling in his sleep. The bedroom door opened, and his grandma ran into the room. She came over and sat down on the bed beside her son.

"It's all right, Tommy," she said, looking down at him. Oh so gently, she began rubbing his forehead with her fingers. "It's all right, Son." The yelling stopped as quickly as it started. Tommy's body relaxed under Alice's gentle touch.

"This is what happens to some of the men who go off to war, Jimmy," she said, as tears ran down her face. "Yes, that's what that war did to my boy. He was the best boy around these parts until he went off to war. It just ruined him. But I have faith, Jimmy, and I know he's going to be all right. I know that to be a fact as sure as I'm sitting here. I know it."

She got up and walked around the bed and sat down next to him. "Lie down, Jimmy," she said, looking at him. He lay down and she covered him up. Bending over, she kissed him on the forehead. "Goodnight, my sweet Jimmy."

"Goodnight, Grandma," he replied.

Getting up, she turned off the bedside light and left the room. Long forgotten memories slowly inched their way into his mind. He recalled other nights in his younger life, when his dad woke him up with his yelling. Closing his eyes, he found it hard to drift off to sleep, but eventually, he did.

When his two tired eyes opened the next morning, he was alone in bed. His dad got up earlier and left without waking him. After he made the bed, he hurried into the kitchen and found everyone sitting at the table.

"Here comes old sleepy head," his dad said, laughing.

"Good morning, Dad," he replied, enjoying the ribbing.

"I've been out back looking at your hawk and her babies this morning, Jimmy," Tommy said. "That mother hawk sure is a beauty. I can see why you won with her. She wouldn't have much to do with me though. She probably knows that I am one of those old pigeon men. I was wondering if you could change her mind. I'd surely like to see you work with her."

"She's easy to work with, Dad," he replied. "All you have to do is show her a little love and affection. She'll let me do just about anything I want. She is, of course, a little bit spoiled."

Strong Feather

"You're right there," Alice agreed. "But I wouldn't say she's spoiled. I'd say it's more like rotten."

Laughter came easy around the Warrior table that morning as they enjoyed their breakfast. After they ate, Jimmy and his dad went out back to the hawk's pen. It wasn't long until Lady Samson was on his fist, and they headed for the open field behind the house. Jimmy began by working Lady Samson with the lure that morning and letting his dad help. He wanted his dad to get used to working with her, and she with him.

While they were resting, they heard someone yell. Jimmy turned to see Mary and her dog, Goldie, coming across the field towards them. "Hi, Mary," he said, when she came running up. "This is my dad. Dad, this is Mary Wilson."

Tommy stuck out his hand and shook hers. "It's good to meet you, Mary," he said, smiling. "Jimmy's been telling me that the two of you are learning how to train the three hawks you've caught."

"It's good to know you, Mr. Warrior," Mary said, shaking his hand. Then without any hesitation, she continued, "That's right. We really enjoy working with Lady Samson and her babies. She makes it easy for us, and we learn from her everyday. Of course, the babies are just beginners. They're just starting to fly, but they're doing real well. We've had problems taking them out of their cage, but we know we have to. They won't learn to fly or hunt, unless we get over the fear that they may not be trainable."

"You two have a small problem, don't you," Tommy said, thinking about what she said.

"Let's show my dad how good a hunter Lady Samson is, Mary," Jimmy said. "We'll worry about the young hawks later."

Strong Feather

"Yea," Tommy said. That was what he had been waiting to hear. The three of them headed towards the creek with Goldie running back and forth up ahead of them. Reaching the other side of the creek, Jimmy removed Lady Samson's hood, raised his hand, and she took flight. With wings outstretched, she swooped down low over Goldie's head, then upward. At first she sailed along like a glider. Then with powerful downward strokes of her wings she gained altitude and speed. When she caught the wind under her wings, upward she went. With the powerful rhythmic strokes of her wings she went higher and higher, until she circled high above them. Mary gave Goldie the hunt command, and off she went, looking for some kind of quarry in the nearby weeds and bushes.

Three eager hunters followed along behind Goldie, all excited. It wasn't long until there was a loud whirring sound, and up from the weeds in front of them rose four pheasants. All heads snapped in their direction, then upward. They saw that Lady Samson started her steep dive. She was descending like a falling rock. Then, at the last moment, she spread her wings and swooped sideways, catching a rooster pheasant. She then fell to the ground with her catch. The three of them ran over to where she flopped around on the ground. Jimmy placed his gloved hand next to her, and she hopped onto it with one foot.

"Give it to me, Lady Samson," he said softly, as he took her catch from her. He then placed the pheasant into his hunting bag. Placing her other foot on his glove, Lady Samson sat there looking at Tommy as if to say, "What do think of that?"

Jimmy removed a small package from his hunting bag. Taking off the outer paper he gave it to Lady Samson, and they watched her eat it. She earned the treat that he brought just for her. Tommy was amazed. "That was something to see, Son," he said, shaking his head. "It's a little hard for me to believe what I just saw. Lady Samson is all you told me she was."

When Lady Samson finished eating, she looked up at Jimmy and blinked. He began stroking the feathers on the back of her head with his finger. She worked as hard as she could at being what Jimmy wanted her to be.

A screech overhead caused them to look upward. The sound came from the top of the old dead tree. As they watched, a small hawk took flight, swooping down, then upward as it flew off. Jimmy and Mary looked at Lady Samson. She sat there calmly on Jimmy's fist watching the young hawk. She seemed to know it was one of her wild babies taking flight.

CHAPTER XIV

Jimmy's pride in Lady Samson grew each time he worked with her. She proved herself worthy of his pride. With three pheasants in his bag, they called it a day. His dad beamed as they walked back to the house. Mary bounced as she walked along beside Jimmy. Lady Samson's hood now covered her eyes as she sat quietly on his fist. Goldie, the golden Cocker Spaniel, ran back and forth up ahead of them, stopping now and then to check out a bush.

The air was clean and fresh that morning. White billowy clouds slowly formed over the mountains to the west, then moved eastward towards the open plains. A turtle dove cooing was heard coming from a tree behind them. A horn honked somewhere in town as they walked along listening to the different sounds. They heard the sound of a train's whistle blow for the crossing on the highway. Then silence returned as they neared the hawk pens.

Alice was on the back porch watching as they crossed the field and headed in her direction. "What a sight," she thought. She watched her son walk towards her. She took a deep breath, held it, then let it out slowly. It was a long time since she watched him come walking in from that field behind their house. As she watched, her eyes focused on her grandson. She marveled at how much her son and grandson looked alike. They were both tall and straight, with Jimmy only a couple of inches shorter than his dad. It wouldn't be long until he would be as tall as his dad . . . maybe even taller.

Alice opened the screen door when they came walking up to the pens. "Lunch will be ready in a few minutes," she said.

Strong Feather

"That sure does sound good, Mom," Tommy replied.

"I'll be right in, Grandma," Jimmy said, opening the gate to the hawk pen. "We got three pheasants."

"That's wonderful, Jimmy," she said, with a twinkle in her eyes.

"I've never seen anything like this hawk Jimmy has, Mom," Tommy said.

"She's been a blessing around here, Son," she replied.

"I can see why," he said, holding the gate open for his son.

"Can you stay and eat with us, Mary?" Alice asked.

"Sure, I'd like that," Mary answered.

"Good," she said, going back inside.

Mary stood outside the pen watching as Jimmy put Lady Samson on her perch. It was a good morning, and she decided that she wanted to get to know Jimmy's dad better. She came to like him that morning, but she didn't know him as well as she wanted. He was a lot like Jimmy, and she liked that.

They were a happy threesome when they entered the back porch. Jimmy removed his hunting bag and put it on the back porch. "I'll leave this out here for now," he said.

"We'll get to those pheasants later, Jimmy," Tommy said over his shoulder as they walked down the hall towards the kitchen.

It was about three years since he saw his dad, and he thought about that as he followed him down the hallway. Most memories of his dad were childhood memories. He had a hard time trying to remember what they did when he was younger. He could not remember the things they did

202

earlier, but he was sure he wouldn't forget the memories they made now.

Jimmy grew some since he came to Mercer. His grandma always told him how much he looked like his father when he was his age. He didn't pay much attention to what his dad looked like when he was younger, and he often wondered about it. But with his dad sitting across the table from him, he saw that he looked a lot like him. It felt good to just sit and watch his dad eat, talk, and laugh.

After dinner, they sat around the table and talked for some time. Tommy looked at his son and said, "I sure would like to hunt with Lady Samson this afternoon, Jimmy" he said.

"That would be great," he replied. Turning, he asked Mary, "Can you go with us?"

"I'd like to, Jimmy," she replied, "but I promised my mother I'd help her clean house this afternoon, so I'll have to be going. Anyway, I think you and your dad need some time by yourselves, so I'll leave Goldie here with you. When you've finished with her, she'll come home by herself; you won't have to bring her. Thanks for the meal, Mrs. Warrior. It was very good."

Alice came over and hugged her. "You come back as soon as you can, Mary. We girls have got to stick together around here."

"I'll do that," Mary said, laughing. She waved as she went out the front screen door. Jimmy and his dad got up and cleared the table.

"You two boys go on and play with your toy out back," Alice said, shooing them away from the table. "I'll clean the pheasants while you're gone. Go on, have a good time."

They both laughed and headed towards the back porch. They took the pheasants out of the hunting bag and

Strong Feather

placed them on the table and were soon next to Lady Samson's pen looking at her. Jimmy took the other welding glove off a nail he drove into one of the pen poles. Handing it to his dad, he put the other one on. Tommy watched his son put Lady Samson's hood on. Jimmy held one of the thongs in his mouth as he grabbed the other thong and tied a knot with his free hand. He was getting good at it. With the hood on Lady Samson, he walked over to his dad and placed his hand in front of his. He then moved his hand backwards until their hands met. Then he moved his hand under his dad's, and when the back of Lady Samson's legs touched Tommy's glove, she stepped backwards onto his hand.

Tommy grinned. "What a sight," he thought, looking at the large hawk sitting on his hand. There was something about having Lady Samson sitting on his fist that made him feel proud. Jimmy opened the gate for his dad. They stepped out of the pen, and he closed it behind them. Goldie ran over to where they were, wagging her tail. She knew it was time to hunt, and she was ready.

They walked towards the creek with Lady Samson sitting like a statue on Tommy's fist. Jimmy marveled at how his dad adapted so quickly to the hawk, and the hawk to him. He, too, was a bird lover, and it showed. Maybe it was the Indian in them that had something to do with it.

When they reached the creek, they ran down one bank and up the other. Goldie trotted along next to Jimmy like his shadow. She knew exactly what was expected of her, and like all good bird dogs, she enjoyed nothing more than hunting. When they topped the far side of the creek, he gave Goldie the command to hunt. Off she ran, sniffing everything in sight. Back and forth she went, looking for any kind of quarry.

Strong Feather

"It's time to take the hood off Lady Samson, Dad," Jimmy said. Tommy looked at his son, not knowing what to do. "Reach up with your left hand and untie the knot. Then gently lift the hood off her head. She won't mind. In fact, she's as ready to hunt as we are."

Tommy reached up and untied the knot Jimmy tied earlier.

"That's it. You're doing great, Dad. Now lift it straight up. There. That's the way you do it."

With her hood off, Lady Samson sat there looking around. She then saw Jimmy standing off to her side. She looked at Tommy, then back at Jimmy. She seemed undecided on what to do. Jimmy took a feather from his hunting bag and walked over to her. He stroked her a couple of times with the feather as he talked to her. His voice, and the movement of the feather, calmed her down.

"When you're ready for her to hunt, Dad, just raise your hand," he said.

Tommy looked at the hawk on his hand, gulped, then slowly raised his hand over his head. Lady Samson spread her wings and took off. Flapping her wings, she rose higher and higher into the air until she was high over their heads. Goldie kept up her busy search of all the bushes. They followed her over three hills with no luck. Jimmy called her, and she came running back to him. He pointed towards the creek and told her, "Hunt."

As she neared the creek bank, she stopped and stood perfectly still. She smelled something. Jimmy ran over to where she stood, and a cottontail rabbit jumped out of the weeds in front of him. Looking upward, he saw Lady Samson was diving. Spreading her wings at the bottom of her dive, she quickly had the rabbit in her grasp. They both ran over to where she was on the ground. Tommy reached down with his gloved hand and she came to his fist. Taking the rabbit from her, he handed it to Jimmy. Jimmy took it and was amazed at what his dad did.

Reaching into his shirt pocket, Tommy brought out the hood he took off of Lady Samson. He raised the hood upward in one fluid motion, slipping it over her head. "I watched you do that a couple of times, son," he said. He then quickly tied a knot in the leather thong, making it look easier than it was.

Tommy felt proud about what he did. It felt good to have such a great bird sitting on his hand, and he was proud of how he put her hood on.

"You did great, Dad," Jimmy said. "I told you she was easy to handle."

Tommy looked at the rabbit in his boy's hand. "Jimmy, you have to be careful with rabbits this time of year. It's about the middle of summer around here, and it's starting to get hot. In another month, it will be even hotter. Rabbits are known to have worms and other types of diseases when it gets hot. Your grandma knows which ones to keep and which ones not to, so be sure and show them to her before you fix them to eat. Pheasants are the best things to hunt this time of year. Later this fall, ducks will be flying over these hills headed south. When winter is upon this land and it is good and cold, rabbits are then the best animals to catch and eat."

"That's good to know, Dad," Jimmy said, looking at him. "You sure know a lot about hunting. Did you do a lot of hunting when you were a boy?"

"I did my share, Son," Tommy replied, looking at the hills about them. "I spent some of the best days of my life right here. I can remember the times when I used to come out here and lay on the side of these hills and watch the world go by. I can remember watching the great hawks like this one circle around and around high above me. My thoughts wandered far and wide as I lay there, and I was the hero of all I surveyed. I now cherish those days, Son, and those memories are precious to me."

They talked as they walked back to the house and put Lady Samson in her pen. His dad dressed out the rabbit, deciding it was all right to eat.

"Now, Jimmy," he said, placing his hand on Jimmy's shoulder, "let's go inside and give this to your grandma, and tell her how I helped catch it."

Jimmy put his arm around his dad's waist and looked at him. It sure felt good to have his dad by his side. "Okay," he said. They were making up for lost time.

The next day Tommy got all of the books he had on homing pigeons. Dragging the bedside chair over next to Jimmy's desk, he sat down. It was now his turn to tell his son all he knew about homing pigeons. As they went through each of the books, Jimmy told him how much of that book he read. His dad was surprised to find out his son read his pigeon books. He closed the book they were looking at, got up, and left the room. When he returned a few minutes later, he had four different books in his hand.

"These are my pride and joy, Jimmy," he said. "Your grandma had them hid in her room. She has always hid things in her room that she likes a lot." When he opened the book on top, a black and white picture fell to the floor. Tommy picked the picture up and looked at it.

"Well, what do you know?" he said slowly, and he handed it to Jimmy.

"Is that you, Dad?" Jimmy asked, looking at the picture. "It looks like me."

"That's a picture of me and my homing pigeon, Alice," Tommy said, sitting back in his chair. "I named her after your grandma. She was one of the best pigeons I ever

Strong Feather

had. She wasn't the fastest homer I ever had, Son, but Alice was the first."

Sitting in their room at the desk, they talked about pigeons the rest of the day, stopping only to eat. Time flew by so quickly and before they knew it, it was time to go to bed again. The two of them really didn't care. They had each other, and it felt good. They even slept together. That's getting real close.

The next day they continued their talk about pigeons all morning long. Tommy explained to Jimmy how to tell the difference between the best pigeons and the almost-best pigeons. While they were eating lunch, Tom came hopping into the kitchen on his crutches. He was getting ready to leave for work in about ten minutes. He didn't need his crutches all the time, but his leg was still sore. He looked at them. It was his polite way of telling them he would like for his son to spend some time with him.

Tommy understood what he meant, and when the meal was over he looked at Jimmy. "I'm going to go help your grandpa clean up, Son. I need to spend some time with him. You read those four new books while I'm gone, and I'll check with you later."

"OK," he told his dad, "I'll do that."

Tom and Tommy headed for the door. When they were gone, Alice went back to washing dishes, and Jimmy went to his room. He quickly separated the four books from the others. He picked up the top book and opened it. The picture of his dad and his pigeon, Alice, slid out of the book onto the top of his desk. Picking it up, he looked at it. His grandma was right, he sure did look a lot like his dad at that age.

When he read two of the four books, he got up and went into the kitchen. Looking around, he asked his

Strong Feather

grandma where his dad was. She told him that they hadn't come back yet. With his dad helping his grandpa clean up the beer joints, Jimmy figured they should have gotten through by now.

Time passed slowly as supper time came, and they still hadn't showed up. Alice was starting to get worried. She tried hard not to show it, but he could tell that it was bothering her. After they ate and were clearing the table, they heard footsteps on the porch. Tom opened the front door and came in holding up his son, Tommy. Looking at his wife, Tom shook his head.

"I got him, Alice, but not before his old friends messed him up. I had to wait until I'd finished cleaning up before I could go look for him. I'll take him back to his room and put him in bed."

Tom walked his son down the hall to his bedroom, opened the door, and went inside with him.

Alice sat down at the table and put her face in her hands. Jimmy moved around the table and sat down beside her and didn't say anything. This was not the time to be talking.

"You know, Jimmy," she said, after they sat there for some time, "Tommy's going to win the battle that's raging within himself one of these days. Those people who call themselves his friends, are really not his friends. They know that my boy has a sickness, and they've got to learn how to help him, not hurt him. They can't help him by buying him drinks, but by not buying him drinks. Only then will they truly be his friends."

Tom came out of the bedroom. "He's going to be fine, Alice. He's been off of alcohol so long that just a couple of drinks hit him hard. This may have been the best thing that could have happened. He now knows what just a couple of drinks will do to him."

Strong Feather

Alice looked at her husband, not saying a word, then slowly she nodded her head in agreement. "I sure hope it does, Tom," she said.

Alice looked at Jimmy and said, "I'd like for you to sleep on the couch in the front room tonight, Jimmy. That way you won't disturb your dad and he won't disturb you."

She got up from the table and went into her bedroom, returning in a few minutes with two sheets and a blanket. She quickly spread them over the couch in the front room, then went back into her room and returned with a pillow. When she finished, she looked at both of them, then went into her bedroom and closed the door.

"Well, Jimmy," his grandpa said, sitting down at the table, "you probably remember a little bit about the problem your dad has. But maybe you've forgotten. It's been a few years since you've seen him. Now that you're a young man, things may look different. I've heard men say Indians are born alcoholics. That's not true, Jimmy."

"Your dad had bad war experiences, which didn't help, but that's really no excuse for him to drink. Lots of men go to war and are not alcoholics." Tom looked at his grandson for a while, thinking about what he said. "You go on to bed, Jimmy. Tomorrow is another day. It'll be a beautiful day, too, just wait and see."

"Okay, Grandpa," Jimmy said. "I sure hope so."

Jimmy went into the front room. Tom sat at the table for some time. Finally, he got up and went into his room. He would have to hold his wife real tight this night. Tomorrow would be another day, and it would be beautiful. He knew it would.

Jimmy got undressed, turned off the lights, and was soon lying between two nice soft sheets. He thought about his dad, and some of the things his grandpa said. He didn't know what to do for his dad, but he wanted to do

210

something. He heard a door open, and light spilled out into the front room. His grandma came out of her room and sat down on the end of the couch.

"I can tell you're worried about your dad, Jimmy," Alice said. "So am I. I worry about my boy a lot. But you know what? I know something that we can do to help."

"What can we do, Grandma?" he asked, looking up at her.

"All Indians know that there is a higher power than man," she said, smiling at her grandson. "All we have to do is ask the Great Spirit for help, and He will give it."

"That's great, Grandma," he said. "Let's ask him to help dad."

Taking ahold of her grandson's hand, she closed her eyes, and so did Jimmy. Turning her face upward, she said, "Great Spirit, we ask that you be with my son, Tommy, Jimmy's father. Take this awful drinking problem he has away from him. We love him so much. Don't let this problem come between him and his son. Not now. Please, Precious Spirit."

Jimmy closed his eyes, but now opened them to see if she was through. He smiled when he saw her looking at him.

"Your grandpa told me it was going to be a good day tomorrow," Alice said, smiling at him. "We'll see. You go ahead and get to sleep, Jimmy."

She tucked Jimmy in, and kissed him on the forehead. He looked at his grandma, then kissed her back. "Thank you, Grandma," he said.

"You're welcome, Jimmy."

She went back to her room. He heard the door close softly behind her, and it was dark again. "He knew that by himself he couldn't do much to help his dad, but with his grandma's help he could," he thought as he drifted off to sleep.

Someone shaking his shoulder caused him to open his eyes. When he turned over and opened his eyes, he saw his dad. Tommy was sitting on the side of the couch looking at him.

"Good morning, Son," he said. "I wanted to talk to you about last night." He paused, then went on. "I've been trying real hard not to get myself into that condition, but it felt so good being around old friends and loved ones. So, I took a few drinks last night. Well, I found out what a couple of drinks will do to me, and I know what it's done to you and my parents. So, I've decided to cut my leave short, and go back to the Veterans Hospital today. I sure don't want to leave, but I know it's the best thing to do. I still need help, and I know it, Jimmy."

Jimmy reached up and grabbed ahold of his dad, wanting to yell at him not to leave. Choking back his tears, he said, "I sure am going to miss you, Dad. But I knew you'd have to leave in a couple of days, so it's all right."

Tommy looked at his son. "I know I can win, Jimmy," he said, slowly. "I know I can. And I'm going to. Just you wait and see if I don't."

Jimmy got dressed, and they went into the kitchen. Breakfast was on the table ready for them to eat. After breakfast, Tommy told his parents that he was planning on going back to the Veterans Hospital. He said he would be catching the bus that afternoon if he could get it to stop. If not, he'd get Mr. Wilson to take him to Longmont. But he felt certain he could get the bus to stop.

They were saddened by the news, but they, like Jimmy, knew that he would be leaving in a couple of days anyway. Alice got up and went to pack her son's things. Jimmy went out back with his dad and looked at Lady

Strong Feather

Samson. Pride rose up within the two of them as they looked at her.

"You keep up the good work, Son," Tommy said. "Don't let anything stand in your way. I don't mean you should walk over others to get your way, but set a few goals that you can reach, and work hard towards them. When you know what you really want, and you know it's right, then work as hard as you can to attain it. Learn as much as you can about what you want to attain. Study hard and keep your word. You've got what it takes to reach any goal you set for yourself."

It felt good to hear his dad say those things to him. The two of them walked towards the creek. Crossing it, they continued walking to the top of the nearest hill. They both enjoyed the view and each other's company. Back along the creek they walked and through the open fields that surrounded the Warrior home. Not much was said as they enjoyed their time together. They both knew it would be a long time before they would walk these hills and fields of Mercer together, but they didn't know when.

Then it was time for his dad to leave, and they headed back to the house. Tom and Alice joined them, and the four of them walked down to the highway. They stood beside the highway talking and laughing as if nothing was going to happen. Then off in the distance they heard the rumbling of the bus as it neared the other side of town. It slowed down as it made its way through town. As it drew near, Tommy stepped out onto the highway and waved. The bus slowed even more, then came to a stop beside him. The door opened, and there sat Sam Brack. He tipped his hat at them and smiled.

Tommy gave everyone a big hug and kiss. Looking into his mother's sad face, he said, "I'll be back before you know it, Mom," and he hugged her again. Turning, he ran up the steps and found a seat near a window on their side of the bus. Sam nodded at them, and closed the doors. Gears ground in the back of the bus, and it started to move. They all waved as the bus passed by, leaving the three of them standing there waving at the back of the bus. When it was out of sight, Alice and Tom put their arms around Jimmy, and they headed for home. Every now and then a tear was wiped away.

Jimmy hugged his grandparents. He remembered what his grandparents said the night before. If this was supposed to be the beautiful day they told him about last night, he wondered when the beauty was going to start.

CHAPTER XV

Lady Samson's fame spread around the state of Colorado. The picture of her and Jimmy in the Denver Post newspaper started it. Then the local papers eagerly joined in on spreading the news of a local boy and his hawk. When the people from Mercer traveled to different cities around the state, they were surprised by their friends asking them about their local boy and his hawk. They, too, helped make others aware of where Mercer was located, which helped some local businesses. A lot of people, from the elderly to the young, now stopped Jimmy on the street just to talk.

That is, everyone except the two guys who hit him in the back with a rock the first day he arrived in Mercer. They spoke only once, and that was it. Now all he got from them were glaring looks like he got at first. They definitely were not overjoyed about the attention he was getting.

The prize money helped the Warriors' finances. Most of the $100.00 went to pay Tom's doctor bills. But that which was left over was treasured, and the Warrior household found itself in good shape.

Then strange things happened. Friends that Tom and Alice hadn't seen in years stopped by, just to talk. They wanted to know about their grandson, Jimmy, and his falcon hawk. Even strangers drove up their lane to see them. They pulled up at all times of the day, got out and knocked on their door. They were just passing through Mercer, and wanted to see the boy and his hawk that won the contest at the Air Force Academy.

One morning while Jimmy was out back working with one of the small hawks, he heard a car pull up out front. He stopped what he was doing and listened. Not hearing any footsteps, he went back to stroking his young hawk with a feather as he talked to her.

He liked for people to come by. It made him feel good. If they wanted to see his falcon hawk, Lady Samson, they were welcome. As he talked to his young hawk, he watched its reactions. It learned well. Placing it on its perch, he hurried out of the pen, leaving the gate open. He went over and stood by the house and waited. There was the sound of flapping wings as both young hawks flew out the gate and headed towards the creek. Letting the young hawks fly around the area was part of their training, as long as they didn't forget where their home was.

He let the wood pile dwindle quite a bit while his dad was here. So he pulled a good size railroad tie off the top of the wood pile and placed it on the X-type sawhorse his grandpa fixed to cut ties on. Walking over to the pen, he removed the large saw from the nail he kept it on. Walking back to the sawhorse, he started cutting the tie into one-foot blocks. "The chores still had to be done, no matter how famous he and his hawk became," he thought. Of course it had nothing to do with his grandma reminding him that morning that the supply of wood was getting low in the wood box behind the stove.

The saw continued to bite into the old tie, as a good size pile of sawdust quickly formed on the ground. Grinning as he sawed, he knew he'd have this tie sawed up in no time. The saw cut steadily through the last part of the tie, and the last part fell to the ground. Laying the saw against the stack of railroad ties, he reached down and picked another tie up off the ground. Moving it along the sawhorse about twelve inches, he set it down. His grandma wanted her firewood cut no longer than twelve inches so it would fit in her wood cookstove.

Strong Feather

As he reached for the saw, he heard the back door open behind him. His grandma stepped out onto the back porch and motioned for him to come inside. He placed the saw back on the nail before going into the house. Inside, he found her sitting in the front room with a long, lanky, red-headed man.

"Yes, Ma'am," he said, looking at her.

"This is Mr. Red Ross, Jimmy," she said slowly, motioning his way. "He's come to get his hawk. He showed me some pictures he has of her, and I'm afraid the hawk is his."

Jimmy dropped onto the nearby couch as his face distorted in disbelief. "But we ran the ad for two weeks, Grandma. I thought she was mine. How come he's here now and not when we ran the ad?"

Mr. Ross started to say something, but Alice raised her hand and he stopped. "Mr. Ross is from Casper, Wyoming, Jimmy. There was no way he could see the ad in the Longmont paper, therefore he had no way of knowing we had his hawk. You must understand, Jimmy, that we cannot keep something that belongs to someone else. You know that, don't you?"

"Yes, Ma'am," he replied, as his chin fell onto his chest. "But it isn't fair, Grandma."

"It's my hawk, kid," Red said gruffly, and pushed some pictures in front of his face. He started to pull them back, but Jimmy grabbed them out of his hand. He looked at each one of them, not really believing what he saw.

"She's my hawk, kid," Red continued, grabbing the pictures out of his hand and putting them in his shirt pocket. He had a large chew of tobacco in his mouth, and he started looking for a place to spit.

Jimmy was devastated. He didn't know what to do or say.

217

Strong Feather

"Her name ain't Lady Samson either, kid," Red growled. "Her name's Strong Feather. I trained her, and she's mine. I also want that prize money you won with her. It's not yours. All I want is what belongs to me, and I want it right now."

"I'm sorry, Mr. Ross," Alice said, "but we've spent almost all of the money."

"What!" Red shouted, swallowing some of his tobacco juice.

"That's right," she said sternly. "We tried to get in touch with you with the ad in the paper. You know that, and I don't think you have a right to, or deserve, any of the prize money."

"We'll see about that, lady," Red replied, desperately looking around. "Anyway, I'm here to get my hawk. Where you keeping her?"

"She's out back in her pen," Alice said, getting up.

The three of them walked down the hall and out the back door to the hawk pens. As soon as Lady Samson saw Mr. Ross, she started screeching. Jimmy looked at his grandma and shook his head. He read in one of the books that hawks don't scream unless they were mistreated by their trainers.

Red finally had a chance to spit, and he did. He spit all over one of the boards at the bottom of the pen. He then took his chew out of his mouth and threw it at his hawk. "Shut up, you crazy nut!" he yelled at her.

Lady Samson's eyes didn't leave him. She watched his every move. Her screeching was beginning to irritate the three of them.

Jimmy opened the gate and went inside. Lady Samson was pacing back and forth on her perch, something he never saw her do before. Putting his glove on, he went over and got her Indian hood off a knob he made just for it.

Strong Feather

He could not believe what she was doing. She wouldn't look at him, which she always did when he was in the pen with her.

Jimmy placed his hand in front of her and she came to his fist at once, but didn't take her eyes off Mr. Ross. He then slipped the hood over her head which stopped her ear-piercing screeching. Looking at his grandma, he shook his head. "She's never done that before," he said.

"That's because you've spoiled her rotten, kid," Red said. "She's the worst hawk I've ever trained. Every time I come around her, she screams like that. I feel like wringing her neck when she does it. I've tried to make her stop, but she just keeps it up. She's not worth making cat food out of."

Red walked over and picked up the extra glove that was laying on the bench inside the pen. Reaching into his shirt pocket, he pulled out a Dutch hood.

"She don't wear that type of hood, kid," Red said, pulling the hood off and throwing it on the ground.

Lady Samson started screeching the moment the hood was off. Red stuck his hand out for her to come to fist, but she just stood there wide-eyed, screeching. Moving his hand back and forth in front of her, he tried to get her to step off of Jimmy's glove, but she wouldn't move.

Grabbing Red's hand, Jimmy placed it behind Lady Samson's tail feathers. He raised Red's hand, dropping his under it. Lady Samson stepped upwards and backwards when Red's glove touched her legs, ending up on his glove screeching at him.

Stepping back, Jimmy shook his head as Red tried to put the Dutch hood on her. Reaching down, Jimmy picked up his hood. He could tell she didn't want to have anything to do with Mr. Ross. Her head bobbed up and down, and back and forth, as she did everything she could to keep the hood off her head. And all the time she continued to screech at him.

With much effort, he caught her just right and jammed the Dutch hood up and over her head. The hood stopped the screeching, but now she quivered.

Jimmy walked over to her and stroked her a couple of times with his finger, as he talked to her. She began to calm down some as she sat on Red Ross' fist.

"Keep your hands off my hawk, kid," Red said, pushing him aside. "I know how to handle her, and she don't need to be petted right now. She needs lots of discipline, and that's what she's going to get from now on." Red walked past Jimmy and out of the pen.

Jimmy and Alice followed him around the corner of the house to where he parked his car. Opening the trunk lid, he placed Lady Samson on a small perch he'd brought. Slamming the trunk lid, he took a couple of steps around his car, then stopped.

He looked at Jimmy and in a gruff voice said, "You can keep the prize money you won, kid. That should be more than enough for your taking care of my hawk for me. I don't want to make anyone around here mad at me. Now that I know she's the best hawk around these parts, I'll win plenty of money with her."

He took off Jimmy's glove and threw it on the ground beside his car. Reaching into his shirt pocket, he took out a packet of chewing tobacco. Taking out a big wad of tobacco, he stuffed it into the right side of his mouth. Putting the packet back in his shirt pocket, he spit on the glove, opened the car door, and got in. He started the car, slammed the door, put the car in gear, and with a loud roar of the engine, let the clutch out quickly, flinging gravel all over the yard and up against the house as he drove away.

Strong Feather

Alice and Jimmy had to duck to keep from being hit. With all of the clatter, Tom came hopping out the front door. He watched the car drive out of the yard and up to the highway. When Red reached the highway, he didn't stop but gunned the car. They could hear the tires squealing on the pavement as his car headed down the main street of Mercer.

"What's going on around here?" Tom asked, looking at them. "I was trying to get some rest."

Jimmy gingerly picked up the glove while Alice told Tom what happened. When Jimmy came up the steps and onto the porch, Tom put his arm around him. The three of them walked into the house and sat down at the kitchen table. "I sure am sorry you lost Lady Samson, Jimmy," he said. "But don't forget, you've got two of her babies. I was out back looking at them yesterday, and they're getting big. They sure look a lot like their mother. It was a blessing when you got a hawk that could hunt right off. I'd say she had a lot to do with your deciding to work with hawks. That hawk helped you much more than you will ever know. Now you can teach her babies all you learned from her. You will have to teach her babies like other trainers do when they catch a hawk. Then, and only then, will you be a true falconer. You'll never be a great falconer without doing it, Jimmy."

He thought about what his grandpa said, and knew he was right. "You're right, Grandpa," he said. "I'm training one of her babies, and Mary is training the other. Mr. Ross said that Lady Samson's real name is Strong Feather. That name fits her, but I believe I like both of them together, Strong Feather Lady Samson."

His grandparents nodded in agreement. Jimmy went over to the refrigerator. Taking a package of meat out, he walked down the hallway and out to the half-empty hawk pen. Opening the gate, he went inside and placed the glove on the table. Coming back out, he walked around the pen to the side where he kept the two baby hawks. He stepped inside their pen and picked up one of the feeding boards. Placing it on the other side of the pen, he opened the package and tied some meat to the board. He then tied the rest of the meat onto the other feeding board on the bench. He went back outside and waited for the young hawks to return for their noon meal.

He released them each morning so they could strengthen their wings. The pen became their home, their shelter, and the place where they came to eat when they were hungry. There was always the fear that they might fly off one day and not come back. But the books said they wouldn't fly away. So with a faint heart, he turned them out that first day. To his surprise, they flew around the house a couple of times and returned to their pen. He was elated with their quick return, and from that day on, he knew they wouldn't fly off. If they did, they wouldn't go far, and if they did, he could always trap them if he had to.

When their mother was in the pen next door, he had no trouble with the two baby hawks. He hoped that would continue. He searched the skies for them, but they were nowhere in sight. It was over an hour, and they were usually back in an hour. They were running late, which started him wondering, especially with it being after noon. They missed their noon meal yesterday, and he knew it was about time he started keeping them penned up. The books said that when hawks miss a couple of meals, they were probably catching their own food. It wouldn't be long until they stopped returning to their pen to eat.

As he thought about the message the hawks might be giving him, Mary came around the corner of the house and over to where he was standing. "Where's Lady Samson?" she asked, looking at her pen.

"A Mr. Red Ross came by earlier and took her," he replied, trying to act as if nothing happened. "I found out her real name is Strong Feather. I like that name, plus the one I gave her. So I now call her Strong Feather Lady Samson. That Mr. Ross sure was mean to her, Mary. I was in her pen feeling so sorry for her, but there wasn't a thing I could do. He had some pictures of her. Sure made me feel bad when he took her. I watched him drive off with her in his trunk. He. . . "

Mary grabbed him by the arm and shook him. He would have gone on talking, but she couldn't listen to any more. Tears filled her eyes as she looked at Jimmy. He looked like he was in shock, and she led him over to the pile of railroad ties. They climbed up on top of the ties and sat down. It was a sad day for the two of them. Then they heard the beating of wings overhead. Looking up, they watched as the two young hawks flew into their pen and started eating.

They sat there and watched them for a while before they climbed off the ties. Jimmy went inside their pen and closed the door. Putting his glove on, he waited until they were finished eating before he took his hawk to fist. Grabbing her jesses so she couldn't fly off, he picked up her feeding board. He then carried both of them over to Lady Samson's side of the pen and placed the feeding board on her table. He then placed his hawk on the limb perch he had made. Placing his glove on the bench, he stepped back and looked at her. "She sure looks a lot like her mother," he thought.

"It's time for us to keep them penned up," he said to Mary. "They missed their noon meal yesterday, and were late returning for their meal today. We can't afford to lose them now, especially with Lady Samson gone. I was thinking it's probably time we got serious about their training."

. From that day forward the training of the two young hawks went into full swing. The first thing they did was decide on a name for each hawk.

"I kind of like Lady in front of the name like you named Lady Samson," Mary said. "I've thought about a good name for my hawk, and I like Lady Joan, after the famous lady, Joan of Arc."

Jimmy thought a long time about a name for his hawk, then smiled. "I'll name mine after a well-known lady also. Her name will be Lady Gwen, after Lady Guinevere, King Arthur's Queen.

They sat there saying the names back and forth a couple of times, agreeing they were both good names. Whether the young hawks liked it or not, they were stuck with those names.

The situation around the Warrior house started looking bad. In fact, it was worse than when Jimmy first came to live with his grandparents. His grandpa's leg wasn't healing like it should. He would have to stay on his crutches longer than he planned. With Lady Samson gone, the money quit coming in. Their savings were soon spent, and it wasn't long until they were out of meat, not only for the Warriors, but for the two young hawks.

That weekend, Jimmy and Mary carried the pigeon cage over to Mr. Miller's barn early one morning, but they didn't have any luck catching pigeons. That afternoon they took the young hawks out into the field to train them. After an hour of working with Lady Joan, Mary put her hood on and placed her on a large log. It was now Lady Gwen's turn to work, so Jimmy took her hood off. They worked with her for an hour, putting her through a lot of different steps in her training.

As they worked with her, they watched her closely. They worked the young hawks with a new lure Alice made. Lady Gwen worked extra well that afternoon.

"Mary," he said, looking at his hawk. "Let's try Lady Gwen without the leash and see how she works."

Mary noticed how well she worked and agreed to take off the leash and see what happened. Unsnapping the swivel from the jess, Jimmy dropped the leash on the ground. Mary swung the lure around and around over her head. Jimmy lifted his hand above his head, and Lady Gwen left his fist with mighty strokes of her wings. She swooped downward, then up at the right moment, and caught the lure in midair after Mary turned it loose. She then fell to the ground with the lure grasped in her talons, waiting for Jimmy to come get it.

"She is working well," he said, with pride in his voice as Lady Gwen came to fist. "Call Goldie, Mary. I'm going to turn her loose and see if she will hunt."

"But, Jimmy," Mary said. "I think it's too early to try that. I don't think we've been working them long enough to do that."

"She's got to start sometime," he said, "and they're out of food."

Mary couldn't argue that point. She motioned for Goldie to come to her side. Goldie was in the tall grass watching. She was around the young hawks long enough for them to be used to her. Mary gave her the hunt command, and she ran a short ways and started running back and forth in the tall grass. Jimmy raised his hand, and away went Lady Gwen swooping down, then up. To her surprise, there was no tug on her leg. She was free, so she continued flapping her wings as she gained altitude.

Strong Feather

It wasn't long until Goldie smelled something and came to point. Jimmy and Mary ran over to where she stopped, and three pheasants whirred up in front of them. They both jumped backwards. Looking up, they saw Lady Gwen diving straight down at the pheasants. It looked like she was going to catch something on her first try, but the pheasant she was after veered off, and she missed. Lady Gwen then flew off a short distance and landed in the top of a nearby tree.

Jimmy ran back and got the lure while Mary ran over to the tree where Lady Gwen landed. When he got close to the tree, he stopped and started swinging the lure over his head. Round and round it went as he walked towards the tree. He then turned the lure loose and it flew high above him and landed a short distance away from him. Lady Gwen just watched him, but didn't come to lure. When he saw she wasn't going to come to lure, he took out the willow whistle his grandma had made for him and blew on it a couple times. He could see her watching every move he made. Again the lure went round and round above his head before it flew through the air. This time she took flight and caught the lure in midair. Running over to her, he placed his gloved hand in front of her, and she came to fist.

That was close. Both of them realized she could have flown away. She probably wouldn't have done so, but she could have. That was enough to put a good scare into them. Mary got her hawk and they headed back to the pens. They worked the hawks all afternoon, and all of them were tired.

With the hawks in their pens, they were about to go inside when they heard a terrible racket coming from the front of the house. They both took off running, and ran around the house to see what happened. As they came around the corner of the front of the house, they stopped. It

Strong Feather

was Mr. Ross. His car slid into the corner of the house. The left side of his front bumper had pushed the lower boards in on the house, causing the boards to be twisted.

Red got out of his car and looked at the damage he did to the house, when Jimmy and Mary came running up. Their appearance startled him, and he gave both of them an irritated look. Red looked back at the mess he made, and his face started getting red. He was mad and it showed.

Looking at Jimmy, he yelled, "Where's my hawk, Strong Feather? I know you've got her here! Come on, kid, tell me where she is! Do you hear me? You'd better tell me if you know what's good for you!"

Just then Tom came out the front door on his crutches. He was mad. He came down the steps at a gallop on those crutches and headed straight at Red Ross. Red stepped over his car's front bumper to the other side of the car to get away from Tom.

"What in the world is the matter with you, man?" Tom yelled, stopping next to the car and looking at his house. "Look at what you've done to my house!"

"I've come back to get my hawk," Red said, angrily. "That boy of yours has her, and I want her back right now. Do you hear me?"

His angry words took Tom by surprise. Turning, he looked at Jimmy. "Has Lady Samson returned, Jimmy? Tell me the truth, don't hide anything."

"No, Sir," Jimmy said. "She's not here. All we have in the back are two young hawks."

Red turned around and looked at Jimmy. "Don't lie to me, kid!" he said.

"If Jimmy says your hawk is not here, Mister, then it's not here!" Tom said, his anger returning to his voice.

Red stood there looking at Jimmy a few seconds before he calmed down. "Okay," he finally said. "If you say

Strong Feather

she's not here, then I guess she's not. I was taking her to a show in Cheyenne, Wyoming yesterday. When I opened the trunk to take her out, she got her hood off somehow. Before I knew what happened, she flew off again, just like she did that first time. But this time I had my shotgun in the trunk, and it was loaded. I got one good shot at her before she flew out of sight. I'm sure I hit her, but I'm not positive. But if I missed, I figure she would probably come back here. But if she's not here, she's probably dead."

Alice also came out of the house to see what made all that noise. When she walked up beside Tom, she heard the last part of what Red said. Her heart sank as she stood there looking at Jimmy. It was hard for her to believe that Lady Samson was dead. Red stepped back over his bumper, and walked past Tom and Alice. Opening his car door, he got in and closed it. He was about to start his car when Tom walked over to the car and grabbed him by the arm.

"You're not going anywhere until you pay to fix my house, fella," he said.

Red laughed. "I've already paid you with my prize money, and if that's not enough, you can have my dead hawk, Strong Feather." He yanked his arm out of Tom's grasp and started his car. Gunning the engine, he backed up fast, turned the wheels as sharp as he could, spun the tires and made a big circle in the front yard. Rocks, gravel, and dust flew against the house and everyone there. They turned around to protect themselves from the flying rocks and gravel. After Red turned the corner and drove down the highway, Tom bent over and looked at the corner of his house. "It's not that bad," he said. Reaching down, he pulled all of the boards back into place. Standing up, he looked at his wife, then back at the house. "I don't believe anyone could ever tell where they were pushed in by his bumper. Can you tell?"

Strong Feather

"No," Alice said, laughing. "Looks like it did before he ran into it."

Looking at Jimmy, he smiled. "Well, Jimmy," he said. "It looks like Mr. Ross' Strong Feather will be yours when she comes back."

"Yeah," Jimmy said. "If she isn't dead."

CHAPTER XVI

Jimmy and Mary worked many long hard hours each day with their young hawks. They learned, but it was slow. It would be some time before they could hunt like their mother. Jimmy had a hard time waiting for that day to come. He wanted that day to be yesterday.

Two young trainers with two young hawks was quite a challenge. The summer days began turning hot. So they worked the hawks early in the morning and in the cool of the evening. The shade of the trees around his grandparents' house became places of relief for the two tired, weary trainers.

One of those trees they loved to lie under was a tree in his grandma's garden. It was a cherry tree, and it turned pink all over about a month after Jimmy arrived in Mercer. The pink blossoms fell off, and in their place was an abundance of green cherries all over it. More than once his grandma told him how sweet and juicy the cherries were on that tree. He found it hard to wait for them to get ripe. Her stories of how good they were caused him to feel them to see how ripe they were each day.

One day when he sat in its shade, he spotted one of the cherries that turned red. He knew his grandma wouldn't care if he ate it. Reaching up, he picked it off the tree and popped it in his mouth. When he bit down on it, its juices flowed throughout his mouth, but instead of a smile, he made an awful face and spit it out. That was the sourest cherry he ever ate.

The next time his grandma mentioned how sweet her cherries were, he told her that he tried one and it was sour. She smiled and shook her finger at him. He gave himself away, recalling she told him not to eat any of them until they were ripe.

230

Strong Feather

"All pie cherry trees have sour cherries, especially Colorado cherry trees, Jimmy," she said. "It takes a lot of sugar to make them sweet and tart. If I remember, that's the way you like them."

That is the way he liked them, but he decided to wait until they got good and ripe before he tried another one. When they did get ripe, he ate a few of them, and they tasted some better. He didn't think they were very sweet at first, but the more he ate, the less sour they became. The robins around there liked them just as much as he did. He continually chased them out of the tree every day. One night after supper his grandma surprised him with a cherry pie. He had a hard time remembering how sweet her pies were. He hesitated before he took that first bite, but it tasted so good he ate that piece and two more. His grandma's cherry pie was still his favorite, no matter how sour they were on the tree.

Before Jimmy came to Mercer, he wasn't an early riser, but things do change in one's life. When the early morning's dew still lay like a glittering blanket around Mercer, Jimmy sat on the back steps of his grandparents' house each morning. He sat there each morning until he was called to breakfast. His eyes eagerly searched the skies for a black dot. Oh, how his young heart tugged at him with loneliness. Each morning when he opened the back door, he expected to see Lady Samson sitting on the top of her hawk pen looking at him. But the secret desire of his heart was never answered. As the days slowly passed, and she didn't return, he faced the likelihood that she was dead. Just the thought of her being dead tore at his insides. Even if she wasn't dead, the thought of her being wounded bothered him. He lay awake at nights thinking about her trying to hunt after being wounded. She would probably starve to death.

231

Strong Feather

After he went over and over this in his mind, he decided that even if Lady Samson hadn't been wounded, how would she ever find her way back to him? He didn't know how far it was to Cheyenne, Wyoming, but it had to be a long way. Then he smiled a little when he remembered she got away from Red Ross once before. She found her way to that old dead tree down by the creek. If she did it once, she might do it again. With that thought foremost in his mind, he went about his daily chores, hoping he was right.

One day stretched into the next around the Warrior house, and things were not getting any better. Tom was now having problems with his broken leg. His running out of the house at a gallop the day Red Ross ran into the house set him back. Not being able to work stopped the flow of money into the household. Jimmy worked Lady Gwen as hard as he could, but she was so young. There were times when she worked really well, then there were others when she didn't do a thing he wanted her to do. It was frustrating to both boy and hawk.

Mary and Jimmy now went over to Mr. Miller's barn every other day. They caught a few pigeons each time they went, but Chuck's pigeons were not that easy to capture. Without the pigeons, the hawks would not progress like they should.

Jimmy did everything the books said to do, but Lady Gwen didn't come along as fast as he wanted her to. It was at this time in her training that he started getting nervous, and it showed in his hawk. She became as nervous as he was.

One morning while Mary watched them work, she stopped him and told him what he was doing to his hawk. From then on, he worked at trying to be more relaxed around her. It wasn't long until she showed much

232

Strong Feather

improvement. She began to calm down and act like she used to.

Mary went to Longmont with her parents one Saturday, which left Jimmy by himself to work with his hawk. It seemed like Lady Gwen perked up a lot when she saw that Mary and her dog were not around. They had the best workout they ever had that day. She came a long way since he first let her try hunting on her own. At the end of their workout that morning, he felt sure she was ready to hunt. With her sitting on his fist, he headed towards the creek. As he neared the creek, he flushed two pheasants, a rooster and a hen.

"This is it," he thought, as his eyes followed the pheasants, noting where they landed. Removing Lady Gwen's hood, he looked around. "The Warriors will have pheasant for supper tonight," he thought. Raising his hand, she took flight, swooping across the top of the tall grass, then upward into the sky. She soon circled high overhead. Around and around she went until she reached the altitude she wanted. Motionless, she looked like she was painted in the blue sky above him.

He ran over to where he saw the pheasants land. He knew they would run some distance after they landed, so he started walking in a big circle. It wasn't long until the rooster took off in front of him. Glancing upward, he saw Lady Gwen spotted the pheasant and was in a dive. With her wings folded along her sides she descended swiftly, heading straight at the pheasant. But the rooster was wise, and veered quickly to the right, causing Lady Gwen to miss. Swooping up, she flew over the tall grass and disappeared over the nearest hill.

"Not again!" Jimmy yelled, as he ran towards the hill. When he reached the top, he saw her fly over the next hill. His legs were tiring when he reached its top. Stopping to catch his breath, he looked to see where his hawk was. Lady Gwen was nowhere in sight. She was gone. She was not in the top of the nearby trees. She was really gone this time. Squinting his eyes, he tried to see better, but he couldn't see her anywhere. He had the sinking feeling that she was gone for good this time.

Losing both of his hawks was too much. His knees buckled, and he fell to the ground on his knees. He sat back on his heels, shook his head, and realized he didn't know what to do. No hawks meant no meat for his grandpa and grandma. Thoughts went in circles in his mind, until his head started to hurt. Placing both of his hands on his head, he tried to stop it from hurting. He began to slowly rock back and forth, realizing this was another one of those bad days in his life. "Why did things like this always have to happen to him?" he thought.

Then he stopped rocking and his body stiffened. He heard something. Not moving, he listened as hard as he could. He heard it again. It sounded like the fluttering of wings behind him. His mind instantly cleared. His hawk was coming back. His heart swelled with pride as he sat perfectly still. Lady Gwen returned just like she had been trained. All of her training finally paid off. Slowly, he moved his gloved hand on top of his other hand and waited.

The beating of wings grew louder and louder until they were directly overhead. Then he felt the weight of his hawk on his hand. The tears of sorrow in his eyes now turned to tears of joy. Slowly he raised his hand off his head, then lowered it until he saw two leather jesses. With his free hand he grabbed a hold of them. With a good hold on the jesses, he raised his head and looked into two big, beautiful, yellow hawk eyes. But it wasn't Lady Gwen. It was Lady Samson! She just sat there wide-eyed, looking at him like she always did. His mouth fell open, and he couldn't believe his eyes as the tears continued to run down his face. Lady Samson came back to him.

He forgot all about Lady Gwen as he looked at Lady Samson. Then he jumped up and ran all the way back to the house. He quickly put her in her pen and ran into the house, yelling, "Lady Samson is back! Lady Samson is back!"

His grandparents were at the kitchen table when he ran in. They both got up and followed him outside. Sure enough, there in her pen sat Lady Samson. She bobbed her head a couple of times at them, but that was it. She seemed to be as glad to be back as they were to have her back. Just her presence in that pen lifted the heavy feeling the three of them had about her being dead. With her back, they knew everything would be alright.

When Mary returned that afternoon from Longmont, she came over to check on her hawk. When Jimmy told her Lady Samson was back, she was overjoyed, and they ran out back. Sitting on top of the railroad ties, they joyfully talked about her return. They both tried to figure out how she found her way back. It would always be a mystery, which they would wonder about for many days to come.

Mary looked in the next pen and saw Lady Joan sitting in the other pen by herself. "Where's Lady Gwen?" she asked, wondering why she wasn't with her sister.

Jimmy forgot all about her. Hanging his head, he told her what happened. How she flew away, leaving him by himself on top of the hill.

"Let's go find her, Jimmy," she said. "I doubt if she's gone very far. She's been raised around here, and I doubt if she'd fly off. I'd say she's probably somewhere around that old dead tree. Let's get our stuff and go see."

Strong Feather

Off they went, running and laughing as they went. It wasn't long until they spotted Lady Gwen. She was in the top of a large tree not far from the dead tree. Mary was close. They saw her bobbing her head up and down as she watched them cross the creek. She acted like she missed them. Taking out his lure, Jimmy whirled it around his head a couple of times and let it go. Down she came, grabbing it in midair, before she fluttered to the ground. He hurried over to her, and she hopped onto his glove.

With her sitting on his fist, they walked back to the house. He placed her in with Lady Joan. Once again, the three hawks were together. It was only then that he realized what happened. Lady Samson was his to keep.

"Lady Samson's mine to keep, Mary," he said, getting excited as he looked at her. "It's hard for me to believe after all that happened lately."

"I know!" she almost shouted. She was getting excited, too. "This is a great day, Jimmy! A great day!"

"Wow!" he shouted, and they hopped and danced around the stack of railroad ties. "It surely was a great day," he thought. It surely was one he'd never forget.

There were very few days that passed that Jimmy, Mary, Goldie, and Lady Samson were not off hunting someplace. They continued to go over to Chuck Miller's farm every other day for pigeons, plus a rat now and then. Chuck told them he had to put poison out to get rid of the rats after Lady Samson left. He sure was glad to see her back. He also let them know he took all of the poison up before they came over. He didn't want her catching anything that might have been poisoned.

Jimmy told Chuck that Mr. Ross had named her Strong Feather. He told him that he liked that name, Strong Feather, as much as the one he gave her. So he combined both names and now called her, Strong Feather Lady Samson.

Chuck agreed with him. "She's definitely a Strong Feather, plus a Lady," he told Jimmy, patting him on the back.

It wasn't long until things around the Warrior house began to look a lot better. People started coming around again to see Strong Feather Lady Samson. Tom's leg finally healed like it should, and it wasn't long until he was off his crutches. Mrs. Wendell continued to buy Strong Feather Lady Samson's extra catch. She even put a sign up next to the meat that read, "Compliments of Strong Feather Lady Samson." It seemed to help her sales. Some people bought it just so they could tell others they'd eaten something Strong Feather Lady Samson caught.

Tom started exercising his leg, and it wasn't long until he didn't have to use his crutches at work. At work, Tom was a celebrity. It seemed like everyone he met wanted to talk to him about his grandson and his hawk. He never passed up an opportunity to tell those who asked.

One day when Jimmy and Mary came in from hunting and sat down at the table, Alice came over and sat down with them. It was the first day of August, and it was a beautiful day outside.

"You know, Jimmy," she said. "When Lady Samson came our way the first time, things around here started to get better. She was the answer to my prayers, and I was happy. Then, when she left, things were not so good. But her return this time has not only been an answer to my prayers, but I believe, both of yours. It seems like everything straightens out around here when she's here, doesn't it?"

"I think you're right, Grandma," he said. "Mary and I were talking about that the other day."

Strong Feather

They realized that Strong Feather Lady Samson brought with her a feeling of security for the Warrior household. Whether it was in their minds, or it was real, it was good to have her back.

It wasn't long until the two young hawks also hunted, and there was an abundance of meat at the Warrior and Wilson households. One day a letter arrived from Mr. Archer. In it he asked how they were doing, and at the end he asked why Jimmy hadn't attended the falcon show at Trinidad, Colorado. With his letter he sent a list of all the shows being held in Colorado that summer.

Bill Wilson took Jimmy, Mary and their hawks to the Denver and Greeley shows, and Lady Samson won first place. Lady Joan was second at both shows. If there had been a third place, they were sure Lady Gwen would have won it.

One evening after supper, they heard a car drive up outside. Jimmy got up from the table and went over to the front door to see who it was. It was Chuck Miller.

"Hello, Mr. Miller," he said, opening the screen door.

"Hello there, Jimmy," Chuck replied, shaking his hand as he came in. Looking into the kitchen, he said, "Hello, Tom and Alice. I've got something out in my truck I'd like to give Jimmy, if it's all right with you two."

Tom and Alice nodded their approval. He hurried back to his truck, returning a minute later carrying two boards. He routed the edges of each board in his shop, and routed something into each board. He walked into the kitchen and placed them on the table, one on top of the other. The board on top had a picture of a hawk carved in it that looked a lot like Lady Samson. Arcing across the top of the board were the beautiful words, "Strong Feather Lady Samson."

Strong Feather

"That's beautiful, Chuck," Alice said, tracing the hawk with her fingers.

"It sure is good workmanship, Chuck," Tom said, looking at him. "You spent more than a couple hours doing that."

Jimmy stood beside his grandma speechless.

Chuck pulled the bottom board out so they could see it. This board also had larger beautiful letters across it that read, "Strong Feather Jimmy Warrior."

The four of them admired the two signs.

"You know something, Chuck," Tom said, taking the sign away from Chuck for a closer look. "You've done the Warrior family a great service. I agree with you that Jimmy is one of the Strong Feathers of our tribe. He was never given a true Indian name, but with this sign, you have given him the name he deserves, Strong Feather Jimmy Warrior. It's a great name for a Warrior."

"I was kind of thinking along those lines, Tom, as I made the sign," Chuck said, looking at him and then at the sign. "His being born in Denver probably deprived him of that part of his heritage. So the idea came to me that he earned the name that was given to the hawk he caught. I've watched him grow strong since he came to stay with you two. Like his grand hawk, he spread his wings and soared beyond his wildest dreams."

Jimmy didn't know what to say as he listened to Chuck, looking at the signs, and wondering if what he said was true. Then he realized the talking stopped, and they waited for him to say something.

"Thank you, Mr. Miller," he said, looking at him. "I surely like that name a lot. Yes, sir, I like it a lot."

"I'm working on two more signs for Lady Joan and Lady Gwen. When you and Mary go off to show your hawks, you'll be able to hang their names under their perches so everyone who passes by will know who they are."

"That's a great idea, Mr. Miller. I . . . "

There was a knock at the front door, the screen door opened, and in came Mary. "Hi, everybody," she said, walking into the kitchen. "What are all of you doing?"

"Look at these signs Mr. Miller made for me, Mary," Jimmy said, picking up the one with the picture of a hawk on it.

"Why, that is gorgeous, Jimmy," she said, looking at it. Tom showed her the sign with his name on it. "That's true," she said looking at him, then Jimmy.

"That's not all," Tom said. "Mr. Miller is going to make two more signs, one for Lady Joan and one for Lady Gwen."

Mary squealed and ran over and gave Chuck a kiss on the cheek. "Thank you, Mr. Miller," she said, grabbing him by the arm and squeezing it.

"That makes this all worth while," Chuck said, laughing. That broke the spell, and they all laughed. "Well, I just wanted to stop by and drop these signs off. I'll be going now."

Mary and Jimmy walked him to the front door, thanking him each step they took. Opening the screen door, Chuck stopped and looked at them. "What you two and Lady Samson have done for me is worth a lot more than a couple of pieces of wood that I did some work on. I think you know that. What I did is just a token payment for what you did for me. So it's me who should be thanking you. I'd appreciate it if the two of you would thank Strong Feather Lady Samson for me."

"Sure," Jimmy said. "I'll do that first thing tomorrow morning."

Strong Feather

Chuck shook his hand and left. Returning to the table, Mary sat down beside Jimmy. They both picked up one of the signs and looked at them.

"I'm going to put these two in my bedroom," he said, getting up and heading for his room with Mary right behind him.

Alice followed them all excited, while Tom looked for a hammer and nails in the cabinet drawers. When he found them, he hurried down the hall to Jimmy's room.

The signs were placed all around the room before it was agreed that they looked best over the dresser. Tom soon had two nails in the wall over the dresser. Placing the signs on the nails, he stepped back to see how they looked. "They look good hanging there," he said, proud of his work.

"Now when you go to a show," Alice said, "you two will be the only ones with your own signs. They sure do look good, Jimmy."

"They sure do," he said, looking at his grandma.

"Let's celebrate with some cherry pie," she said, looking at the three of them.

"Now you're talking," Tom said. "Signs are signs, but pie is pie."

The four of them laughed as they headed for the kitchen and the cherry pie.

A week later Chuck Miller brought the other two signs by. The next weekend they used them at the falcon show at Fort Collins. Jimmy found himself thinking about the day when there would be more than three signs over his dresser. The two Mercer, Colorado falconers were soon known as two of the best in the state. Their fame was even spreading outside the state. It seemed like everywhere they went someone knew them.

Strong Feather

Jimmy was pleasantly surprised one night when he sat down to eat. His grandma fixed spaghetti, his favorite food. She then topped the meal off with cherry pie, another favorite of his. When he ate all he could eat, he sat back in his chair and smiled at his grandma. Alice got up and went over to the cupboard. When she returned, she had a neatly wrapped package in her hands.

"This is your birthday present, Jimmy," she said. "It's from your Grandpa and me," as she gave him a big hug.

"Thanks Grandma and Grandpa," he said, surprised. "I'd forgotten all about this being my birthday. So much has happened lately."

Opening the package, he found a new leather billfold inside. It was just what he needed to put his money in, money he earned from working, not from begging.

"It's kind of hard for me to believe all of the things that happened to me since I came to live with you," he said, looking at both of them. "It turned out a lot better than I thought it would." His voice quivered a little. "I've found a home here with both of you, and I want to thank you for taking me in."

Tom looked at his wife. "Alice, I think our grandson is trying to tell us he loves us."

"I believe you're right, Tom," she replied. "I know that's what we're trying to tell you, Jimmy, with that present. You've made us so proud of you."

There were a couple more hugs before he sat back down and looked at his new billfold. His grandparents sure were good to him, and he wanted to thank them, but didn't know how to say it. Finally he said, "Your Strong Feather Warrior has found a home where he is really wanted. He'll never leave."

Strong Feather

Tom and Alice looked at their grandson with pride showing through their misty eyes.

"We're glad you feel that way, Jimmy," Tom said.

"That's true," Alice agreed, with pride in her voice.

There was silence as the three of them thought about what was said.

Jimmy looked at his grandma and grandpa and slowly said, "Could I have another piece of cherry pie, Grandma?"

"Me, too," Tom said, grinning at his wife.

The three of them laughed as Alice got up and cut the remainder of the pie into three pieces. She liked cherry pie, too.

A young Strong Feather sat in the house laughing, while outside, another Strong Feather sat on a perch listening to her master laugh. Both Strong Feathers found what they looked for, a home where they were loved.

Printed in the United States
R2597800003B/R25978PG59263LVSX5BA/25-27

9 780977 222162